Bernard Levin

Bernard Levin was born in 1928 and educated at Christ's Hospital and the London School of Economics. He has been a book, television and theatre critic, and for many years now he has written a regular column for *The Times*. In 1990, he was awarded the CBE.

His first book, THE PENDULUM YEARS, was published in 1970, and since then several collections of his journalism have been published. He is also the author of three travel books which were linked with Channel 4 television series – HANNIBAL'S FOOTSTEPS, TO THE END OF THE RHINE and A WALK UP FIFTH AVENUE – and most recently A WORLD ELSEWHERE, on the subject of Utopias.

SCEPTRE

I Should Say So

BERNARD LEVIN

SCEPTRE

Copyright © Bernard Levin 1995

First published in 1995 by Jonathan Cape
First published in paperback in 1996 by Hodder and Stoughton
A division of Hodder Headline PLC
A Sceptre Paperback

The right of Bernard Levin to be identified as the Author of
the Work has been asserted by him in accordance with the
Copyright, Designs and Patents Act 1988.

10 9 8 7 6 5 4 3 2 1

A CIP catalogue record for this book is
available from the British Library

ISBN 0 340 67187 4

Printed and bound in Great Britain by
Cox and Wyman Ltd, Reading, Berkshire

Hodder and Stoughton
A division of Hodder Headline PLC
338 Euston Road
London NW1 3BH

Contents

Acknowledgments

Once again, I thank my indispensable friend and secretary, Catherine Tye, for all the countless things that I forget and she remembers. Once again, I turn to Oula Jones for the index, knowing that she is an indexer beyond rubies.

Alas, the two friends who have always read the proofs, Brian Inglis and Bill Rolph, have died. That very tiresome chore is now done by Liz Anderson, who not only did it, but actually *asked* to do it.

Tom Maschler, of Jonathan Cape, was his usual helpful self, as were all those at Cape who were involved, most particularly Jenny Cottom.

Mike Shaw, my literary agent, was as always a tower of strength. And many of my colleagues at *The Times* gave most helpful advice.

My thanks, also, to Christian Solidarity International, for the translation of Mehdi Dibaj's letter. (See "In the Holy Name of God").

Introduction

By profession I am a journalist, and I am a successful one. I put the "successful" in, not for boasting, I assure you, but for a reason that sometimes wakes me from sleep, shuddering with terror, not to close my eyes till dawn comes as a soothing mercy.

I shall explain this lurid problem in a moment, but before I do so, allow me to introduce myself – again, truly, not for vainglory. For twenty-three years, I have been on *The Times*, as a columnist; I have full *carte blanche* to choose the subjects I write about, and I take that licence so much to heart that over those twenty-three years I must have written on literally hundreds of subjects. When I joined *The Times* (William Rees-Mogg was then the editor and, incidentally, I am now on my sixth) I was invited to write once a week. After a time, William asked me to write twice a week, then thrice.

That "thrice" was very nearly final for me, because, one day, looking in the bathroom mirror, I was startled to find a haggard nonagenarian staring out at me, his hands shaking, his eyes rheumy, his hair grey and with barely the strength to step on the scales, albeit they were all of one inch high. I took some time off (a considerable time, it turned out to be) and when I came back, re-freshed, to the fold, I swore a mighty oath that I would never write regularly more than twice a week, and I have kept my vow. Mind you, I could hardly believe that I was the man singled out by St Luke, saying that joy shall be in heaven over one sinner that repenteth, more than

over ninety and nine just persons which need no repentance.

But I never thought of giving up journalism, and that
brings me back to my apparently boasting words with
which I started. For in a sense I am a journalist *manqué*; it
is nothing but the truth when I say that if I had not
discovered journalism I would have starved to death. For I
can do nothing else. I could not be a businessman or
financier; I could not be any kind of an artist; I cannot sing,
or play any musical instrument; I could not make anything
with my hands; I could not keep ledgers and their like; I
could not be any kind of a teacher, and certainly not
an actor; I could not do anything with animals – but you
get the point. The *only* thing I could do, I discovered,
was journalism, and I had the luck to fall on my feet in
my prentice days, where I learned my trade, and learned
it sufficiently to make a good living. The good living
from journalism remains, and I hope will see me out,
but the nightmares I mentioned earlier are still at work,
and they lay out all the countless varieties of work, bar
one.

Away, clouds! I have, as I say, done well out of my pen
(well, it was a pen when I started), but I have to add that I
have enjoyed it enormously. And why should I not? It is a
trade in which friendships are made and kept, and it is a
trade astonishingly unenvious. Not long ago, it was discovered (by my secretary, of whom more later) that my
2000th column was approaching; I was most generously
fêted, but I tried, with very little success, to add up all the
words I had written in all my journalism. I included not
only *The Times* (and remember those three-a-week articles
which, incidentally, were very much longer than they are
today), but also the *Daily Mail*, where I spent a good many
years before I moved over to *The Times*. (I wrote *five* times
a week for the *Mail*, and I was its theatre critic at the same
time.) Nor was that all; I had had a good few years before
the *Mail* – the *Spectator*, the *Guardian* and more. Shall we

say five million words? Six? Seven? Surely not *ten*? I wouldn't be surprised.

I wouldn't be surprised, and even if I were, it is quite certain that my secretary, Catherine Tye, would not. For it was she who spotted the imminent 2000th column, counted the lot, and alighted upon the right one. Happy the man who has an infallible assistant; thrice happy the man whose assistant is not only infallible but a beloved friend.

Never mind the tall and beautiful trees (or the ugly ones come to that) which have been felled to feed my – well, is it my vanity? Surely, I do not believe that my words, which must certainly be highly perishable, are bound for immortality? And, if we are being pessimistic, we remember what the adage says: you read it today, and it wraps the fish tomorrow.

So why do I do it? Not only because I would starve if I did not; perhaps. But why ask such questions in the first place? Does it matter where and why and how I write and others read? Indeed, to tell my readers even to look out for this or that passage is an impertinence. So, with no particular idea in mind, I have, every two years or so, selected from the three or four hundred articles I have written in that time, some fifty or sixty that might entertain, amuse, even enlighten, and put them in a book. *I Should Say So* is the eighth such culling. The first was *Taking Sides*, published in 1979, followed by *Speaking Up* (1982), *The Way We Live Now* (1984), *In These Times* (1986), *All Things Considered* (1990), *Now Read On* (1991), *If You Want My Opinion* (1993), and now *I Should Say So*.

Over the years, I have, as most people have, watched for signs of real change, in our land and its temper. I have used my series of volumes to that end; asking what is happening that would have been otherwise a year or two ago, and if it is beneficial or the contrary. In my most recent volume before this one, *If You Want My Opinion*, there is a passage that asks the question point-blank: the answer goes like this:

I have browsed through the seven previous Introductions in compiling this one, to see whether there is even an illusory feeling of a series, of continuity, of torches being handed. Think of the possibilities of revolution in attitudes, politics, entertainment, speech, international affairs, crime (and laws), health, travel, food, drink and the list could go on for some time. Does *b* follow *a* in our ordered alphabetic world?

And I answered my own question: Oh, my word, *no*.

Only two years have passed since I said my vigorous no, and said it in italics. Yet few, I think, would feel the same today. What has changed, changed, that is, in matters sufficiently important to be noticed in the first place?

In the previous volume, there was much discussion of violence; no one could have been ignorant of the rising tide. But today, few would deny that that rising tide is now higher than ever, and gives many signs of drowning us all. Indeed, discussing the very many changes that only two years had brought, very many would have ignored most of the great differences that had been seen, and if asked for their *most* pressing worry would say as their first thought, simply "violence". But some would go further and say "random violence"; others would go further still and say "violence that is out of control"; I would say, and I do so, that the *kind* of violence we are seeing now is new and far worse than anything that has happened to us since something like a hundred and fifty years ago. Nor should anyone believe that we are discussing Britain only; the savages of war and oppression have always been with us, but surely not to the level they have now reached, which allowed Caroline Moorhead, in launching the new-format *Index on Censorship*, to say that "Not only has violence reached catastrophic levels in many parts of the world, but the contempt of governments for the rights of their citizens seems never to have been higher."

Of course, it is not only violence, and many changes are manifestly changes for the better. Look at 'A giant goes home' (p. 33) and think back to those years in exile, an exile that only a few of us believed would end, and went on believing until it came true. Go a step back in time with 'The feel-good factor' (p. 42) and see me relish the fellow-travellers and their like being beaten to their holes.

I pick and choose, as I picked and chose the columns that went into the books. There is no attempt to put them into a meaningful order, and anyway no two readers would agree on the meaningfulness.

As with books, so with everything else; to give one umbrella answer to the question of what is happening now that did not before is probably a waste of time. If violence holds centre-stage, what is waiting in the wings? I think the key-word is "disintegration". Oh, our society is not going to break into fragments, never to be put together again, though perhaps 'To do with everybody' (p. 60) is here a tiny pointer to something that is all too likely to become less tiny. But disintegration can take a variety of forms, and we see many of these forms daily; from dirt to marriage, from civility to ignorance, from vacuity to unemployment, from culture to rubbish – "What, will the line stretch out to the crack of doom?" The answer is: yes, probably. My 'The hunting of the shark' (p. 84) made mock of a stickler for perfection, and he was ribbed accordingly. But in a different context something much more important and even terrible might happen. It does; take, for instance, 'To die will be an awfully big adventure' (p. 9), which tells the story of a pop singer who wanted so badly to die that his wish was granted when he was twenty-seven. Or 'In the Holy Name of God' (p. 65), which speaks of the fanatical and murderous fundamentalist Muslims, or 'Before the savages came' (p. 70), which speaks almost the same words, this time of the torturing and killing in Tibet by the Chinese invaders. If that is not disintegration, what is it?

Well, as I say; it takes many forms. Take 'Capital punishment' (p. 144), a tale of our times that is getting more familiar every day. I do not believe that any of us would have guessed, a few years ago, and *only* a few years, that by now huge armies roam the land to find things that do not matter and then make them matter by – well, the usual practice is for the snoopers to come first, to show the way; then, armed with bundles of regulations, the thought police pounce upon the law-abiding figure who has been tagged, and finally take the innocent individual to court. (Where, I regret to say, the judges don't even criticise these bullies, let alone denounce them as steps towards the Gulag.)

Take the smoking saga. I have said before that the United States give us their very best things and their very worst things, and sometimes we get the two. At the present time, they are giving us their worst intolerance. Some of the outbreaks of intolerance in the US have been truly appalling; McCarthyism ruined thousands of innocent people and indeed killed many. You would think that, with such a dreadful warning, the US would have been eager to break down barriers, encourage laughter, fly the flag of relaxation. And for a time, that was what did happen. I remember the warmth and lightness of step America showed in those days (and not only in San Francisco). Alas, it did not last. A new McCarthyism arose in the form of PC (there have been suicides already).

This kind of absurdity is usually hooted off the stage immediately, whether or not it takes root later; those who can read omens, however, shivered, for these grim, terrible two letters leaped into the forefront at a single bound. We, or more precisely our forefathers, should have known, and everyone should have known, that tolerance in the United States can be the best in the world and also the worst. When we read history books and learn about Prohibition (which also had a massive death-rate), we shake our heads in wonder, that such things could happen in such a country. But then, only a few decades later, we are celebrating toleration at its highest. It could not last, and did not. McCarthy came, and took a long time going. Back swung the pendulum, and no one had to look over his shoulder. But now?

It is no joke being a smoker in the United States; it will, a few years hence, be a criminal act. And we should remember the adage. The United States sends us its best and its worst.

I dwell on this historical see-saw because there is very little about the US in this volume, and what there is could be shelved only under the title Greatness in Human Beings, as a reader will see from 'Arms and the man' (p. 115) and 'Face to face' (p. 119). But greatness can be found anywhere, and no one needs a ticket of admittance to gaze upon it, as witness 'The men who did their duty' (p. 207), wherein there is a tribute to two heroes, each of whom would reject the title of hero, and each would say that they were only doing what a human being must.

Watchman, what of the night? The watchman saith: the morning cometh. There is also very little in this volume about the collapse of the Soviet Union and the end of its evil, but there is a reason. I suppose that from all the articles I have written, there is one subject that dominates all the others, not just any one of them, but all of them put together. For some forty years, without a break, I denounced the evils of Stalin, his successors and his terrible achievements. I was jeered at, patronised, told I was a Fascist, but I never wavered in my knowledge – knowledge anyone could have had – that Stalin was another Hitler, and Hitler was another Stalin. (And, which doubled the fury of the fellow-travellers, I also did not cease to attack the vileness of the rulers of South Africa.)

"And the rain descended, and the floods came, and the winds blew, and beat upon that house; and it fell: and great was the fall of it". *Annus mirabilis* had come.

And not long afterwards, it went. No one, I am sure, thought that the change from tyranny to democracy was going to be easy, or even bloodless. There were too many buried hates to dig up, too many scores to settle. But that the Soviet Union had broken into fragments of mutual hate, and instead of the rejoicing and rolling up of sleeves there was news of internecine fighting, was enough to break hearts, and to want breaking heads. Surely, Stalin must have been laughing foully in Hell when he heard the final news: Grozny.

I suppose that I have never, in all my days, had such a disappointment; it is not an exaggeration that it has scarred my life for what remains of it. Shakespeare, as usual, has a word or two for it. "Be friends, you English fools, be friends, we have French quarrels enow, if you could tell how to reckon." But Corporal Bates couldn't reckon.

War alles falsch? asked the Kaiser, as he went into exile. Did I do everything wrong? And did I waste those thousands of spoken words, and throw away those hundreds upon hundreds of pages?

A gloomy note, but how else could I feel, given the hopes and what has happened to them? And in any case, the horror of a dashed ruin is by no means confined to the Soviet Union and its aftermath. For if you think that you have heard the end of wickedness, I can only respond with *Sancta simplicitas*! Try 'Before the savages came' (p. 70), where you can find quite enough murderous persecution to suffice any level of blood and torture, the blood and torture being suffered at the hands of the Chinese invaders. Then there is 'It will have blood' (p. 149), which starts with the murder of a girl whose lover stabbed her sixteen times, and ends with the murder of a policeman who was trying to save the girl.

We live, do we not, in a disturbed universe? But even the most disturbed universe must pause for a moment to take breath, and it is then that the lighter side of life can be heard among the uproar. 'Heads in the sand' (p. 28) tells the story of a lady who was by choice and pleasure a runner in marathons, and one day, when she was in training for the next long run, she came face to face with a very angry ostrich (the cause of its anger was never revealed, though the *marathoneuse* denied teasing it), and – well, have you ever, dear reader, taken out time for ostrich wrestling?

As I have said, I am happily in the position of choosing my subjects; years ago, someone suggested that I should be psycho-analysed, the object being to find some common thread between, say, 'Blind eye to murder' (p. 173), which denounces a communist rogue who looked upon mass murder and found it good, and 'The Balun Declaration' (p. 163) which chronicles a sturdy American who killed a rat, and chased away a busy-body who was trying to have the rat-catcher prosecuted. Or where do these columns meet (or are supposed, subconsciously, to be meeting): 'The Queen of England' (p. 14) which wallows in the sybaratism of my only crossing of the Atlantic by sea, and 'What's in a word?' (p. 245), which is dedicated to the careless word which ruins an empire?

I think that the psycho-analyst would be driven mad long before I would, yet there must be some connection, else how did I choose *these* columns for this book, rather than *those*?

One theory, at least, can be traced, but it ends in sorrow. Anyone who reads anything of mine will sooner or later find me at the narrow end of some group of people who are being ill-treated, and who have come to me to defend them. An example: I am not a Freemason, nor am I interested in the doings of Masons, but I have found myself writing in defence of the Masons. How? And why? Because I had discovered that in some of London's boroughs Masons were being dismissed, not for any misdemeanour or failure in their work, but only because they *were*

Masons, and I was asked to speak up for the Masons, precisely because I wasn't one. Exactly the same thing happened with the smokers; I was singled out for defending the smokers' rights, *because* I had never smoked. And then came the homosexuals with their plaints (and in those days homosexuals were not only jeered at, but frequently beaten up), and again I was roped in to defend a cause that was not mine. (Mind you, all I got for it was good reviews of my books in *Gay News*.)

But I said that this quixotic galloping to the rescue of those who needed rescue (it was never a beautiful maiden, alas) would end badly. And it has ended badly, very badly indeed. When I defended homosexuals who were being ill-treated for their sexual nature and *only* their sexual nature, almost all of them behaved as anyone else would, and most were content with their lot. There was, after all, no need to proclaim anyone's sexual nature, homosexual or heterosexual.

And now? The odious blackmail that peaceable and innocent people are suffering because they wish their sexual nature to be private is now a threat to any homosexual; at any moment he can find himself "outed", which means dragged into the limelight to feed the vanity of those who spray publicity about like spittle. And, of course, the homosexual cause is set back years; no matter, the fanatics have got their pictures in the papers.

What a world! No, we cannot hide behind the wickedness, cruelty and dirt of the world, for it was we, and we alone, who made all the wickedness, cruelty and dirt, and added, for good measure, the lying, the violence and the aimlessness. And sometimes – no, often – I begin to think that the aimlessness is the worst of all. And that may be no coincidence, because aimlessness is the breeding-place in 'I heard it somewhere' (p. 93), when terrible rumours, entirely empty and with absolutely no evidence, came very close indeed to starting a pogrom. When will human beings all become rational? When it is proved that the moon is made of green cheese? Not even then; for many will agree that the moon is indeed made of cheese, but scorn the belief that it is green, insisting that it is blue, or at a pinch, purple.

I have wandered somewhat in writing this Introduction for this, my eighth selection of my newspaper columns, but perish the thought that I should put them *all* in a book, not least because the book would be almost exactly one yard thick. (Alas, that may be the last time I use the word "yard" in a book or anywhere else; for – though it will be difficult for you to believe what I am just going to say – the ancient measures are to be abolished, and *the use of them is to be a criminal offence punishable with a fine of up to five thousand pounds*.)

I know, from long experience, that my readers will hotly disagree with my choice of columns; the usual cries of "Why did the idiot include *that* one, and leave out *this* one?" will be heard wherever any two readers of *I Should Say So* come together. That, I have always believed, is as it should be. If there is one thing above all that a columnist should shun, it is conformity within his work. G.K. Chesterton once said that it would be a wonderful thing if a tube-trainful of passengers bound for Waterloo, coming out of the tunnel, were to find themselves arriving instead at Sloane Square.

People often ask me, sometimes in tones of awe, how I can find ideas for my next column, let alone the ones looming on the horizon. I shouldn't be giving away trade secrets, but I feel I must get away from any idea including awe. The truth should be obvious, and I am truly amazed when it is not, for the answer is the one that Sir Christopher Wren gave: "If you seek my memorial, look around you." There is virtually nothing at all in the world that cannot be commented upon, argued about, examined, felt, touched, tripped over, be hit on the head by and astonished at. More trade secrets: I keep a stock of small white cards in my wallet, and I jot down on those cards ideas that might turn into a column. But there are *never* fewer items than ten on the card.

Try it; I particularly beseech those who bring awe into it. For why go round the world to seek the treasure, when you only have to stand on your own doorstep and watch the world go by.

Then, all I have to do is to take the clay and turn it into some sixty-odd columns, culled from the harvest. And how do I turn that clay into life, you ask? Come, come; I can't give away *all* the trade secrets, can I?

November, 1995   B. L.

Arabian days

I DON'T KNOW WHY novelists bother; anyone capable of throwing a bag of peanuts out of the window can be sure of hitting at least a dozen people who, from their own experience, can tell stories very much more remarkable than the latest dreadful Booker winner.

Just read this nearly invisible news item:

Mr Roger Johnson, a former American airman who stole a cycle while stationed at Polebrook, Northants, during the second world war, will make amends today by presenting 90 new ones costing nearly £10,000 to local children.

Thirty-six words, and a thousand and one Arabian nights to make magic tales out of them! There is not another word of explanation, no promise of further revelations, no startling denouement to await. So much the better; we can speculate freely, unhindered by facts.

Imagine the young airman (no veteran he), perhaps including in his duties nightly sorties over Germany; he would certainly have noted the number of aircrews – many of them his friends as well as his colleagues – who did not return. Next time might be his last; if life itself is as cheap as that, surely bicycles should be given away free?

Why did he want a bicycle, anyway? That's easy: he was in a strange country, and being an imaginative young man, wanted to fill his few leisure hours by exploring his surroundings. He couldn't run to a car (and even if he could, petrol rationing precluded sightseeing); I don't know Northamptonshire's rural delights, but I assume that they were sufficiently interesting for him to pedal about in them. Did he come from a sleepy rural state, so that what he saw he could recognise, or from the heart of downtown bustling Detroit to find woods and fields all around him? I have assumed, so far, that his theft did not greatly disturb him. Did he have a qualm, though, when one of his mates, or a senior officer, asked where he got it? Surely not. He, his friends and his superiors all had more things on their minds than the provenance of bicycles.

Some of these things on their minds concerned neither bicycles nor bombs; what about the young ladies of the area? Did he have a girl back home in Kansas or New York? And if so . . . well, did he have something more significant to feel guilty about than bicycles? Or did he have a photograph in his breast pocket, which he took out and kissed, particularly when he was taking off for a journey that might be his last? For that matter, did he have a rabbit's paw in one of his other pockets? (Jeer not, you beastly rationalists; I read once of a wartime airman who never flew without a pair of his girlfriend's stockings around his neck, and he lived to tell the tale.)

Well, the war ended, and our hero survived it. He went home, and made a life for himself. Presumably he married and had children. Clearly, he prospered. But, as with the princess and the pea, there was something amiss. Did the theft of the bicycle get into his dreams? Did he think that if he died abruptly, say in a car crash, he would not have time to seek confession and absolution? More dramatically, had he long ago forgotten his trivial crime, when suddenly, because of some oblique mental association, it leaped into his mind?

Yet there is a great gulf between remembering a peccadillo from half a century ago and determining to put it right. And how handsomely right! Ten thousand pounds-worth of brand new, state-of-the-art bicycles, to be distributed among 90 of the children of Polebrook, Northants, where Christmas comes twice this year.

A child at the time of the Great Bicycle Robbery would today be about to draw the State Retirement Pension (the Old Age Pension it was called then, though later that was felt to be too downmarket); two or three generations have grown up since someone limped home on foot, and the world has gone round nearly twenty thousand times. Yet are not five sparrows sold for two farthings, and not one of them is forgotten before God?

In this case, however, God made no sign; the sinner took it upon himself to make amends. No matter that Polebrook had obviously forgotten the sin a week after it had been committed; no matter that the Polebrookers would have looked upon the American airmen as heroes coming to the succour of the old country; no matter that if he had asked politely for a bicycle, a dozen would have been proffered; fifty years on, Jiminy Cricket gave a little whistle, "and always let your conscience be your guide". Mr Johnson's conscience is clean; truly, it was hardly even smudged in the first place. And 90 Polebrook children will be sporting handsome new bicycles. All's well that ends well.

We all have dim corners in our lives, and most of us have one or two that are not just dim, but truly dark. Most can be illuminated somehow, but a few cannot, and we must take them to the grave. But Mr Johnson has turned his into a shining triumph. Remember, he didn't rob a bank or break a head. He stole a bicycle, lived with the knowledge, and made amends exactly 90 times over. Polebrook should honour him in a fitting manner. Why not an explanatory plaque on the village fountain, with a bicycle chained to it? Surely no one would steal it.

The Times, 2 July 1992

Lara's theme

SHAKESPEARE SAID "The evil that men do lives after them, / The good is oft interred with their bones", and Shakespeare will be relieved to know that I entirely agree with him. And even I didn't, I would be hard pressed to get round the latest manifestation of Shakespeare's comment. But if we wish to understand it in full we must go back to events that took place in 1957; a good deal of water has gone over the dam since then, more than a third of a century has passed since the events I shall recall, yet they are not forgotten, and indeed the wounds are bleeding afresh as I write.

When did you last read *Doctor Zhivago*? I did just now, because Pasternak's masterpiece is central to my theme today, but surely it has its place for ever in Russia and the Russian language. (In a sense, we are exchanging compliments; *Doctor Zhivago* was translated into English by Max Hayward and Manya Harari – a labour of love if ever there was one, considering the extraordinary circumstances of the translation – and Pasternak had translated Shakespeare into Russian.)

Pasternak was a poet first and a novelist second – last indeed, because he wrote the book in 1955 (it was his first and last novel), and spent two fruitless years trying to get it published in the Soviet Union. He died in 1960, his end hastened by what he then had to suffer, which included not only the banning of his novel (and his poetry as well, though it could in no way be classified as subversive), threats to his life, and reminders – as if anyone in that terrible country needed such reminders – that the Gulag's gates could swing open at the press of a button. We must remember that Stalin was only four years dead and the Khrushchev speech only one year past.

Khrushchev speech or no Khrushchev speech, *Doctor Zhivago* was classified as "a hostile act" (do you remember how Khrushchev was fawned over by every sleazy fellow-traveller in Britain?) and it had to wait decades for its debut in Pasternak's own country.

And what, you ask, brings all this nostalgia to my pen? It is the discovery that, although Pasternak has been dead for 34 years, his Lara is still alive, in her eighties. And she is not only alive, she is in fighting mood, and it behoves me to take her side in the battle she is waging.

I shall come to the battle, but there is much to say about Lara before I do so. Lara, you must know, was not her name; she was Olga, but Pasternak had based his heroine on his love (they were never married) and called her Lara, and Lara she was and is.

Khrushchev did not dare to have Pasternak murdered, so great was his name and fame outside the Soviet Union. He could have had Pasternak exiled as, many years later, Brezhnev (equally fearful of murdering the terrible human thorn of truth which would not be blunted) threw Solzhenitsyn out of the Soviet Union; but Khrushchev probably knew that Pasternak had not many years to live.

Hurrying Pasternak to his grave was not enough vindictiveness by Khrushchev; as soon as the great man died, his Lara was arrested and sent to one of the concentration camps in the Gulag. Ironically, she already knew what it was like, for she had been one of Stalin's victims, thrown into the Gulag in one of his insane round-ups of thousands – eventually many millions – of innocents. (She was pregnant, by Pasternak, when she was arrested; the baby was stillborn in the camp.)

Her second visit to the Gulag lasted four years. Until the Soviet Union collapsed she remained in fear of being sent back. Now she faces another kind of struggle. When she was arrested, immediately after Pasternak's death, the KGB thugs who came for her robbed her apartment. Among the things they stole were papers, letters, manuscripts and other material that made up so great a part of her life; and she wants her life back. She could have it, because the materials were not destroyed; they were kept in an archive, and there they stay, to this day.

There are problems. Pasternak had relatives (and, remember, a wife), and some of them hated Lara. This hatred has seeped into the story, and there is a tug-o'-war between the parties. (I must say that Russians who hate other Russians do go to great lengths to live long, the better to do their hating.) There is a Pasternak Museum, but Lara is not welcome at it, though Pasternak's son urges conciliation. The division of the relics, it seems, cannot be calmly organised, and I am in no position to adjudicate. But I cannot forget this heart-tearing story. I saw the film soon after it came out, and I have not seen it again, but the "Lara theme" has made its way into the ears and hearts of millions of people who neither know nor care who Pasternak was.

I suppose there are thousands of stories within stories, but what gives this one its unique quality is the way it blurs the divisions of the book, the man and the woman. The man is dead; the book is not, and never will be. But the finite woman permeates book and man. Among the treasures the KGB men stole when they came to take Lara away is a version of *Doctor Zhivago* in manuscript, dedicated to her.

I tear up all versions of everything I write. My biographers will go pale when they find that I have not even kept the typescripts of my books. (Nor any diaries, for that matter.) But I can understand that a work of art, as it grows to completion, goes through many stages, and those stages are the steps to something that is not like anything else. Mind you, I do not write fiction (and you wouldn't like me if I did), and collecting the stages of what I write seems ridiculous.

Well, yes, I would tremble if I found in manuscript a play and realised that it was indisputably from Shakespeare's hand, but it would be the text that made me tremble, not the orthography. Nevertheless, it must be different for Lara. I never met Shakespeare, so the discovery by me of a new play would go no further than surprise. If, when I was holding it in my hand, Anne Hathaway came up to me and engaged me in conversation, I would listen closely, and Lara must feel something similar when she contemplates their all-consuming love, and lives to tell the tale.

And then, Lara has a letter from Pasternak (or perhaps *had* a letter, for there is no indication as to whether it is in the archives or beneath her pillow) which reads "I am bound to you by life, by the sun shining through my window, by a feeling of remorse and sadness, by a feeling of guilt". How many of us have received a letter like that from the hand of a great genius? Traditionally, love from a great genius leads to an unquiet house, but perhaps it is only tradition that makes us think so. What did Anne Hathaway say when, as the will was being read, she learnt that he had left her his second best bed? Jests galore have been made of Will's will, but for all we know Anne might have shed tears of pure love and joy, if that was the bed in which they first made love.

"They should just give me back my papers. They are keeping the most precious part of my life." Thus speaks Lara, but it cannot be literally so. However many trinkets, documents, letters, jewels, pebbles picked up on an early morning walk, these cannot be "the most precious part of my life" – the very word "life" argues against it. A woman who has been held in the passionately loving arms of Boris Pasternak has kept something more than tangible objects. Did she, when she was in the Gulag after Pasternak's death, call upon objects to strengthen and complete the sacrifice?

A rabbit's foot to stand for Boris Pasternak? Surely not. What she remembered was the day he dropped the samovar on his foot and limped for weeks, the day that they got the tiny flat they wanted, the day that they hid in a cupboard, thinking that the KGB had come for them, only to find that it was Boris's mother-in-law banging on the door.

It is an impudence for me to tell her what to feel, but I shall be impudent. Dear Lara, love has touched you in the form of one of Russia's greatest artists. Be comforted, be proud, be rich in memories, and tell the bureaucrats that they can go and strangle themselves in their own red tape.

The Times, 21 June 1994

To die will be an awfully big adventure

RARELY DOES A month go by but a pop singer dies young, usually from drugs or drink or both; ephemeral as their music is, their lives are no less insubstantial. They clearly court early death; one day they are holding thousands of young people in trance, and the next day the obituaries are out, so premature as to puzzle the actuaries. Some of the posthumous *réclame* remains, but not much and inevitably not for long.

The latest was Kurt Cobain, who shot himself at the age of 27, as far as I can see for no better reason than *Weltschmerz*. (Obsequies in these matters can take various forms; one of Cobain's followers, Eddie Vedder, some weeks after his hero died, felt so bad that "I was in a hotel room in Washington D.C., and I just tore the place to shreds . . . then I just kind of sat in the rubble, which somehow felt right".)

I am not quite sure why I am taking an interest in the death, by his own hand, of the leader of an American "rock group". Experts in these matters insist that Cobain's suicide was a particularly great loss, though no one has made clear why his ending was different from the now familiar decline and fall. The hoodoo seems to be impartial, and whether they kill themselves, or die by their excesses, or live on after their brief span, the Brian Joneses and Sid Viciouses and Jimi Hendrixes and Keith Moons and Janis Joplins almost invariably die young or badly or both.

Kurt Cobain trod the now well worn path; stuffed with booze and heroin, he was not likely to see old bones, and indeed he made clear that he wouldn't and didn't want to. It is not for me to judge him, though there must be a grave heaving somewhere.

But I had sufficient inquisitiveness to go down to London's biggest record store and, donning a false beard, asked rather timidly for some albums of Nirvana, which was the name of the Cobain group. Skilfully led through the thousands of products by a most helpful assistant who pretended not to notice the false beard, I took two albums, called respectively *Nevermind* and *In Utero*, and went home with the knowledge (I had already done some homework) that the albums of Nirvana sold not by millions but by tens of millions, and presumably wherever young people are to be found.

I played my acquisitions through. For those even more ignorant than I was, I should say that the team is guitar-led, though unfortunately not by Segovia. (No, dear, Segovia is not another "rock band".) I expected a great deal of raucous noise, and got it, but listening carefully, I realised that this stuff is not just shouting, and is even up to making a musical point. Yet I knew that it would fail the crucial test; I do not believe that I would or could continue to listen to such music, and the reason is surely obvious: it is ultimately without roots. I heard Brendel playing five Beethoven sonatas the night after I had listened carefully to *Nevermind* and *In Utero*, and I am in no doubt which evening was eternal. No doubt these players, and their millions of followers, would reply that they were not in the business of eternity, so the comparison breaks down.

That, of course, does not settle anything; there is permanent music and there is music born in the morning to die at night, and both have their virtues. Nevertheless, even virtues can be ranked. But it was the lyrics that settled matters. Try the number tastefully called "Rape Me". It goes:

> Rape me, my friend
> Rape me again

I'm not the only one
Hate me
Do it and do it again
Waste me
Taste me, my friend
My favourite inside source
I'll kiss your open sores
Appreciate your concern
You'll always stink and burn

That is fully typical of the 13 items on the *In Utero* album, and a cynical reader of those lines might conclude that since no one could possibly deduce the words of these songs by listening to them (which is certainly the case), the creators of them could shove anything down, confident that no one would be any the wiser. (I had to take a very powerful magnifying-glass to the lyrics, printed on the inner wrapping.)

Now I have not come here to despise this stuff, much less despise those who admire it and follow it. *Anything* that ten million people want to buy must have something in it that for some people has a meaning. Perhaps very few of the ten million could say what that meaning is, and not only because they would be incoherent. But obviously almost all of the purchasers responded to Kurt Cobain and his music; his public performances brought out thousands to see as well as listen to their hero.

And hero he obviously was, even (shouldn't that be particularly?) when boozed, coked and violent (very violent – he was apparently given to smashing furniture, recording-equipment and people indiscriminately). For his young followers he was a god, and I doubt if any of them thought it strange, let alone amusing, that although he lived for only 27 years, and became prominent only four years before his death, he had already been the subject of a biography. (His biographer said that Cobain was "a very sensitive person, sweet and bright"; well, perhaps not to the furniture, recording-equipment and people he smashed up.)

It would be pointless as well as unkind to tell those ten million followers that they will have forgotten him in a year or two, and that he will be replaced in their affections by a similar figure, who in turn will succumb to booze, coke, adulation and biographers. But the obituarists ought to be ashamed of themselves. One began "Let no one underestimate Cobain's importance", and went on to say that there is "an eternity now left to consider the songs on Nirvana's four albums", and another said that "punk rock . . . created a kind of community of outcasts; it provided a refuge, one Cobain compared to the Buddhist concept of nirvana . . ."

The heathen in his blindness bows down to wood and stone. Don't laugh; we all need idols, and some of us find them in the most extraordinary situations. Why should not ten million youths find their idol in a foul-mouthed, brutish, violent singer-guitarist, drugged to the eyebrows and hating himself and his way of life? (Hating so deeply that he eventually killed himself, remember.)

Tentatively, I have a suggestion; it is, of course, a long time ago that I was a youth, and assuredly the idols we worshipped were a very different kind; for that matter, the young people who did the worshipping were very different from today's ten million. But it is the difference that must be explored.

When and where and why did hate – and a new strain of hate – come into the consciousness of the young? Some still say it was violence on television, and others will insist that the young *demanded* the violent television. The appropriate volume of the second edition of the OED does not include "lager-lout", though the book was published in 1989. Is there today any issue of any newspaper that does not carry details of some kind of killing somewhere in the world – killing, more often than not, without intelligible reason? Leave out the killing for a moment, and consider the smashing and wrecking – "running riot" it used to be called. Who has not seen or read about a gang "trashing" a quiet street, solely because it was a quiet street? Who has not seen the wreckage of such a street in a foreign country, through which "fans" have rampaged to and from the football ground? There is an "organisation" that calls itself Class War and says that it is fighting such a war; probably it is a bunch of likely vandals feeling bored. But even a bunch of vandals feeling bored can inflict much damage, and do.

Yet remarkably, whenever the fans' young gods are performing, something is missing. The thousands do not fight, kill or maim. Very rarely indeed do we read of mayhem at those gatherings. Have we found a kind of solace amid the carnage, a solace dreadfully noisy but with the anger drained?

Shall we have to go to our children to learn how to make a noise but not fear that the noise was a gunshot? Shall the young lead us back to sanity via the howling and screaming of the pop singers? Shall Kurt Cobain be remembered not for the terrible blackness that drove him to his death but for the realisation that he had another, and much more important, task to do on this earth?

The Times, 14 May 1994

The Queen of England

A TINY NEWS ITEM caught my eye, and I caught my breath. The *United States* – the ship, not the country – was to be broken up and sold for scrap. You have to be as old as I am to remember the majestic transatlantic liners – the very word "liner" came into existence to denote the ocean-going ships and the "line" that owned them. And the *US* was the last of them.

For centuries, and by common consent, British ship-builders were recognised as the kings of the trade, and the Clyde rang, day in and day out, with the sound of yet another ship being built, christened and launched. (To the end of the shipbuilders' world, the same moving words were used as the vessel moved down the slipway: "God bless this ship and all who sail in her".)

The *Queen Mary* was a queen indeed; her sister the *Queen Elizabeth* did not stir the heart so. But America was not content to bow to the great Cunarders; the *United States* was to be the Atlantic's reply. The gauntlet was taken up; the *United States* was built, and now there was only one test, one championship, one prize to win. It was the Blue Riband of the Atlantic, and it went to the ship that crossed in the shortest time. Just as the jet aeroplane was being born, so soon to kill the great ships, the American challenger, on July 3, 1952, set out on her maiden transatlantic voyage, and docked three days, ten hours and 40 minutes later. The Blue Riband was hers, and it was never to be taken from her.

The fate of these great beauties was sad; the *Queen Mary* was bought as a tourist attraction by the city of Long Beach; the *Queen Elizabeth* caught fire and capsized (in Hong Kong harbour, as I recall), and the *United States* had the most pathetic ending of all. When her days as a liner ended, the shipping line which owned her had no use for her, and left her virtually abandoned, being moored at one berth after another, the last a mere coaling pier. Finally, the owner failed to pay the mooring charges and the ship was put up for sale by auction. Scrap merchants gathered, but even as the gavel fell, a white knight, Fred Mayer by name, bought the great lady for $2.6 million, declaring that he would restore her to her ancient glory. I doubt it.

What days they must have been! Some lines had four classes – First Class, Cabin Class, Tourist and – my dear! – Fourth. (And never the twain shall meet; when the *Titanic* was going down, some lower class passengers were trying to get forward in the hope of survival, when shocked stewards pointed out that they were not allowed in that part of the ship, and would they kindly go back to their quarters. Those were the days: they did as they were told.)

Both the *Queens* did great service in the war as troop-carriers. As soon as the war ended they were refitted and plied the Atlantic again, even as the planes were rolling off the assembly lines. At last there was a mournful announcement from Cunard to the effect that the next transatlantic voyage of the *Queen Mary* was to be her last. Yearning to know what that pre-war world had been like, I prevailed upon the editor of the newspaper I then wrote for, the *Daily Mail*, to send me both ways on the great ship's last voyage. (Mindful of the fate of those unfortunates on the *Titanic*, I insisted on First Class.)

It turned out to be one of the most astonishing experiences of my life, largely because my dream of getting a glimpse of the past came entirely true: there was *nothing* to see, to hear, to eat, to drink, to play, to dance, to exercise, to read, to dally, that could remind us we were living in the late-Sixties, not the mid-Thirties.

I discovered as much on the first evening out. My steward (he had been one before the war and returned to *Queen Mary* service as soon as he was demobbed) laid out my dress clothes. Well, any expert valet would do that; on the *Queen Mary*, however, they went somewhat further. The hanger on the jacket hung from the wardrobe knob; he had buttoned the braces on to the trousers, and laid them, perfectly pressed, diagonally on the bed, so that they hung down a few inches from the floor; exactly beneath the end of the trousers were my (perfectly shined) shoes, each adorned with a sock, the top of which had been carefully rolled down a few inches. The only possible meaning of the layout was that I was expected to climb on to the bed, put my legs into my trousers, and, as they emerged from the ends, automatically find them entering first my socks and then my shoes.

It went on like that for five days each way. If, on the boat-deck, I moved a finger, a deckchair was instantly provided, rug and all; at 11 am precisely, a cup of bouillon (no, sir, we do *not* call it soup) was offered, and at noon a pot of caviare. Quoits, sir? Deck-tennis, sir? Ah, a stroll round the ship, sir, most invigorating. On the parade I met two white-haired twin sisters, clearly pre-war habituées of the ship. I asked them if they had a rough estimate of the times they had gone there and back: they bristled, "We know *exactly*," said one; "Thirty-four," said the other.

A naval officer was shaking his head sadly; perhaps we had hit a rock? No; but if this were his ship, he said, there would be courtsmartial all round. "Good gracious," I said, "what on earth is wrong?" "Wrong?" he cried, "Good heavens, man, look at that rust! Look at that paintwork!" I murmured something about the ship being some 35 years old, but he was not to be mollified.

The evenings were even more Thirties than the rest of the ship. There was the bet on tomorrow's speed (I looked round for the naval officer in case he wanted it translated into knots), there was Lotto (oh, no sir, they may call it Bingo on shore, but it is Lotto here), there was dancing, as ballroom as could be, and on the last night there was the funny hat competition, for which I was enlisted as one of the judges.

I am very glad that I touched hands with a unique and glorious past, even as that past was coming to an end. But three days out there was one more event, and this one to moisten the driest of eyes. The *Queen Elizabeth* had a few more years before her, but this was the last time that the sisters would pass each other in mid-Atlantic. It was night, but of course nobody had gone to bed. A speck of light on the horizon grew larger, larger still; now we could see the ship. As the two separated for ever, the lights of both ships were blazing from end to end, and the sirens cried goodbye to the heavens.

Ah, yes; I did have a shipboard romance. Oh, no; I will certainly not disclose the lady's name. After all, this *is* the *Queen Mary*.

The Times, 4 May 1992

Old foss is the name of his cat

I AM NOT QUITE sure how many cats I have, which is as
it should be; the notorious independence of a cat easily
encompasses any number of changes of location, nor does
it find any difficulty in being in two or more places at the
same time, or even nowhere. When I last counted I lost
count, and I made a resolve to catalogue the entire collection, so I might as well try again now.

There is one made of tin. It is white and looks smug,
with a pink bow tie; strictly speaking, it is one side of a
jardinière, but who ever knew a cat to speak strictly, or
suffer for long the indignity of being two-dimensional? At
the opposite end of the range, there is one made of the
very finest and heaviest Baccarat glass, not so much the
figure of a cat as a sculpture of one. Curled up, it has just
been disturbed, and is looking calmly over its shoulder.

Another (made of a wood that never grew in Europe)
has its proportions awry, its ears being almost as big as the
rest of its face; if it were not for its tail it almost might be
a dog. It sits on my desk, in a most uncatlike position, and
is somewhat sinister, so I put my figurine of Hans Sachs
beside it, to exorcise any evil spirits it might conjure up.
(They do, you know.)

Here are two more wooden ones, both carved to show
the same beautiful grain; I think the larger is the mother of
the smaller, a belief reinforced by the identical way they
are holding their tails. A third, in a lighter grain, though
no less beautiful, is cut in such a way that it *must* be on the
edge of a table, or anything that has an edge, for it won't

balance unless it is peering over. All three sit on the television.

These tails tell a tale. All three came from that wonderful shop in Marylebone High Street, the Casson Gallery; I could not count the number of beautiful and lovingly made objects that I have bought there for presents and for myself. Then one day, Pan Henry, whose empire it was, told me that she was closing it. The reason? The rent was going up so preposterously that she had to give up.

Mark the sequel. The Casson Gallery premises have been empty from that day to this, rotting away for more than three years, and the idiot who had (has?) the lease has got not a penny from it in all that time. (The ruin of Marylebone High Street is now almost complete; there will soon be more shops shut than open – indeed, some have been empty longer than the gallery.)

There are two more wooden ones; both from foreign parts, one from the Philippines. It is extraordinarily light, almost as light as balsa, and bears a disturbing likeness to Nigel Lawson. The other is one of the finest of the whole collection; a kind of ebony, its tactile quality and graceful lines demanding to be held in the hand. Then there is a range of cloth, stuffed and plywood ones, ruled over by a huge and lazy chinchilla, which thinks it's real. And my latest, an adorable little toy, with black and white fur and a pink nose, and a tail as long as its body.

But never a real cat to rub itself against my leg, to sleep in my lap while I listen to music, to stretch out its chin to be tickled, to be stroked so long that the purring is as loud as a car's engine, to demand to be let out and to change its mind and insist on being let in.

That sounds rather mournful, and I suppose it is, for I would dearly like a cat on the premises. But that very change of mind precludes it; if I am not in, there is no one to attend to the creature (a fifth-floor cat-flap is, after all, out of the question) and I deem it impermissible to the point of cruel to keep the beast shut up all day. While I am hovering on the brink of mournfulness, I had better get the obvious question out of the way: no, I do not love cats because I cannot love human beings, and a cat, for me, is not a substitute anything, let alone a wife. I do assure you that you don't have to be a bachelor to love cats.

I have loved cats from infancy; I am certain that I have been one in an earlier existence, perhaps several times, and I take no notice of the pathetic fallacy – there is a place for them, too, in heaven. But why do I love them so much?

A foolish question; can a human lover answer it even when the loved one is also human? No, but very few humans, very few indeed, love the entire human order; well, we real cat-lovers love them as a race, and truly encompass the entire feline world. Beethoven had a word for it: "*Seid umschlungen, Millionen: Diesen Kuss der ganzen Welt!*" But he was speaking metaphorically twice over, for even he could not really bring himself to embrace the millions and kiss the whole world – look at the nephew who gave him all that trouble, for a start. But real cat-lovers, like me, love the very essence of cat, and can see the souls of them, so there is no room to make exceptions.

A cat – we must learn this early in the relationship – will not give its whole heart to anyone. (No, the Siamese is *not* the exception; it does indeed give that impression, but it is a carefully calculated one, and the rule holds.) We must therefore resign ourselves to give more love than we get – an experience not entirely unknown in the human being. But that very frustration fires our love and binds the object of it to our hearts. Have you ever heard of a real cat-lover falling out of love?

Come closer to the creature; look at those eyes, full of the mysteries of long-past centuries, the steady gaze that invites drowning. Look at the flanks, calmly going in and out like the softest bellows in the world, refusing our wish to stroke them until we have paid the admission price of stroking the back, from head to tail-tip. Look at it going to sleep, instant and conclusive proof that it has been on Earth for millions of years, as it turns round and round to flatten the primeval grass. Look at the paws, practising the *marcher sur place* for a surface it has reason to suspect. Look at it feed. There is no abasement of thanks, no thanks at all, and the clue lies in the kitten; in its innocence, it displays gratitude, but when it grows up it demands its right. Cats are not haughty, though, except those who are taught to be by humans, entering them for shows.

That only a kitten needs to play is a fallacy, for the grown cat's need is similar, albeit more mature. Once, walking in France, I met a cat, a handsome tabby; we sat down together on a bench, and had a long conversation. After a time, my companion indicated that it was time we got on to something more profound. I suddenly realised that nobody had played with the cat – presumably a farm one – for years, and the unthinking cruelty of such a deprivation gave me a stab. I led him a dance in and out of the long grass, in and out of the trees, and he flung himself into the game, bursting with joy; by the time I had to leave the purring could have been taken for a tractor. But there was another lesson in our frolic; fools will call it mawkish, but in truth the cat and I had exchanged love.

Why not? If two humans can experience love at first sight, why not one human and one cat? There is no need for the human to take on the lineaments of the cat; we can exchange vows while being quite clear that two species are involved. But the point I am making is that we can love cats without either demeaning ourselves or fantasising. And, incidentally, in case you were wondering: no, it is not impossible, or even difficult, to love a human being, at a level far above cat-love, yet not need to expel the cat from your heart.

Oh, but I forgot the teapot! I have a china one which *is* a cat; it is sitting up with one paw poised, and that paw is

the spout, while its head is the lid. But I didn't forget
Swinburne: what cat-lover could?

> *Stately, kindly, lordly friend,*
> *Condescend*
> *Here to sit by me, and turn*
> *Glorious eyes that smile and burn,*
> *Golden eyes, love's lustrous meed,*
> *On the golden page I read.*

The Times, 21 March 1992

Fore and after

YOU WOULDN'T THINK, to look at me, that I once played a round of golf, would you? The circumstances are still in my memory, so I might as well recount them now.

In those days – hundreds of years in the past – I was a parliamentary sketchwriter-cum-commentator, which meant that I had to go to all the party conferences – Tory, Labour, Liberal (as it was in those days) and even the TUC.

I measured the horror by venues; the best of them all was Scarborough – a town that knew (I trust still knows) how to treat human beings, for there was a first-class restaurant and hotel, owned by no less a figure than the brother of Charles Laughton. From there, though, it was downward all the way, and the downward was very down indeed. Bournemouth was dreadful, and I have no reason to believe that it has ceased to be so; the Isle of Man was, if that place *was* the Isle of Man, no better; but the wooden spoon, year after year, was taken by Blackpool. Until I discovered St Anne's, a more or less civilised place a few miles from the dreaded Blackpool, and commuted, I shuddered at the thought of all those hours in the place, and longed for the moment that the chairman finally banged the gavel that said we could all go home.

Once – the scars on my soul have never fully recovered, but bleed afresh every time I think of it – *all* the four conferences were in Blackpool, and I had to stay something like a month in the place; my hair was then a beautiful nut-brown when I arrived, but by the end it was a grey so deep that several of the ladies refused to run their fingers through it.

One year, when the Labour Party was in conference at Blackpool, they had a closed session, I think to discuss the party's finances, and the press had to leave for the rest of the afternoon. O blessed release! Before I could think about what I might do with the time, a group of my friends announced that they were going to play golf. "But what about me", I cried, "I can't play golf!" Very well, they said, we shall teach you. The outcome was that I went round in 282 strokes, and ruined a pair of brand-new suede shoes. And I vowed never again to touch a golf-club, be it a driver, a putter, a five-iron, a niblick, a mashie or (I think someone was pulling my leg with this one) a sand-blaster.

Which, of course, brings me to the sad tale of Mr John Buckingham, and I might as well kick off with my now world-famous apophthegm: "You've never seen a thin lawyer or a fat litigant."

To start with, *how* can anybody cheat at golf? Surely nobody has invented a golf-ball in which is embedded a miniature engine, guaranteed to send the ball flying for miles before it slows down and floats on to the greensward? On the other hand, why would anybody want to cheat? If the ball comes to rest just *here*, what would be the difference if instead it had come to rest just *there*? There are, of course, mysteries that I cannot plumb – there is something called "the rough", and something else called "two over par", and a man called a "caddie" (which I always thought was a thing you keep the tea leaves in), but to lay out no less than a quarter of a million oncers to establish what was what and who was who, which was what Mr Buckingham did, is surely coming it a bit too strong.

For that matter, why aren't the holes made bigger? Quite apart from helping short-sighted players, they could make them the size of an upturned dustbin-lid, which would diminish the shocking displays of anger, together with the charges of cheating, and the contestants would get round much more quickly, thus giving them more time to get happily sloshed at what I am told is "the 19th hole".

But it is when I see a headline reading "When golf becomes a matter of honour". I begin to twitch in a rather unpleasant manner, realising as I do that the matter of honour usually concerns nothing more than a bunch of idiots getting themselves at best stinking colds, and at worst severe rheumatism, by wading into wet grass two feet high, solely to go wandering about with no better purpose than to whack a ridiculous white ball with an equally ridiculous bent stick.

I ask the world again, for the thousandth time, knowing that I shall never get an answer: *why* don't we all get together, agree that what we are quarrelling about is not worth the effort, and *starve all the lawyers to death*? Here, for instance, is poor Mr Buckingham (well, actually rich Mr Buckingham), jabbering about honour on the golf course, when the lawyers – who, I assure you, are just as amazed at the suckers – have mopped up the money.

Honour? In whacking a little white ball about? Falstaff had the right idea about *that*, and it is a shame that Mr Buckingham is not as well acquainted with the Bard as he might be. If he was (or if he was familiar with Verdi, who set the passage wonderfully) he would say:

"Well 'tis no matter: honour pricks me on. Yea, but how if honour prick me off when I come on? how then? Can honour set to a leg? no: or an arm? no: or take away the grief of a wound? no. Honour hath no skill in surgery, then? no. What is honour? a word. What is that word, honour? air. A trim reckoning! – Who hath it? he that died o'Wednesday. Doth he feel it? no. Doth he hear it? no. It is insensible, then? yea, to the dead. But will it not live with the living? no. Why? detraction will not suffer it: – therefore. I'll none of it: honour is a mere scutcheon: – and so ends my catechism."

But apart from starving the lawyers, they are surely in some measure to blame here, unless Mr Buckingham is so monumentally stubborn that he had rejected the obvious advice the very distinguished (not to say expensive) lawyers must have given him. Mind you, the lawyers don't really need to talk like that – "like that" being what Mr Milmo, for the plaintiff, came out with, viz; "If your evidence is correct this was just about the most blatant piece of cheating in golf that has ever happened", nor does Mr Hartley, who was for both Mr Rusk and Mr Dove, need to say that "Goldfinger was one of the richest men in the world, and it does not matter how much money you have if you are cheating at golf. For some people it is the winning above anything else." No doubt the bystanders could not join in at that point, but at least the judge could have thrown a jug of water over both of them.

I find it difficult to imagine any circumstances which might lead *me* to sue anybody for libel, or indeed for anything. True, I have an opportunity in my column to give as good as I get and, I flatter myself, a good deal more. But it is the sheer absurdity of libel actions above the level of a butcher who is said to sell poisoned meat that first gives me giggles and then causes me to throw up. This ridiculous case should never have come to court for a number of reasons, but one of these stands out, and it is the one that stands out in every libel case.

Today most libel cases are for nothing but gain; so crazy have juries become that libel has turned into an open-cast gold-mine. But, as I said, there are a few genuine cases, people who go to law not to scoop the jackpot but for honourable though misguided reasons, and Mr Buckingham's seems to be one of them. He sued, not for money but for his reputation, but what he did not know, and what all those innocents who want to prove their innocence do not know, *is that those who sue for honour, find their honour run through the mire.*

It should not be so. But it is. In a year or two, possibly much less, anyone who remembers the Buckingham libel action will be immovably certain that there was a Mr Buckingham who cheated at golf and for good measure robbed the blind man on the corner of his matches. Mr Buckingham has done neither, and would not do either, but the crooked tongue of distance shouts louder than the whispers of the sweetness of the truth. For those who treasure their unstained escutcheon, the first rule of going to law must be: don't.

The Times, 29 April 1994

Heads in the sand

FROM TIME TO time, I feel compelled to remind you that I do not make the news, nor even report it; I comment on it. The result, unfortunately, is that it gives too many opportunities for disbelief, and however many times I remind you that there is nothing in this world so strange as to be truly unbelievable, the cries of "Come off it" resound right through breakfast. But, after all, when a story is published in both the *Daily Telegraph* and the *Sun*, who am I to cast sidelong glances and wink? Here goes.

The story, which took place in South Africa, in the small town of Harrismith, Orange Free State, concerns a lady of 45 years, a Mrs Annalie Pieterse; she weighs only eight stone, and I would be obliged if you would kindly keep that figure in mind during what follows, for − as you shall learn − it is vital to the unfolding scene. Mrs Pieterse is a marathon runner (well, I suppose marathon running is better than jogging, though not all that much), and she was out for a training spin, happily lolloping along the trail, and no doubt dreaming of the day when she breasts the tape at Atlanta to take the gold medal, when, all of a sudden, an ostrich strolled into view.

Now despite the attempts of the experts to explain that ostriches are real birds (albeit flightless), practically everybody is convinced that they are not to be found in the South African bush, but in newspaper and magazine cartoons, invariably standing in rows with their heads stuck in the ground. Nevertheless, the lady refused to believe that the beast would soon come up with a caption, and was right in her supposition, because the first thing the ostrich did when he caught sight of her was to give her an almighty kick, which knocked her flat. (I should say here, heedless of the last shreds of my credibility, that the correct zoological name of the ostrich is *Struthio camelus*, presumably because the first man who ever set eyes on one exclaimed "Struth, it's a camel!")

As any ornithological expert will tell you, if you have the misfortune to be kicked to the ground by an indignant ostrich, the second best thing you can do (the best is to be somewhere else, preferably a long way away) is to lie still. Lying still, and trying to make no sound, is probably the manoeuvre best designed to persuade the bird either to stick its head in the ground or go away. But in any case, the victim was most unlikely to be in any condition to exchange pleasantries, having been half stunned by the thing's first blow.

In fact, she was unlikely to be in any condition to do anything, not least because all her attempts to persuade the creature that she was dead (her first ruse) had been received with considerable suspicion. As you may imagine, the winged terror's incredulity did little or nothing to improve the situation, but for some time it happily contented itself with marching round and round our fallen heroine like Achilles dragging the corpse of Hector round the walls of Troy. After some time, however, our spirited eight-stoner became sufficiently cross (and, no doubt, sufficiently unconcussed) to get up. This rash decision, no doubt based on the reasonable belief that she could not stay indefinitely where she was, turned out to be a serious mistake, because the bird kicked her to the ground again, this time breaking several of her ribs, puncturing one of her lungs, and causing her to suffer a variety of cuts and bruises.

Two throws: whether ostrich-wrestling follows the more familiar method I do not know, and I suppose that she didn't either, but the gallant lass, perhaps determined to get the Lonsdale Belt as well as the gold medal for marathon running, spat on her hands and essayed the third bout. No go; the thing, tiring of kicking her, tried stamping on her, with considerable success. (Yes, I know it's only a bird, but going tweeter-tweeter-tweeter and holding out a palm full of nuts to a bird that can – and frequently does – grow to a weight of 300lb will not advance matters very far.)

By now you might think that the lady would be ready to call it a day. Not so. Indeed she was only getting into her stride, and if the maddened bird thought it could now devour her at leisure, he had a nasty shock coming, and about time. Those years of aerobics were not wasted, for – in her own words – she took the war to the enemy, saying "I rolled on my back and kicked him three times in the chest *before getting up and grabbing him by the neck*." (If any ostriches are reading this, I beg them to adopt a low profile; I have no animus against them, but it would be straining belief to suggest that the lady would, if she survived the experience, still go on leaving a nightly saucer of milk outside the back door for any stray ostriches.)

By now, I am sure, you have ceased to believe a word of all this; a story about eight stone of woman against 300lb of ostrich would be greeted with scepticism even if it were told by an archbishop: yet I do but speak the facts as revealed. The trouble is that you have noticed that ostriches in Disney and similar films, in cartoons by the thousand, in comic-books and in children's television, always have knots in their necks, and by now you are firm in the belief that real ostriches also have the telltale sign. To be jeered at when telling nothing but the truth is painful, but even more distressing is that in this case the scoffers plainly prefer the absurd fiction to the bald reality.

But, believe it or not (and I have no illusions as to which you have chosen), I have to go even further in this story, every step of it perfectly true, yet every step of it inevitably rejected with sneers of disbelief and even clods of earth, half-bricks and dead cats. For the eight-stone marvel with broken bones and a punctured lung got to her feet and essayed, with astounding courage and fortitude, to grab the ostrich, and this time *she got hold of the thing and tied the knot*.

Well, not literally, of course. Hear the lady herself, and shame on you for doubting her: "I kinked his neck, gave it a few twists and, to my surprise, he dropped dead." Well, I should damned well think so; if you and I had our necks kinked and then given a few twists, dead is the thing we would be likely to drop. But a word of warning, please, to our new Florence Nightingale, the lady with the iron hands; it is unlikely that the Animal Liberation Front would approve of a woman who, if she doesn't go as far as eating an ostrich for breakfast, certainly strangles them at teatime, so there is danger there. But don't, any of you, try to emulate her feat of valour; much better stay at home, watch children's television, and when the ostriches come galumphing on, with the standard knot in their necks, listen to them ticking. Yes, ticking, because just as everybody believes that ostriches have knots in their necks, so everybody is certain that ostriches tick, because they are forever swallowing clocks.

Staggering home, our bravest of the brave must have been – for all the damage she had sustained – greatly pleased with herself; she was certainly entitled to be. But from headquarters, that is to say the ostrich experts, came a sombre warning, though it is not entirely clear whether the warning was directed to the lady or the ostrich, for the word was that "The toenail of an ostrich slices like a blade: it can kill a human being".

An ordinary human being, possibly, but not Mrs Pieterse, our ostrich-conqueror. There is, or was, a man who made a living on the music-hall stage by *eating* razor-blades – real ones, too – it was no fake. But *our* girl eats ostrich toenails, and what is more, she eats the ostriches, too.

Cherchez les femmes, at any rate if you want ostriches beaten up. It is believed by the experts that the beast's original hostility sprang from its protective role – it had a pregnant ostrichess to look after. Perhaps: but if so, there is an unconsolable ostrich-widow somewhere in the vicinity. Somehow, I do not think that our heroine will undertake the role of midwife.

Before we part today, can anybody say why ostriches cannot fly? If you ask the experts, you will be told that in the course of evolution, their power of flight atrophied and disappeared. Yes, but why did that happen? After all, pigeons didn't find their powers of flight waning, and a considerable nuisance they have always been. Perhaps, over the centuries, there were not only ostriches, but a breed of Mrs Pieterses, too.

The Times, 6 April 1993

A giant goes home

WE HAVE IT on Shakespeare's authority, no less, that the whirligig of time brings in his revenges. But can there ever have been any revenge so sweet, or any revolution of the clocks so meaningful, as the news that Alexander Solzhenitsyn is shortly to return to his homeland, Russia, after almost exactly 20 years of forced exile? And what a homeland!

> I met a traveller from an antique land
> Who said: Two vast and trunkless legs of stone
> Stand in the desert. Near them, on the sand . . .

The day he was expelled from the then Soviet Union was one I still remember vividly; it was in 1974, and Brezhnev, coward to the end, dared not have him killed, so great was his international stature by then. But nor could the giant be put back into prison or concentration-camp, if only because he would find a way of getting his words out; by then, the expansion of *samizdat* had gone so far that anything heard on the vast complex of grapevines with which the country was bestrewn would be common knowledge before sundown. And above all, Solzhenitsyn could not be allowed to live his own life in his own way, because most of that life and way would be a series of demands for freedom for his country, varied by denunciations of the regime and its actions. Nor was that an empty threat; the man who wrote *The Gulag Archipelago* and circulated it, *sub rosa*, in his own country, making sure that it would also reach freedom, was not a man to be intimidated by a crew of thugs, none of whom dared to let any of the others out of sight, so trustful of each other were they.

Half sunk, a shattered visage lies, whose frown . . .

So what did Brezhnev do? He sent a posse of his KGB to Solzhenitsyn's home; they flung him into a van, drove him to Moscow airport and bundled him into the next plane that was going anywhere outside Brezhnev's empire. The plane was going to West Germany, and a few hours later (if Brezhnev didn't have the spunk to kill him on Soviet soil, he certainly lacked the bottle for having the plane shot down) Alexander Solzhenitsyn was in exile.

And wrinkled lip, and sneer of cold command,
Tell that its sculptor well those passions read . . .

The Germans came up trumps, treating their unexpected visitor like the hero he was; so did the French, more surprisingly and thus more commendably (Sartre was still – not that he ever stopped – eager to lick any boot worn by any Soviet criminal); so, from afar, were the Americans. Only our country was shamed; the ranks of fellow-travellers, not least in Parliament, took to sneering at the giant, and the BBC shamed itself as well as Britain. When Solzhenitsyn was interviewed on *Panorama*, the conditions of secrecy surrounding the broadcast meant that only a small number of people saw it; there was no trailer. But, almost unbelievably, there was a strong faction in the BBC arguing against a repeat, lest more people should see and hear the terrible truth. (The faction did not prevail, and the repeat was seen.)

Whatever the in-fighting in the BBC, the people – the ordinary people, who know the difference between right and wrong, and prefer right – made clear that the giant's message was understood. Unvarnished, it said that we, the West, were responsible for the evil in the Soviet Union, because we had never had the courage or indeed the wish to face the enemy eye to eye.

The ordinary people showed their betters an example; a substantial quantity of the text of the broadcast was published in the *Listener*, and for the first and last time in its history that magazine had to be reprinted, so great was the demand for the giant's words. And those searing words of truth challenged the lies from which he had been forcibly ejected; we can be certain that he knew, from brave men and women who risked everything to keep him informed, that his message had been delivered to the country that dared not hold him.

Which yet survive, stamped on these lifeless things.
The hand that mocked them, and the heart that fed . . .

Alexander Solzhenitsyn had three burning and unswerving ambitions. They were, first, to see the Soviet Union crumble into grimy dust; second, to finish the mighty epic story of its rise and fall, chronicled in the series of novels on which he has been employed for more than a quarter of a century; third, to go back to the land of his birth, now cleansed of the detritus of communism, and live there for the rest of his life, with his wonderful consort, Natalya.

So he swore three oaths; they corresponded to his three ambitions, and all three oaths said the same thing: I shall not die until I have accomplished what I set out to do.

Nor will he. He will find, when he lands at Moscow, that he has come home to a bleak and barren world, a world of strife – even murderous strife – and poverty, a land where bickering too often takes the place of advancement. Will he be disheartened? Come: this man lay six years in Stalin's Archipelago and survived, survived not by stealing his comrades' rations (and they were pitiful enough), nor by stoolpigeoning for the guards, but by the fire in his breast, which no one and nothing could put out until those three ambitions were satisfied.

And on the pedestal these words appear:
"My name is Ozymandias, king of kings:
Look on my works, ye Mighty, and despair!"

Where did he get that faith, that unlimited faith that his vows would not be broken? It was easy for me to predict the fall of the Soviet Union, for I wasn't living in it; imagine not just living in it, but living in it year after year, decade after decade, generation after generation, with nothing to conjure hope, no glimpse of melioration, never a moment not filled with lies. And that of course was merely for those who suffered in silence, who did nothing and had nothing done to them. But think of the millions slaughtered in Stalin's frenzied genocide, think of a world where an official would find on his desk a memorandum ordering him to round up the population of half a dozen villages with, say, a few thousand people in each, and ship them immediately eastwards, never to return.

But of course it was much worse than that. From outside they came, the dupes and liars, the fools and rogues, the simpletons and the wicked; often the two ranks were indistinguishable one from the other, nor did it much matter where the Soviet slaves were concerned, for I suppose it hurts no more or less if someone is telling lies or being lied to. But imagine liar and lied-to, hand in hand, peering into the cage, while a thousand devils laugh uproariously, and more than a thousand go home and tell their neighbours what an exciting and happy country the Soviet Union is.

One down, two to go, but it cannot be long now until the other two account books are for ever shut. The Soviet Union is no more; Solzhenitsyn is still at work on his gigantic *roman-fleuve*, and now he has promised to return to the earth that bore him. He had already stipulated that all the false charges brought against him before corrupt witnesses, and even more corrupt judges, must be formally overturned. They were, in 1991, *Nihil obstat*.

> *Nothing beside remains. Round the decay*
> *Of that colossal wreck, boundless and bare . . .*

And yet perhaps the people of his country need him even more than they think, perhaps more than he thinks himself; perhaps there is another duty waiting for him for when he disembarks from the plane, and this one the greatest yet. It would be reasonable to make him a noble figurehead – a president, say, or a roving speaker of all the parliaments, or a mighty, nation-wide ombudsman. These things would befit his dignity and his faith, but there is a more urgent task for him. The constituent parts of what had been the Soviet Union fell, one by one, off the dying body of that most wicked rule. Could it not be Solzhenitsyn's last great blessing on his country – that country he loved in the Gulag and in exile – to mend the broken borders, to unite the chafing and warring groups, to bring the single nationalisms into one, yet keeping the distinction of each? Then, his three ambitions fulfilled, he might contemplate the past as well as the future, that past drenched in evil, and wonder how human beings could do such things to other human beings.

> *. . . The lone and level sands stretch far away.*

The Times, 4 June 1993

The jeans of China

How many of you know that my middle name is Autolycus? I have just snapped up a couple of ill-considered trifles. They are both what in newspaper parlance we call "Nibs", which is an acronym for "news in brief", and brief these certainly are. Here is the first:

> Supplies of condoms to Egypt have been cut off by the United States after reports that millions were resold as balloons.

And here is the other:

> Chinese officials have seized 170,000 pairs of fake Levi jeans in a crackdown on counterfeiters.

Let us consider each of these items calmly. First, the condoms. We must all begin by admitting that we did not know that the United States had been sending millions of condoms to Egypt – so many, indeed, that there were millions left over to use as playthings. But it is not clear *why* the United States has been showering Egypt with condoms.

Perhaps the manufacture of full-strength condoms is but in its infancy in Egypt, so that the more advanced United States has taken pity on the backwardness of the recipient. But there is another puzzle. The statement said that the condoms were "resold" as balloons. But surely the American generosity does not consist of giving with one hand

and taking back with the other; did they really *sell* them to the Third World? That would only deepen the mystery, for if the Egyptians bought the condoms, they could thereafter do whatever they liked with them.

There are no clues as to who was selling the balloons, much less who was buying them. It is all very well to say that balloons are popular, harmless and beloved of children and of the children in all of us, but we are dealing here with *millions*; has the entire population of Egypt gone plain barmy about balloons, now spending all its time blowing them up, knotting the necks, and throwing them into the sky for the passing currents to take them whither they may? If so, it is no surprise to learn that Egypt is not only unable to make or even buy its own condoms, but inexcusably frivolous as well.

Let us leave this conundrum for a moment, and go on to an item that may well prove even more odd than the Great Condom Mystery. It is the news from China not only that the authorities have seized 170,000 pairs of fake Levi jeans, but that they have done so as a warning to counterfeiters.

First of all, what *is* a fake pair of Levi jeans? As I understand these matters, jeans are the simplest and most egalitarian items of clothing. Why would somebody counterfeit them? More extraordinarily still, *how* would they counterfeit them? What, indeed, can counterfeit *mean* in this context? Apart from anything else, if somebody is counterfeiting them how is it possible for anyone to know which is the genuine article and which the copy. Don't say "the label", for heaven's sake; if someone can counterfeit a couple of yards of cheap cloth, he can surely have thought one step further and counterfeited the bit which says "Accept no imitation". But then it gets like a hall of mirrors; which is the real thing and which the fake, and which faked label is being put on which real (or imitation) pair of jeans?

But that is only scratching at the surface of the enigma; if there are such things as counterfeit Levi jeans, and the

Chinese authorities go so far as to worry about this trade, what did the counterfeiters think they were doing with no fewer than 170,000 pairs?

I do not wear jeans; but inquisitive I am. When I heard about this, I took from my wardrobe a pair of linen trousers which I guessed must weigh roughly the same as a pair of jeans, and weighed them. Then I multiplied the result by 170,000. The answer was more than 75 tons, and as for the volume, it was stupendous. Where did they keep such quantities, and how did they think they could conceal their fakes?

Then again, assuming the storage problem could be solved, what about the retail side of the business? I have never been to China, but I have seen many photographs and television programmes featuring Chinese people, and the standard dress from the waist down does indeed seem to be something like a pair of jeans. Now I cannot believe that a pair of regular jeans, honestly come by, would cost more than a tiny sum. But if I cannot believe that, I have a very much greater leap in incredulity to take, because if the ordinary Chinese cheap jeans in the stores are available, and someone thinks it would pay him to make 170,000 pairs of fake Levi jeans, the only possible conclusion is that your average Chinese peasant is so fashion-conscious that he or she ignores the state-run emporiums and flocks to the under-the-counter contraband, there to buy a fake pair of real Levis with which to go one up on the neighbours.

Let us go back to the balloons, *nés* condoms, for a moment. It occurs to me that if a pair of cheap Chinese jeans would cost no more than a trifle, then *a fortiori* a balloon, whether a real one or a condom makeshift, could only have on it a price-tag so modest that it would hardly be worth the retailer's trouble to stock it. Now if the mystery of the jeans comes down to the wearers insisting that they must be absolutely *à la mode*, can it be that there is status to be got in Egypt with a condom for a balloon instead of the more traditional toy? If so, we shall all be obliged to revise our impressions of the Third World pretty sharpish, lest we shall be travelling in, say, Africa, and stop to inspect a grass hut, only to be told by the proud owner that the grass came from the cuttings of Wimbledon at championship time.

Is there any way the condom-sellers can get together with the jeans-fakers, with mutual profit to them both? For instance, it is well known that the Chinese are keen on kites, and adept at flying them; could some sweet-talking Egyptian salesman convince them that condom-balloons are even more fun? Or look at it the other way: if we can tempt the Chinese authorities to turn a blind eye to the jeans-faking ("mind you, I've said nothing"), and content themselves with, say, a 15 per cent rake-off, Levis indistinguishable from the real thing could be the newest Egyptian fashion sensation, which would obviously be good for trade between China and Egypt. As for the Americans, who started this, they need not fear an unsaleable quantity of condoms; all they need to do is to rain them down on Colonel Gadaffi.

The Times, 20 February 1992

The feel-good factor

I HAD NOT BEEN in Berlin for many years, and the shock was considerable. The greatest cities always get worse, though I don't know why; in particular their great boulevards are steadily ruined – not by traffic or shoppers but governments. Can you remember the beauty and elegance of the Champs Elysées before it became a hideous refuse dump? I can; and I can also remember the Kalversstraat in Amsterdam, where today a jostled walk down it would cause you to shudder, even before the drugpeddlers began to tug at your sleeves; and nearer home, what about the vile thing that is Oxford Street?

So I steeled myself to revisit the Ku'dam, and needed all the steeling I could find. Berlin, though, has a better excuse than most. The fall of the Wall was one of the greatest moments in all history, but it has brought dreadful problems with the rejoicing. I was staying in the *ehemalige* East Berlin, which seems to have spread its sullen misery over the West, though surely it ought to be the other way round. Roadworks are everywhere, but the streets of the East still bear the names of the great swines of communism; imagine having to admit that you live in the Grotewohlstrasse – even Marx-Engels Platz would be preferable. Along the Unter den Linden the women of the Yugoslav refugees sit begging, while their menfolk have revived – of all things – the three-card trick.

And what was I doing in Berlin? Well, first, I wanted to walk freely through the Brandenburger Tor, which on my last visit had been made impossible by the edicts of wickedness. But my main purpose was to take part in a conference titled "A Last Encounter with the Cold War". And those in the conference, assembled in the Palais am Festungsgraben (made much more delicious for the knowledge that it used to house the Soviet Friendship Society), were the motley army which, without a shot fired, fought for the truth against lies, for reality against mirages, for steadfastness against capitulation, for civilisation against barbarism, for the peaceful word against the brutal blow, for applauding courage against excusing cowardice, for – put most simply – democracy against tyranny. And we were right: entirely, completely, provably, joyfully, patiently and truthfully right. One of the leading figures in the army of the truth was Norman Podhoretz, who summed it up:

"We said – and never stopped saying – that communism was . . . no less evil than Nazism. We said – and never stopped saying – that communism had brought nothing but murder, political oppression, cultural starvation, and economic misery to the countries forced to suffer under its rule. We said – and never stopped saying – that no people had ever freely decided to live under communism, or ever would if given a choice. On all these points . . . we were not only opposed but were sneered at, ridiculed and defamed . . . "

And now we could rejoice, however many fearsome problems and horrors have come to the surface from the collapse of communism. Our ranks, alas, had been thinned by death; men like Sidney Hook, Tibor Szamuely, Arthur Koestler, Charles Douglas-Home, Raymond Aron are no more. But as I looked around the conference chamber, I saw a host of those who fought the good fight.

The heavy artillery came from Robert Conquest; his massively authoritative book *The Great Terror* documented Stalin's maniac slaughter. The infinitely staunch Leo Labedz, with his meticulously accurate magazine *Survey*, poured more fire on the enemy. From the Antipodes (the

Australians were particularly staunch) came Peter Coleman
with the splendid magazine, *Quadrant*, a rallying-place for
the truth. From the United States, where – more than
anywhere else – cowardice, mendacity and dishonesty
joined hands to do down the truth, came Irving Kristol,
Gertrude Himmelfarb, Richard Pipes, Edward Shils; from
Hell came Vladimir Bukovsky; and it was particularly
moving to see the frail form of François Bondy, helped on
to the platform, his fire still burning bright. And we must
never forget the men and women of Radio Liberty and
Radio Free Europe.

And over the revels, there presided Melvyn Lasky his
beard sharp enough to stab any fellow-traveller, his mighty
archives shelved in his head, and the reason we were all
there.

Mel was for almost all its life the editor of *Encounter*, the
proverbial tiny candle that no amount of darkness could
put out. It is often regarded as a wholly political, even
polemical, organ, but that is an illusion; culture in its
widest definition described *Encounter*, and particularly the
culture that our enemies would destroy. Among the graver
questions of the hour he published short stories, poems,
the battles of historians, a vast range of literary discoveries;
among his many "firsts" were the first full texts of the
broadcasts which P.G. Wodehouse gave in Nazi Germany,
and from which Wodehouse got dreadful and long-lasting
opprobrium, though they were as innocent as he was.

Mel was emphatically one of those who fought the good
fight, and though he is 72 there is no sign of flagging in
him; the way he handled the contributors to the sym-
posium was masterly, not least because the enormously
wide spectrum of participants was even wide enough to
encompass a figure who had been one of the oppressors in
East Germany. I was invited, I suppose, as a representative
of the Cold War PBI. Among the brass, I was a mere
footslogger, but I had had the good fortune to serve under
editors wise enough to let me have my head, and over the

years I must have written not scores but hundreds of articles upholding the democratic values in the faces of those who would replace them with totalitarian evil.

Let me go back to Norman Podhoretz's summary of *our* rightness and *their* wrongness: "We were told that it was nothing short of blasphemous to see communism and Nazism as . . . morally equivalent. We were told that in some respects (economic security, health care, etc) conditions under communism were better than life under our own rotten system. And we were told that the communist regimes did indeed have the support of their peoples. *It is important to stress that we were told these things not only by the communists themselves but by good liberals and social democrats* . . ." The italics are mine. And it is that particular battle that I have been engaged in for what must now be nearly 40 years. Can it be true that orders for my demob have been issued, that even Mel Lasky can call it a day? Well, communism has not only been overthrown, but its unmitigated emptiness has been demonstrated beyond argument. But even as I bend down to take off my boots, the bugle sounds. I had forgotten China; at this very moment a huge throng of commentators on these matters are preparing to argue that although *Soviet* communism is indeed disgraced, *Chinese* communism is different – permitting free speech, giving its people a high standard of living, and without the cult of personality. Fall in; you too, Mel.

The Times, 15 October 1992

The jewel in the crown

ANYONE WHO KNOWS me even slightly, and indeed anyone who reads my books and articles will know the depth and breadth of love that I have for India. I fell under its spell, that maddening but wonderful country, many years ago, but I have never wavered in my feelings towards it and its people, and I have been blessed in the making of Indian friends.

Very early on in my Indian days, I was in Hyderabad, and I was going on to Bombay, where a dinner for me had been arranged. My ticket was plainly stamped OK, but in those days I had not fully taken the measure of Indian Airlines and its schedules, and when I was told that my ticket was not valid for the flight, I behaved as I would in Western Europe – that is, I made a gigantic scene. One of the villains came out from behind the check-in desk: I was ready to murder him, when he said, in the most soothing tones, "Come, come, sit down over there, and I will bring you a cup of tea".

As I opened my mouth to scream imprecations, something happened in me; I realised that I was in India, not England, and that India was not at all like England, and above all that my friends in Bombay would not mind if I were late, not least because even then I had discovered that in India everything is always late. I took the tea, but that was not the end of it; a vast, warm feeling swept over me, engulfing me in the love that India exudes, and from that day on, I was India's. Indeed, whenever I am going to the Near or Far East, I make sure that I drop down for at least

two or three days in India. And if the break is even a few
more days longer, I have one visit that I never miss, one
that I would never let myself miss, one friend I must see,
one friend I must salute, one friend I must bow to. It is at
Agra, and it is called the Taj Mahal.

Let me remember for a little while, until I come to the
point of the remembering. This was my first visit, and this
is what I wrote:

The Taj Mahal has a great deal to live up to. So much,
indeed, that there can be few thoughtful visitors today
who, knowing something of its reputation, do not fear
the betrayal of expectation. How can *anything* justify the
rhapsodies, the descriptions, the history, the legends, the
very photographs?

I confirm that it was in such a spirit, almost with
fingers crossed behind my back, that I paid my two
rupees, passed through the outer arch, and approached
the inner, which serves, when you have advanced to the
right point, as a frame for the picture before you.

Fear nothing; the sight that there swims into view
surpasses everything you have heard or seen or read or
imagined, and almost the only intense emotion you will
not experience as the frame fills is disappointment.

They told me that the Taj Mahal is beautiful, and they
were right. They also told me that it is white, though
there they were wrong, for white is almost the only
colour it is not, except for a few minutes immediately
after the sun goes down; at that point all the delicate
blues and greys and yellows and pinks are drawn from it
and leave it like a ghost, until it takes on its evening life
and becomes as rich as the moon.

I have quoted at length for a purpose, and I have mentioned the vast palette that the Taj displays for its visitors
to reinforce the purpose. Because I learn that the Taj
Mahal, that monument to perfect love and perfect beauty,

is dying, and in not many years it will be dead, so that where it now stands there will be nothing but rubble, and dirty rubble at that. Unless, that is, the Indian Government soon – very soon indeed – stems the rot. (As I write, there is no sign that the Indian Government is doing anything at all about it.)

I can say, I suppose, that I have seen that glory many, many times, and to the rest of you, I can say "too bad", but such selfishness would be almost criminal.

What, then, can be done, and what is the problem that bids fair (foul, actually) to destroy the Taj? It is the pollution in the filthy air of Agra, made filthier by the factories and an oil refinery, and multiplied by the acid rain that fills the atmosphere. (A single figure will give you an idea of the problem: the refinery alone pours a thousand kilos of sulphur dioxide into the air *every hour*.)

Well, says the well-fed occidental, there's no problem there: all you need is to close the factories, shut off the refinery, and clear up. What's the problem? It is that if anything like that was done, something like a hundred thousand men and women would be thrown on to the streets, and anybody who has seen an Indian street will know that it is not the most comfortable place to lay one's head. Leaving the employment question for a moment, I must bring good tidings: very many factories in the vicinity *have* been shut down by order. Well, says the occidental, that's a good start isn't it? No, it isn't, because for every factory that is shut down by the courts, one or more illicit "ghost" factories spring up.

And now for the worst. The worst is that in and around Agra and its immortal treasure (soon to be very mortal indeed, if nothing is done about it) most of the people who live there manifestly do not care if the Taj Mahal lives or dies. How did the jingle go? "If every man sweeps before his home, the village will be clean." Alas, it is not thus in Agra.

*

There are exceptions. Once, many years ago, I was wandering about the Taj, when a bearded Methuselah beckoned me to sit beside him and learn about the treasure. He told me that he came always once a week – the day on which there is no entry fee (two rupees!) – and in the few hours we talked, he taught me more about the Taj than all the guidebooks together.

But he taught me more from the storehouse of his age; he talked of serenity, he spoke of life and death as two friends, he demonstrated how he had learnt not to care about poverty. He must be long dead, my sage at Agra. But I am glad that he did not live to see the death of that precious jewel, and mourn.

Or perhaps his serenity would stretch far enough to encompass the terrible irony of the crumbling Taj. All that lives must die; nowhere is it written that that truth does not include stone and jewels. For assuredly it includes love.

Meanwhile, the Taj is rotting, and perhaps long in the future, when that wonder has gone to dust and the dust blown away on the wind, the guidebooks will record nothing but that Jim Callaghan said that sitting on the steps got his bottom cold.

There are, of course, many wonderful sights in India; anyone who has wandered about the stones of Fatehpur Sikri is unlikely to forget the experience. But the Taj Mahal is truly unique, and it therefore behoves us to save it. I say us, but by that I mean the whole world.

Already, the crumbling goes on ever faster, and the wholly untrained workmen who are trying to clean it are making it dreadfully worse. And – it had to happen – souvenir hunters are now breaking bits off.

Yes, it is the whole world's misfortune, and it is therefore the whole world's duty to put it right. But India cannot hide behind the money and experts that will come to Agra; hide, that is, India's shame. For this catastrophe was not like an earthquake or a terrible explosion; it was caused by Indians, by Indians who were too lazy, too indifferent, too wasteful, too ignorant, to look after a precious – unimaginably precious – treasure, that was given to India some 350 years ago.

And the rest of the world cannot leave the Taj to its fate, but must rally to its misfortune, because although India does not deserve the Taj, the world still does, and cannot do without it. Let us hope that we are not too late; very soon, the experts must gather and measure the shape and size of the misfortune, then get to work on it. And if it is saved, there should be these words carved on a stone plaque just outside the Taj: "India would have let it die: the rest of the world saved it."

The Times, 20 December 1994

How his genius struck me

JOHN OSBORNE NEVER hit me, though he threatened to do so frequently. He threatened all theatre critics (I was one when he was in his heyday), all managers, all agents, all theatre owners, all directors, all journalists, almost all of his wives, all teetotallers and for good measure all Irishmen. But as far as I know he didn't actually hit anybody, and the closest he got to doing so was giving instructions to people in the news who were being plagued and chased by gossip-columnists: "If physically possible," Osborne said, "push them out of the way."

But, oh, he could hate. And *how* he could hate. Perhaps the hate was to drain off a rage that otherwise would boil over and issue in bodily violence; perhaps, but I have never known anyone (with the single exception of Lee Kuan Yew) so devoted to keeping the hates alive.

Why? The answer cannot be that his later plays were failures, so that he became embittered; he was already hating vigorously (at 26!) when his first play, *Look Back in Anger*, was staged at the Royal Court and applauded to the heavens by Kenneth Tynan. But he was hating long before he put pen to theatrical paper, for he hated – the word must be used, because he used it – his mother, nor did he wait until she died to proclaim his hatred; indeed, his first volume of autobiography was studded with opportunities for cursing his mother, all of which opportunities he gladly took.

I dwell on the mother-hatred not only because he does, but because many people have hated their mothers, for good or bad reasons, but very few have proclaimed the hatred while the object of it was still alive. Nor, of course, was he shy of denouncing his four discarded wives (the fifth marriage endured to the end); one of the nicest things he said – publicly – of Jill Bennett was that "she was the most evil woman I have ever come across – she was a bitch", and he said it immediately after she had committed suicide. And then, in an interview with Lynn Barber, he was asked why he had a reputation for being nasty:

I don't understand it at all, I really don't. I suppose it's because of the style in which I write. Everyone expects me to be . . . I certainly don't *try* to be unpleasant.

The almost incredible thing about that remark is that it is quite plainly true: he pisses in his once-beloved's grave, and he is really astonished when people find him unpleasant. This, surely, makes John Osborne a very singular person, does it not? We must dig more deeply.

He says, at the end of his autobiography, that his life had been ruled by passion; yes, but there are very many kinds of passion. Here is one: you have 33 guesses for the reason he takes off his signet ring when he meets the mother of his only child – Nolan, by Penelope Gilliatt. Give up? It is that he used to make a point of removing his signet ring whenever Gilliatt was around, for fear he might hit her and disfigure her for life. And, in his own words, "I never did hit her, and thank God I never did, but I came very close to it once or twice."

Look Back in Anger: Osborne looked back, forward and sideways in anger, but it is possible – indeed, almost certain – that the anger fuelled the genius and that without it we should never have had the body of work.

I used the word "genius"; should I have done so? Well, there is a test, and an uncannily apposite one, which may settle the question. No one, I think, would deny the substantial quality of our most regular, interesting and memorable contemporary playwright, David Hare. I now never leave the theatre after one of his plays without taking time to digest what I have heard; I take my time because I know that there are rewards for doing so, as Mr Hare digs more deeply into his theme. And yet, and yet: put Hare beside Osborne – is not something vital missing? And that something is the burning bush that Osborne swallowed many years ago, and which tore his guts until the end, pouring out poisonous venom and at the same time pouring out plays that will be staged for very many decades to come.

It was a pity that *Look Back in Anger* was his first play; it tagged him as a "kitchen sink" playwright. (I still remember the poor devil on the *Daily Mail*, where I was then working, who was sent out to find more disgusting plays to denounce as fit for nothing but Sodom and Gomorrah; he was a man who never went to the theatre, but who found *Look Back in Anger* rather interesting; nevertheless he managed to rustle up the required *Daily Mail* denunciation.) But it took years to teach the theatregoing public (to say nothing of the *Daily Mail*) that a new and immensely gifted star had risen over the British theatre.

Just turn to *Who's Who*; if run in place of this column, his credits would occupy fully a third of the space, from *A Cuckoo in the Nest* (in which he acted), to *God Rot Tunbridge Wells!* (which he wrote and meant). But never mind the price, feel the quality. It must have put him in a rage when he had finished *Luther* and staged it to have featherbrains saying "that's the *Look Back in Anger* man", but his retort was always there in his catalogue. The pages flutter: *The Entertainer, Luther, Under Plain Cover, Inadmissible Evidence* (for me, his masterpiece), *A Patriot for Me, West of Suez, Hotel in Amsterdam, The End of Me Old Cigar* and *Watch It Come Down*.

What went wrong? Did the stream dry up? Remember, a flop is only a play that too few people go to see; this does not mean that it is a bad play. His rancour, true, grew worse, not necessarily because his later plays failed, but the other side of the burning bush within him blazed anew, and some of his tirades were hardly coherent for the rage that he felt; his targets became the ordinary ones of the Home Counties, saying that the country is going to the dogs. Illness was added to disappointment, and when he collapsed, more than once, because he had forgotten his insulin injection, it was all too easy to categorise the falls as drunken, for the descendants of those enemies of yesteryear, the gossip-columnists, their teeth long since drawn. (Mind you, he could never be tagged a teetotaller, illness or no illness.)

Towards the end, he mellowed. He denounced the modern world, but there was no real rage behind it. His fifth marriage had stood 16 years, and he learnt to laugh at himself – something he had always found difficult. I admired him immensely, for his genius first, of course, and what it had given the world, but then for his iron-clad refusal to conform. Some of his shouts and murmurs (many more shouts than murmurs) were silly, but he didn't care if they were, he went his ways – very many ways – annoying people who deserved to be annoyed, together with many who didn't. As I said when I started, he threatened to hit me and others but never did, but I have one such battle honour: on a railway station he declared that he would push me under an incoming train, but in the end he didn't do that either.

The fire in the bush has now burnt out, and we are the poorer for it. We have his works, which will endure; he blazed across our sky like the comet he was, and there aren't many like him left. (No, dear, Mr Alan Clark will *not* do.) We shall miss him; even those he singed will miss him. I never spoke words as deeply felt as those I speak now, when I say of John Osborne: "May he rest in peace."

The Times, 27 December 1994

Crash, bang, wallop

WE ALL HAVE absurd and impossible aspirations, and unless we allow ourselves to believe that we can achieve them, and behave as though we can, no harm is done. I used to dream of singing Hans Sachs at Covent Garden or marrying Princess Anne, or preferably both, but when those imaginary worlds of bliss faded under the extreme improbability of it all, I transferred my dream to chess, and imagined myself challenging the world champion (and beating him, of course). I bear Nigel Short no grudge, and indeed I was cheering him on when the first half of his own dream came true – to challenge the real world champion; I shall be cheering all the more loudly when he sits down at the table with Gary Kasparov on the other side. But I still wish that it had been me.

That reminds me of a moment, so many years ago that I was still a schoolboy, but which I have remembered all my life, so poignant and deep was the impression it made upon me. At my school, Christ's Hospital, the uniform was extravagantly recognisable, and one day an elderly man, worn, shabbily dressed and I would guess hungry, stopped me in the street to touch the dark blue gown. All he said was "I should have gone there, if I had been done right by," and he walked on. Again and again, I have wondered whether it was true, and somehow he had been cheated out of an education that might – surely, would – have changed his life. Perhaps, though, that was *his* unattainable world, and over the years he had come to believe his dream, like Thurber's moth. But I still have one more imaginary life to live, and I have been imaginarily living it for many years. Who tugs my sleeve?

I love reading about gigantic financial disasters, so long as they do not involve my own hard-earned savings or the savings of those unequipped for catastrophe. That being so, you may imagine my delight when I heard the news of IBM's world record crash-bang-wallop: this august organisation, which must have at least one product in practically every home of the advanced world, has gone into the red for *five thousand million dollars*.

Here is an American one-dollar bill; it measures, from end to end, six and one-tenth inches. If, then, all the dollars in the above-mentioned smash were put end to end, the ribbon of dollarity would stretch approximately 481,376 miles, which is almost exactly the distance from the Earth to the Moon and back again, provided that I have done my arithmetic correctly – which is unlikely.

The *schadenfreude* induced by this magnificent achievement was enough to make me choke on my breakfast with pleasure when I read about it, and I imagine most people without shares in IBM would feel something of the same. But I had a special, a very special, further longing; *I* want to go smash for five thousand million dollars.

It is a curious kind of envy, I admit, and the psychiatrists would have a marvellous time working out what it means, but I have had it as long as I can remember. I read the financial pages not so much to find tips for the best way of increasing my savings, as to come upon a huge concern (preferably a bank, of course) which has gone down the hole without even time to say glug-glug-glug. As you may imagine from that confession, I am an avid reader of the doings of the great financial rogues, the Ivar Kreugers and Robert Maxwells and their like, and I regret to say that I am more often than not to be found nervously admiring the scoundrels, and urging them to be even more scoundrelly before they go bust. It doesn't matter much whether the crash comes from the crooks, like those two and the master-swindlers of the BCCI, or from the strictly respectable IBM, but whenever I hear the first rumblings of a huge empire in frightful trouble, my heart lifts, and the only cloud in the sky is my wistful longing to be not just a spectator but the boss of the whole troubled empire.

And IBM gave me a vicarious thrill so powerful that it was all I could do not to rush out into the street and dance among the traffic. The experts tell me that the IBM's day of doom easily beats the previous record for any such smash, but that in itself gives me only a small part of the pleasure: it is the noise of the earth caving in that gets me a-trembling.

What about Canary Wharf, then? I was sorry when the Reichmann brothers went smash: I disliked considerably the gross and ill-proportioned phallus that still looms over London, but I have to say that on my only visit to it, I admired enormously the meticulous handsomeness of the interior (to say nothing of the stupendous views).

But what can be done with it? I have the solution, though nobody will listen to me. Anyway, here is my plan. We carefully lower Canary Wharf to the ground, pyramidical top-knot and all; then we put it on a long row of specially strengthened barrows, and we trundle it through the streets – giving ample notice for those who want to watch it pass – and when we get to Folkestone we stuff it into Sir Alastair ("Blame someone else") Morton's Tunnel. But will we do it? No fear, only when, some years ahead, everybody is sorry, will they admit that they should have listened to me in the first place.

How do you get into a position from which you can lose five thousand million dollars? Is there an exam an aspirant loser has to take? Or do you just have to be the managing director's nephew? Or do you listen to the experts? Whichever it is, I bet there are already a dozen books with titles like *How to lose five thousand million dollars without anybody noticing*.

That word "noticing" deserves a comment. The IBM splosh, five billion dollars deep, did not, I take it, happen in a moment, nor, if it did, was it so careful as to choose the moment at which the accountants opened the ledger. (Ledger! As if there were such things any more, in this perfect world of computers – IBM computers, naturally – which work out to the last cent how the business is getting on, so that if any imbalance or danger is sighted, the troublesome matter is immediately put right.) But although I followed the delightful IBM story, and learnt that the problem was that the firm was still doggedly turning out mainframes, whereas the computer-buying folk had already got as many mainframes as they needed and perhaps a few over, I never could understand how IBM failed to notice this shift.

I ruled out, as you may imagine, the absurd possibility that the trouble might have been that the people running IBM are quite amazingly stupid, and plumped for a very much more likely explanation: that little green men – lots and lots and *lots* of green men, plus a good many purple ones – had crawled down IBM's chimney and deliberately messed up the figures. But I must reconcile myself to the truth: I shall never have the chance to lose five thousand million dollars, and must content myself to do it in my day-dreams.

Very well, I shall do it in my day-dreams. In the safety of these comforting shadows I shall pile up great unrepayable loans, monstrous skyscrapers of debt, billions of pounds of wholly imaginary collateral; I shall buy huge banking networks just as they are about to collapse, I shall revel in the knowledge that by the time I am finished I will have broken every record for ruin, and I shall sit on the windowsill (just before jumping off it), to watch IBM go by and shout "cheapskates!"

Who will join me in this limitless imaginary financial scam? I cannot be the only man whose dreams fill the bankruptcy courts, and I call upon those who dream to such good purpose. And we have Shakespeare's blessing:

"They say he is already in the forest of Arden, and a many merry men with him: and there they live like the old Robin Hood of England. They say many young gentlemen flock to him every day, and fleet the time carelessly, as they did in the golden world." *Golden* world, you note.

The Times, 26 February 1993

To do with everybody

I HAVE BEEN ENCHANTED by the story of Sir Bernard
Ingham, Crookfinder-General to the nation. The story
was played out some time ago, but the issues involved
continue to echo.

I have no personal acquaintance with Sir Bernard,
though I could hardly have escaped all knowledge of him
in the years in which he served Margaret Thatcher as her
press secretary. On that subject, all I wish to say today is
that the fidelity, care and unstinted service he gave the
then prime minister make a notable and permanent high-
water mark on our political system, though perhaps I
might add that when he was dealing with the press it
would have been the height of folly for anybody to believe
anything he said without independent corroboration,
preferably including at least two bishops.

For those who missed the episode or have forgotten it, I
must rehearse the course of justice that Sir Bernard
followed. Travelling on the London Underground, he
saw a crime being committed. It was not much of a
crime: to wit, the offence of travelling without a ticket
and with intent to evade paying. The offender had il-
legally pushed through the automatic gates, which should
flip open only when the ticket is inserted. Sir Bernard saw
the miscreant at his miscreanting, and called out, "Hey,
you shouldn't be doing that, you should be paying your
fare."

The miscreant now made his first and last mistake; he
said to Sir Bernard, "What's it got to do with you?"

To the miscreant's question, Sir Bernard replied with a crisp lecture entitled "Why it has got to do with everybody", which by all accounts held the audience spellbound. A policeman appeared and took over; Sir Bernard outlined the events of the day, and later on all these happenings were discussed in court. Bernard the Avenger gave his evidence, and the scofflaw was fined not only for cheating the Underground, but also for using offensive language. (He had no money, so he couldn't pay the fines, and anyway he didn't turn up to the court, but none of that detracts from Sir Bernard's hour of uprightness.)

There are items which need examining. For instance, Sir Bernard, giving evidence, said that the villain "started to intimidate me". It is well known that I am a particularly trusting and unsceptical man, but even I cannot believe that the most intrepid fare-dodger in history would be so foolish as to try to intimidate Sir Bernard Ingham. Moreover, it transpired that during the events, Sir Bernard "wasn't frightened"; since a runaway steamroller would be needed to make Sir Bernard even mildly nervous, that must be the most otiose statement made in the entire business.

By now you must be thinking that there is something important amid the hilarity. It is, of course, the question we all ask ourselves in such circumstances, *viz.*, would we do what Sir Bernard did? It is all very well to say that wrong-doers should not get away with their wrong-doing while the bystanders do nothing, but Sir Bernard, after all, did not know whether the offender had a knife in his pocket or, if he had, whether he would use it. These days, too, we are all well aware of drugs and of what people can do to get their poison; this time the fare-dodger turned out to be a fare-dodger, but again, Sir Bernard did not know that he was not facing a junkie desperate for a fix.

But leave out the dangers. We can all agree that he was public-spirited in what he did; what I want to test is ourselves. The criminal was obviously committing a very small crime, one that would not cause real damage to our society, as a crime would that involved violence or a robbery of a substantial sum. So why not slip away? After all, to start a scene can be embarrassing; many, I am sure, when they heard the shouting, believed that the red-faced man was drunk, and hurried off without knowing that red-faced man was anything but drunk. And of course, Sir Bernard must have known at the time he took action that London Underground would not come to a permanent halt, or even an intermittent halt, if it were cheated out of 90p.

Very well; 90p and *we* turn our heads the other way. But then we must climb the ladder. A trivial fare-dodge is one thing; what about seeing a traveller, all oblivious, having his pocket picked? Do you go up to the thief, Ingham-wise, and confront him, or do you tap the robbed man on the shoulder, whisper the news, and point out the thief? The first course is braver, obviously, but the less brave is at least drawing attention to the crime, even without taking direct part in any attempt at apprehension.

Another rung up the ladder: what about violence? We are a peaceable people; it is all very well talking about the rising crime rate, but what happens when you find yourself inside the rising crime rate looking out? Are obvious villains violently attacking an obviously innocent man? We hesitate, and as we hesitate we climb another rung of the ladder: what about a woman being attacked with violence?

Now, for me the very thought of violence to a woman is so pathologically horrific that it must have some more profound psychological aspect, though I cannot recall anything in my life which would give a clue to such feelings. But of one thing I can be sure: if I did have the courage to go to the rescue of a woman who was being attacked I would instantly throw away any thought of the Marquess of Queensberry: I would go in, boots and all, and if I crippled the villain in doing so, I would have not so much as a twinge of remorse. For me, and I should hope for most men, it also works the other way round: there are no circumstances in which I might even contemplate striking a woman.

Yes, but for that matter, there are no circumstances in which I might even contemplate diddling the Underground, let alone British Rail. I have told the story of the sticky sweet in Woolworths, but I don't think I have told the one that goes with it.

I once entered the Underground at a Tube station that I had never used before, and discovered that the steps went down to an entry without a ticket office, though the trains stopped there. (This was before the new system with automatic gates and tickets.) I got into the train. As the doors shut I realised I had not paid. *I was travelling on the Underground without a ticket.* I took money from my pocket, put it in my palm and held the hand right out as though my arm was paralysed; if an inspector had come along he could not possibly have thought I was bilking the system (though he might – probably would – think I was mad), but though no inspector came, I shook throughout the journey, and practically danced with joy when I got to the barrier at my destination and flung far more money than was necessary at the startled booking-office clerk.

We must go back to the beginning, to the truly trivial crime of 90p bilked from the Underground, and we find to our dismay that we are on an escalator. There is no break between the 90p and the thousands of pounds stolen or the robbery with violence. We cannot promise to try to stop a murderer, but by failing to stop a fare-dodger we may have set him on the road to murder. Sir Bernard, we conclude, was twice a hero. Well, well.

I failed once. Two young boys emerged from Debenham's, one of them stuffing a scarf under his jacket; it was quite clear that they had stolen it. I should have grabbed them, lectured them, and sent them back into the shop to put back the scarf as surreptitiously as they had taken it. I did not do so, and perhaps I then set two children on the path of crime: I can only hope not. I thank my stars that there is in me a horror of even the tiniest and most insignificant law-breaking – a horror, that is, in its intensity, close to madness. Indeed, there is one story from my childhood, at the age of nine, as innocent as anything could possibly be, which I have never told to anyone and never shall, though I am convinced that it has permanently damaged my life.

We have come far from Sir Bernard's admirable action, but we might, all of us, benefit by thinking a little longer about it. Mind you, if we think long enough, we shall start wondering why Sir Bernard, who can hardly be short of a few bawbees, was travelling on the Underground, rather than in a car or a taxi.

The Times, 24 September 1993

In the Holy Name of God

*T*HERE ARE DIFFERENT *kinds of savages. Perhaps the worst of them are those who believe – or, rather, claim to believe – that they have been given some kind of message from their deity which permits them – indeed orders them – to demand that those professing a different faith must renounce it, on pain of ostracism, expulsion, imprisonment or ultimately execution. Such people now rule Iran.*

There is a man there named Mehdi Dibaj, who long ago embraced the Christian religion, and has ever since followed his master Christ. For this, and only this, he has been imprisoned for nine years, has recently been threatened with hanging, and has only now, after a worldwide campaign on his behalf, been released.

We shall see what becomes of him, and others in a similar situation. Meanwhile, I seek enlightenment. Why has one of the world's most beautiful and profound religions, Islam, been turned into a monstrous charnel-house of fanaticism, by the people who sought the death of Mehdi Dibaj, and nearly got it? And why do these same people spit in the face of the Prophet (peace to his name)?

I await answers. But when Mehdi Dibaj was awaiting his fate, he wrote his final testament, addressed to his jailers. I reproduce it here in its entirety.

In the Holy Name of God who is our life and existence. With all humility I express my gratitude to the Judge of all heaven and earth for this precious opportunity, and with brokenness I wait upon the Lord to deliver me from this court trial according to His promises. I also beg the honoured members of the court present to listen with patience to my defence and with respect for the Name of the Lord.

I am a Christian, a sinner who believes Jesus has died for my sins on the cross and who by His resurrection and victory over death, has made me righteous in the presence of the Holy God. The true God speaks about this fact in His Holy Word, the Gospel. Jesus means Saviour "because He will save His people from their sins". Jesus paid the penalty of our sins by His own blood and gave us a new life so that we can live for the glory of God by the help of the Holy Spirit and be like a dam against corruption, be a channel of blessing and healing, and be protected by the love of God.

In response to this kindness, He has asked me to deny myself and be His fully surrendered follower, and not fear people even if they kill my body, but rather rely on the creator of life who has crowned me with the crown of mercy and compassion, and who is the great protector of His beloved ones and their great reward.

I have been charged with "Apostasy"! The invisible God who knows our hearts has given assurance to us Christians that we are not among the apostates who will perish but among the believers so that we may save our lives. In Islamic Law an apostate is one who does not believe in God, the prophets or the resurrection of the dead. We Christians believe in all three!

They say "You were a Muslim and you have become a Christian." No, for many years I had no religion. After searching and studying I accepted God's call and I believed in the Lord Jesus Christ in order to receive eternal life. People choose their religion, but a Christian is chosen by Christ. He says "You have not chosen me but I have chosen you." From when? Before the foundation of the world.

People say "You were a Muslim from your birth." God says "You were a Christian from the beginning." He states that He chose us thousands of years ago, even before the creation of the universe, so that through the sacrifice of Jesus Christ we may be His! A Christian means one who belongs to Jesus Christ.

The eternal God who sees the end from the beginning and who has chosen me to belong to Him knew from everlasting whose heart would be drawn to Him and also those who would be willing to sell their faith and eternity for a pot of porridge. I would rather have the whole world against me but know that the Almighty God is with me, be called an apostate but know that I have the approval of the God of glory, because man looks at the outward appearance but God looks at the heart, and for Him who is God for all eternity nothing is impossible. All power in heaven and on earth is in His hands.

The Almighty God will raise up anyone He chooses and bring down others, accept some and reject others, send some to heaven and others to hell. Now because God does whatever He desires, who can separate us from the love of God? Or who can destroy the relationship between the creator and the creature or defeat a heart that is faithful to His Lord? He will be safe and secure under the shadow of the Almighty! Our refuge is the mercy seat of God who is exalted from the beginning. I know in whom I have believed, and He is able to guard what I have entrusted to Him to the end, until I reach the Kingdom of God, the place where the righteous shine like the sun, but where the evil doers will receive their punishment in hell fire.

They tell me "Return!" But from the arms of my God, whom can I return to? Is it right to accept what people are saying instead of obeying the Word of God? It is now 45 years that I am walking with the God of miracles, and His kindness upon me is like a shadow and I owe Him much for His fatherly love and concern.

The love of Jesus has filled all my being and I feel the warmth of His love in every part of my body. God, who is my glory and honour and protector, has put his seal of approval upon me through His unsparing blessings and miracles.

This test of faith is a clear example. The good and kind God reproves and punishes all those whom He loves. He tests them in preparation for heaven. The God of Daniel, who protected his friends in the fiery furnace, has protected me for nine years in prison and all the bad happenings have turned out for our good and gain, so much so that I am filled overflowing with joy and thankfulness.

The God of Job has tested my faith and commitment in order to strengthen my patience and faithfulness. During those nine years he has freed me from all my responsibilities so that under the protection of His blessed Name I would spend my time in prayer and study of His Word, with heart searching and brokenness, and grow in the knowledge of my Lord, I praise the Lord for this unique opportunity. "You gave me space in my confinement, my difficult hardships brought healing and your kindnesses revived me." Oh what great blessings God has in store for those who fear Him!

They object to my evangelising. But "If you find a blind person near a well and keep silent then you have sinned" (a Persian poem). It is our religious duty, as long as the door of God's mercy is open, to convince evil-doers to turn from their sinful ways and find refuge in Him in order to be saved from the wrath of a Righteous God and from the coming dreadful punishment.

Jesus Christ says "I am the door. Whoever enters through me will be saved." "I am the way, the truth and the life. No one comes to the Father except through me." "Salvation is found in no one else, for there is no other name under heaven given to men by which we must be saved." Among the prophets of God, only Jesus Christ rose from the dead, and He is our living intercessor for ever.

He is our Saviour and He is the Son of God. To know Him means to know eternal life. I, a useless sinner, have believed in His beloved person and all His words and miracles recorded in the Gospel, and I have committed my life into His hands. Life for me is an opportunity to serve Him, and death is a better opportunity to be with Christ. Therefore I am not only satisfied to be in prison for the honour of His Holy Name, but am ready to give my life for the sake of Jesus my Lord and enter His kingdom sooner, the place where the elect of God enter everlasting life, but the wicked to eternal damnation.

May the shadow of God's kindness and His hand of blessing and healing be upon you and remain for ever. Amen.

With respect, Your Christian prisoner, Mehdi Dibaj.

The Times, 18 January 1994

Before the savages came

WHEN PEOPLE ASK me what I do when I cannot think of anything to write about, I tell them, in my modest way, that that is the only problem I never have. But that is not because I am enormously clever, but because even if the flow of ideas should dry up, there is one subject from which I can always – always – draw sustenance, in the certainty that its fountain will never dry up. It is, of course, man's inhumanity to man.

So, although I have many subjects to write about, I now choose three columns on the subject, starting with this one, to appear on Tuesday 18, *deo volente*, with the other two appearing shortly.

And so, I must first announce that the rape of Tibet continues; the Chinese savages, it is clear, will not cease their destruction until that tragic and beautiful land ceases to exist. And still the mystery remains – the mystery, that is, of why the savages want to wipe it from the globe and from the memory of mankind. After all, we do not have to wear magic spectacles to see that the Chinese forces have a hundred times the fire-power needed to put down any imaginary insurrection from Tibet, particularly because armed resistance on the part of the Tibetans ended many years ago, largely by the persuasion of the Dalai Lama, who will not countenance violence even against his people's oppressors. Yet the Chinese behave as though they were sitting on a mountain of explosives, awaiting every moment the Tibetan match.

As for the proof that the Chinese do want to see Tibet disappear altogether, we do not need to go so far as Tibet, for the proof is ready at hand in sober print, here.

Two American tourists, Karen and Karl Aderer, were interrogated for four days and then deported, after giving a Buddhist monk a cassette of the teachings of the Dalai Lama. They had been given the tape by a Buddhist friend and made three copies before they left. They also brought photographs of His Holiness and gave three of these to other monks.

Their tour group was later stopped at a police road-block that had been specifically set up for them. Hear the Aderers: "Every day we were forced to go to the police station where we would undergo interrogations, listen to threats and sign 'statements', saying we distributed pol-itical propaganda. Our guide (a Tibetan) was also inter-rogated" [God help him when the Aderers finally left]. Their passports were confiscated, their room was searched and the remaining copies of the Dalai Lama tape and photographs were impounded. After days of waiting, the couple were given a police escort to the airport hotel . . . before being put on the plane back to Kathmandu.

Well, contemplating the lengths the Chinese authorities go to when a pair of obviously harmless tourists give an obviously harmless cassette to an obviously harmless Budd-hist, it must truly be madness that the sight of a peaceful, gentle, holy and vegetarian monk causes in a Chinese official. For us, he is comical, but what follows is not comical, not comical at all, because lying on my desk there is a document that would freeze the smile off anyone human, except of course a Chinese official seconded to the Tibetan women's torture-chambers. Those of my readers who have a squeamish nature should have something strong to drink before I continue, and something much stronger after.

Dogs were set on us while we were naked, lit cigarette butts were stubbed on our faces, knitting needles jabbed in our mouths . . . kicked in the breasts and the genitals until they were bleeding . . . made to hang from trees and beaten on bare flesh by electric batons. Containers of human urine were poured over our heads . . . I was hung up from the wall with my legs up and beaten with electric prods in the genitals and the mouth. After this I could not even go to the toilet.

That was the testimony of Nima Tsamchoe; the above was what she experienced. Or rather, it was some of what she experienced.

Reports of women being raped by cattle prods are numerous. There are also reports of women being attacked by specially trained dogs whilst in prison . . . Tibetan nuns have been singled out for particularly brutal treatment. They are regularly subject to solitary confinement, which is rare among prisoners in Tibet given the number of detainees that exist. "The soldiers made us show our private parts and told us we were like dogs and pigs . . . They also forced the nuns to come out naked and prostrate themselves in front of the monks."

Incidentally, this treatment is not for torturing information out of prisoners, not that it would be any less barbaric if it were. But it seems that these horrors are routine in Tibetan women's prisons, and there is another gruesome aspect of what is called (the things I have to know!) "gender specific torture". For these tortures and other sexual indignities are not typical of the experience of *male* prisoners.

I could go on like this for some time: well, come to think of it, I shall. It is unlikely that many of my readers have heard of Phuntsok Nyidron, but they should have, because she holds a record, and we all like to hear about people who can do remarkable things. In this case, however, it is not really *her* record, but that of the Chinese authorities in Tibet; Phuntsok Nyidron was sentenced to 17 years as a political prisoner in Drapchi Prison, and so far her record is unlikely to be surpassed. What is more, she was at first sentenced to a mere nine years, but copped another eight. And now I shall tell you what dreadful crime she has committed, to have been so severely punished.

Already she had been, in company with 13 Tibetan nuns, behind bars as a political prisoner, and she, with the other nuns, composed and recorded patriotic songs and poems on a tape-recorder that had been smuggled in to them. These dooms-day weapons were enough to have all the nuns' sentences increased by another eight years, thus bringing up the record of 17 for Phuntsok Nyidron. Nor are such sentences particularly rare; for shouting a single forbidden slogan, the average sentence is roughly seven years. And yet those unimaginably brave nuns can say – do say – "Our enemy is our greatest teacher, teacher of patience and compassion. Imprisonment is our greatest test of faith".

It had better be. But there are two imponderables in this strange and terrible story. One is the brutality of the Chinese usurpers, and the other is the courage of the Tibetans. And both need elucidation. (Strictly speaking, there is a third; it is the way that almost all of the rest of the world ignores the wickedness of the intruders and the courage with which the sufferers have faced it.)

The first, the apparently pointless savagery against the peaceable people of Tibet, may be a long-sighted fear of their own people. The flood towards the cities can hardly be called an insurrection, but that is not the point; it shows that demand for obedience is no longer instantly heeded. Do the rulers of China look that far? They would be wise to. Tiananmen Square is not forgotten, and next time it might be very different.

As for the people of Tibet and their heroism, it is almost without compare in all history. It is all very well to say that the quietism of the Buddhist faith teaches that one should not raise a hand in anger, let alone strike a persecutor (or, for that matter, knowingly tread upon a beetle); the only comparison I can think of is the persecution of the early Christians.

But remember that before the savages came to Tibet, the Tibetans had had a very long time to study the world and their part in it, and to perfect their contemplation – it is believed that Tibetan Buddhism had taken root in the 7th or 8th century. Such roots not only go deep, but they stabilise what is on the surface – surely, those wonderful temples that the Chinese savages destroyed, had enough time to end time, and would have done so, but for the savages.

One belief – I have never heard a better – is that the Chinese savages know just enough of their own history to know that China was once one of the greatest and most profound civilisations the world has ever held, and that the brutal and brutalised empire that these their successors have made it must at all costs banish the comparisons.

Over the centuries, there have been many attempts to destroy entirely a culture, a set of beliefs, a physical reminder of eternity; many have succeeded in such engulfing. But surely the genocide of Tibet, among all the countless destructions of history, must rank very high in the claims of evil.

The Times, 18 October 1994

Ashes to ashes

HAVE YOU EVER noticed that whenever a new quango is created (there are, by the most recent count, 4,381, all of them leeching on the body of our society), its personnel go through a series of predictable steps?

The first is wonderment, when they see before them suites of handsome offices, smart filing-cabinets, secretaries and press offices, even pleasant dining-rooms and attractive carpets. They move in, and the second step is reached; in this, they go about with their eyes cast down, and are heard sharpening pencils which are already well sharpened. In other words, they have realised that if they are honest (and I have no reason to think them otherwise), they really have nothing to do, and in most cases never will have anything to do.

A flurry, and the third stage has been reached. They are not, of course, going to sack themselves in the light of this revelation; no quangoid has ever resigned because he or she has realised that the entire enterprise is a Potemkin village, nothing but the front wall. Nor has any quangoid ever been sacked because he or she was redundant; indeed redundancy is a word unheard in the corridors of a quango. On the contrary, every opportunity to swell the payroll is taken, and that is the meaning of the third step.

In the fourth, a dramatic change has come over the quangoids. Their early nervousness and embarrassment have disappeared entirely, and a haughty assertiveness is now everywhere to be felt; the quangoids have realised that they *cannot* be sacked unless they are found with their hands in the till, and that is very rare indeed – apart from the fact that they are honest, why steal, when if you can make a good case, the appropriate ministry will shell out more funds whenever they are needed (or, more exactly, whenever they are wanted)?

And now for the fifth and penultimate stage. The number of personnel has grown, multiplied, soared; every day, hundreds upon hundreds of reams of paper pour out in the form of "press releases" (would that the quangoids might be released for ever into the darkness, never to be seen or heard of again) with which, incredibly, they have managed to establish their existences, their positions and their incomes. And, thus armoured in their own esteem, they take the final step.

Facilis descensus Averno. The haughtiness discerned in stage four has been replaced by something very much nastier. Now, they have reached regality; we – all the rest of us – are their subjects, to be ordered about, hectored, shouted down, refused redress, sneered at (a very special supercilious sneer, in which newcomers to the lists are given tuition), and required to do obedience, silence and repentance.

I am caricaturing of course, but there is a bit of truth here. What about Ash?

Ash stands for Action on Smoking and Health, and is ostensibly (watch that ostensibly) devoted to persuading smokers to give up the dangerous weed. You would think (*you* would, because you are an innocent, but *I* don't, because I am a leathery old cynic and I know what people like those who run Ash can get up to), you would think that if they wanted to make their persuasion work they would speak quietly and gently to their clients, giving them a pleasing, soothing picture of what they would feel like when they had signed the pledge, boosting and strengthening the wavering ones, calming the desperate ones, giving three cheers for one who has finally dispensed with the stuff, and being understanding with one who has fallen back into his former life, promising that he would not be abandoned, but on the contrary would be treated like the man in the parable: "I say unto you, that likewise joy shall be in heaven over one sinner that repenteth, more than over ninety and nine just persons, which need no repentance."

And is it like that? Hear Ash on the subject.

"Until now we have adopted a 'softly softly' approach," said Stephen Woodward, Ash's deputy director [*the hell they have* – B.L.]. "We have tried the carrot and now we are going to use the stick." Ash will back moves to have employers prosecuted . . . and encourage actions for negligence under common law . . . Medical and scientific evidence suggests that at least one non-smoker dies every day in Britain from lung cancer as a result of inhaling others' smoke . . .

Whoopee! Let's have lots and lots of litigation to keep the lawyers in *foie gras*! But did you spot the weak link? Don't be abashed if you didn't; even I, inured to the antismoking lobby, missed it twice, and saw it only on the third reading. Ash says that the "Medical and scientific evidence suggests that at least one non-smoker dies every day in Britain from lung cancer as a result of inhaling others' smoke . . . " But "Medical and scientific evidence *suggests* . . . ", means that Ash would not go so far as to say something untrue, so it slips in "suggests" to get around the truth – the truth that nobody has yet proved that anybody has died by "passive smoking".

But Ash is thus far only warming to its work; now it really starts.

Ash believes that it should now start a more aggressive campaign, believing that the threat of substantial compensation payments will force businesses to look anew . . . We believe that the number of workplaces . . .

where smoking is banned would escalate considerably
with more litigation . . .

I bet it would. But it is now time to say that it is
becoming difficult to distinguish between Ash and a gang
of imperfectly house-trained pirates. Can these quangoids,
puffed up to bursting in their righteousness, get into their
heads that they are talking about British citizens, not
escapees from a Mississippi chain-gang? And as for the
screaming hate that was poured out in my quotes, it
seriously suggests that there are people in Ash who should
be seeking psychotherapy. For among those British citizens
of whose existence Ash is apparently unaware, there are
seventeen million who smoke. I wish there was none; but
until the day dawns, they have rights. (Incidentally, Ash
gets money from public funds. The 17 million British
smokers have the right to see that their share of that money
is not used to hound, abuse and confine them.)

As for the lunacy, the *Spectator* got the story first, from
Avril Munson, and it is going the rounds, but I think it
should have a hearing in *The Times*:

> The fine for smoking on a London Transport bus is
> now £1,000. Under the sentencing guidelines issued
> recently, you can do the following . . . television licence
> evasion (black and white), £20; drunk and disorderly,
> £20; speeding 30 mph over the limit, £28; obstructing
> a police officer, £32; theft from a vehicle, £60; cultiva-
> tion of cannabis, £60; drunk driving, twice the limit,
> £72; burglary (non-dwelling), £80; assault on a police
> officer, £100; burglary (dwelling), £120; possession of
> class A drugs (e.g. cocaine), £120; grievous bodily harm,
> £160. The total comes to £872 . . .

The clown who thought a £1,000 fine was a right and
proper penalty for smoking on a bus, when that catalogue
of real offences fell well short of LT's £1,000, was plainly

in the grip of PC: it is just what the dregs of American PC look like when they have been used and discarded. (I haven't got the clown's name – they wouldn't give it, I am sure – but I know what he looks like: very neat, given to putting his finger-tips together, dark blue suit, hair somewhat thinning.)

And yet there is a real danger staring at us. *The Times* campaign demonstrates that air pollution is worse than any cigarette: we can usually avoid smokers and their cigarettes, but no one can avoid the air we have to breathe. And a day's breathing our air, with its benzene pollution, is *equivalent to* 15 cigarettes a day. (But I have not heard denunciations of benzene from Miss Anne Diamond – perhaps the stuff is not PC enough.) Meanwhile, we see, more and more frequently, bicyclists on the streets of our cities wearing masks which the wearer hopes will filter out the filth.

As for Ash, its spokesmen, shoutsmen and screamsmen should remember that the cigarette business brings in, by the taxes on tobacco that Britain imposes, no less than £6.5 billion a year; would Ash care to make a list of the things that that sum now buys and would have to cease buying? Oh, horror! Suppose the Government, in those straitened circumstances, decided that Ash should go? Can you not hear the squeals, as first the suites of offices go, then the permanent tenure, and finally the right to sneer? Why, the very thought of it would be enough to make every member of Ash reach for a cigarette.

The Times, 8 March 1994

It can't be true, or can it?

THERE IS A bizarre notion going about that scientists are scientific; does anybody know where this absurd belief got into circulation? I ask because of the extraordinary business of Dr Nicholas Humphrey.

Dr Humphrey is undoubtedly a scientist, indeed a justly well-regarded one, and he has recently been appointed a research fellow in parapsychology at Darwin College, Cambridge. As Alice Thomson explained in her recent *Times* interview with him, £100,000 had been left to the college for such an appointment, a gesture that was by no means unanimously welcome there. This looking a gift horse in the mouth (and a £100,000 horse at that) was caused by the hysterical terror that seizes so many otherwise rational people when anyone suggests that there might be things in the universe that cannot be detected by sight, sound, smell, touch or taste, yet have an effect, even a physical effect.

The two men most extravagantly terrified of the possibility that that may be so, are the truly eminent editor of *Nature*, Mr John Maddox, and the hardly less expert Mr Adrian Berry, science correspondent of the *Daily Telegraph*. Mr Maddox keeps heterodoxy at bay by a careful refusal to study anything that might shake his certainty, and Mr Berry, faced with a similar suspicion, goes into a series of frightful seizures culminating in the *arc-en-ciel*, which must be significantly shortening his life expectancy.

I shall come back to this phenomenon, but first I want to pick up Dr Humphrey where I left him. Darwin

College (shame on them with such a name!) hesitated to carry out the joint benefactors' wishes, lest such a seat of learning might become a laughing-stock among those who are quite sure that Hamlet was wrong when he pointed out that there were more things in heaven and earth than were dreamt of in Horatio's philosophy. A neat compromise was arranged; the bequest specified a research fellow in parapsychology, but the post was offered to a man who plainly has nothing but contempt for the very idea of parapsychology, and from Dr Humphrey's comments in the interview it seems that he is determined to outstrip both John Maddox and Adrian Berry in their horror of anything they cannot hear, see, touch, taste or feel.

"An extraordinary amount of people do still believe in the paranormal . . . But the most important work to be done in this area is to expose the fallacies . . . Roman Catholicism without the paranormal would be nothing . . . But then who needs Catholicism? Praying has no paranormal benefits . . . After 100 years . . . they have come up with nothing convincing . . . I want to show not only that these things don't happen, but they are logically impossible."

No wonder Dr Humphrey's interviewer commented demurely, "Not exactly what the people who left the money intended."

Now a scientist who says, "I want to show not only that these things don't happen, but they are logically impossible", must be a very peculiar scientist indeed. Take the simplest and perhaps most familiar paranormal belief, telepathy. There is much evidence that such communication exists, but of course Dr Humphrey is at liberty to insist (well, he would, wouldn't he?) that it is all coincidence; and so it may be. But what kind of a scientist is he to think that he can prove that it *can't* be true? Has he ever read a page of Sir Karl Popper? Or does he think Popper, too, is a piece of pseudo-ectoplasm, ripe for exposure?

I come back to the extraordinary terror which seizes otherwise perfectly sensible people when the subject of the paranormal comes up. On this subject, I have asked what history, I trust, will call Levin's Question, and I have asked it again and again and yet again and once more again; nay, not content with that, I have even halloo'd it to the reverberate hills, and I am perfectly willing, if it would help, to stand on one leg for a week and then ask it once more, but as yet, from those who reject in manifest dread any possibility that the paranormal might exist, I have never had a coherent answer.

Here, then, is Levin's Question. It is: If the paranormal does exist, and acts upon us in reality without our knowing how the effect is made, *what would be so dreadful about it*?

And the dreadfulness is no metaphor. I have repeatedly induced shaking rage in those who deny the paranormal, not by baiting them or jeering at them, but simply by asking Levin's Question and pressing for an answer.

The more I examine the unscientific rejection of the paranormal, the more I wonder why it should be so complete and unquestioned. A few years ago I was a guest at a lunch at which one of the other guests was a scientist whom I admire, not least because of his book about science itself. The talk turned to the work on the paranormal by Dr Brian Inglis, who is this country's leading figure in the field; he has written a dozen books on the subject, and their meticulous scholarship is outstanding. The scientist dismissed Dr Inglis's entire *ouevre* (though he did so calmly, pleasantly and with no suggestion of charlatanism) as nonsense; but under pressure from me, he gaily admitted that he had never read any of Dr Inglis's books.

We shall see, in due course, how Dr Humphrey gets on in his new post; I would be sorry to think that so much of his time will be given to shrieking at the paranormal that he will have little time to examine the evidence. It is no use reminding him that he is the research fellow in parapsychology at Darwin College, because he made his position plain before he took up the post; no double-crosser he – for him, research in parapsychology seems to mean knocking it down and stamping it into the ground.

Stamp on, stamp on, good doctor, and do not burst into tears if you come across a phenomenon that you cannot explain with the normal tools of science; just ignore it. "We have a duty to accept responsibility for our own actions," he says, "and to have an alternative to superstition." Quite; but what is his stance if not pure superstition? What would *you* call an apparently ironclad determination not to examine more than one half of the evidence? Yet Dr Humphrey is a rightly respected scientist; whence my opening question – who spread the rumour that scientists were scientific?

When you think how little humankind knows about the way the world goes, from the mystery of why the anopheles mosquito came into being to the mystery of what love is, it is surely an impertinence to behave, as Dr Humphrey does, as though all mysteries, large and small, are either already solved or very shortly will be. Tell me, good doctor, what song the Sirens sang, or what name Achilles assumed when he hid himself among women? After all, we have Sir Thomas Browne's assurance that though these are puzzling questions they are not beyond all conjecture. But I bet Dr Humphrey doesn't know the answer to either.

The Times, 4 June 1992

The hunting of the shark

I START UNKINDLY, I fear, by saying that Mr John Power, who is chairman of the planning committee of Oxford city council, might do well to go and boil his head in a light stock with a *bouquet garni* and perhaps a teaspoonful of sherry.

This discourtesy is provoked by Mr Power sounding off in no uncertain manner: " . . . a victory for anarchy . . . a slap in the face for the decent and respectable people . . . seeking legal advice . . ." And what has brought him, in his municipal character, to such a state? Has someone opened a brothel next door to Balliol? Has the Sheldonian been taken over by meths-drinking dossers? Or has a band of undergraduate scofflaws had the impudence to debag Mr Power himself and paint his bottom purple?

No such luck. What has brought Mr Power to the very edge of bursting is the decision of the public enquiry into the Hunting of the Shark. Over the six years of battle, you must have seen photographs of the famous fish which adorns the roof of the Oxford house of a Mr Bill Heine (to whom goes the Diamond Star and Sash of the Order of They Shall Be Mocked and With Good Reason); made of fibreglass, it is sited to look as though the shark dived headfirst at the roof-tiles and crashed through up to its gills. It makes a delightful, innocent, fresh and amusing sculpture, and people come from far and wide to see it, to admire it, to photograph it, and to smile at it.

But there is nothing about smiling in the analects of the planning committee of the Oxford city council, and that august body ruled that it must come down, giving as the reason that it had been put up without planning permission, or more likely just because it *was* delightful, innocent, fresh and amusing – all qualities abhorred by such committees. Mr Heine (if he is descended from Heinrich Heine, it is another reason for me to shake his hand) fought heroically through the years as the battle swayed this way and that, with the authorities getting more and more indignant at the impudence of a mere person defying the might of a planning committee.

It had to go to a public enquiry, and eventually did, whence the sound of corks popping at 2 New High Street, Headington. For not only did the planning inspector of the Department of the Environment, Mr Peter Macdonald, rule that the shark can stay where it is, but the decision was couched in language so human, so intelligent and so wise that it ought to be painted in enormous letters on the pavements (both sides) of Whitehall. Here are some of his conclusions: "I cannot believe that the purpose of planning control is to enforce a boring and mediocre uniformity . . . Any system of control must make some space for the dynamic, the unexpected and the downright quirky, or we shall all be the poorer for it. I believe that this is one case where a little vision and imagination is appropriate." Whereupon, Mr Power made it clear that he would "try to challenge the decision", a threat that brought from Lord Palumbo, chairman of the Arts Council, this mild but appallingly true comment: "Most politicians do not know how to lose graciously."

When I am Ruler of the Universe, one of my earliest decrees will lay down that anyone who uses the words "What if everybody did it?" will be fed to Sirius, the dog star. It is the last resort of the fun-killers, the oriflamme of the pursed lips brigade, the buttress of those whose motto is "Go and see what Johnny is doing and tell him to stop it". Anyone but a prize nana would have seen that Mr Heine's splendid lark (I pause here to commend the sculptor, Mr John Buckley) was an exact definition of delight, particularly Shakespeare's kind "that give delight and hurt not".

But it hurt the planning committee no end, whence the six years of battle and the preposterous comments (". . . a slap in the face of the decent and respectable people . . .") of its chairman when the battle was finally lost and won.

It is not difficult to see how people get things so devastatingly out of scale; indeed it is one of the most thoroughly studied of human frailties. I poked fun at the Oxford council planning committee and in particular its chairman, but that was largely because I had a measure of that body – useful but nothing more. Now suppose you have worked hard and honestly at your job (useful but nothing more), and you dream, or once did dream, of making a mighty stir, of climbing to the heights, of being Someone. What is the inevitable knowledge that goes with what has happened to those dreams, and what can be done about it? The knowledge, of course, is that the dreams have not come true; what can be done about it is to exercise that tiny corner of the world in which you *do* hold sway.

Man, proud man, dressed in a little brief authority . . . Shakespeare knew humankind, and knew that the briefer the authority the greater the vigour with which it is employed. The chairman of the Oxford council planning committee does not have the power to have anybody's head cut off, nor to have anybody exiled to Outer Mongolia, nor even to compel anybody to do penance in a white sheet for seven days and seven nights. But he and his council *do* have the power (exercised, I am sure, only in strict compliance with the law) to order a man with a 25 ft fibreglass shark on his roof to take it off. And when he finds that higher authority has overruled him, he is fit to burst – whence the slap in the face for the decent and respectable people – because even that little authority has been, at least for some time, taken from him.

Shun power, shun it fiercely, if you want to sleep soundly in your bed. If it is real power, the power to compel others to do your bidding, your dreams will be haunted ones. If it is the mock power of the chairmanship of a municipal committee in Oxford, you will wake to disappointment. I am not going to quote Acton, but here is Hazlitt, who in this context is even more apposite:

The love of liberty is the love of others; the love of power is the love of ourselves.

You do not have to be a bad man to want power. Our chairman is plainly an honest and scrupulous man, certainly to be numbered among the decent and respectable people who have figured so largely in this story. But he has forgotten the old and tried proverb: "A man with a stuffed shark on his roof is eccentric, and quite possibly in breach of the planning rules; a man who tries to take the shark off will run no danger of being bitten, but will almost certainly make a fool of himself."

The Times, 11 June 1992

The yes man cometh

JUST LISTEN TO this: "If you tell the man in the street, funds are available, he understands that there is a pile of cash next door. But when a corporate financier says it, it does not mean quite the same. Most people in the City know that."

Oh, they do, do they? Then be so kind as to classify me as the man in the street, one of the peculiar band who believe that "funds are available" means that funds are available. And just in case there is any doubt about the matter – after all, the story I am to unfold hinged on that very question – I have left a document with my solicitors, which states that, in my opinion, the words "funds are available", even painted on the pavement in Threadneedle Street – nay, set to music in the key of D minor – means that funds are available.

The story, found in the Pink'un and growing mushrooms by now, is about one Ian McIntosh. When the curtain rises, Mr McIntosh is head of corporate finance, whatever that might be, at the firm of Samuel Montagu. (I once, very many years ago, met the then head of Montagu, and I had an uneasy feeling that things might go wrong, because he made clear that he didn't understand how the pools work. Well, I mean . . .)

Anyway, some incomprehensible deal was going through, and it seems that this Mr McIntosh was in charge. All was going well, until Mr M was asked whether the client he was steering had the funds – oh, those funds, we shall meet them more than once before this story is over! – to complete the purchase that was about to be clinched. And Mr McIntosh said "Yes", just like that. And now (I leap over the intricacies in one bound), somebody has been ordered to pay somebody's damages to the tune of a hundred and seventy-two million smackers. I could do a lot with that.

I have always kept in mind the precept that warns against trying to do things which are manifestly beyond our powers. But that's easy, at least fairly easy. The real test comes when you persuade yourself that you could, say, become an expert bungee jumper, and the next thing you know you fall into the River Severn and are never seen again.

But take me; no such fate will befall me, because no such folly would I ever commit. For instance, I have never sat on any part of any horse, and the horses – noble beasts that they are – have reciprocated by never sitting on any part of me. And that will be the situation to the end, where I am concerned.

So it is with high finance, and so it shall remain. There was never any danger, for instance, of my becoming a Name at Lloyds and being ruined, because so far from understanding how Lloyd's works, I cannot remember which is the Lloyd's with the apostrophe and which the Lloyds without it, as indeed you can see from this paragraph.

Be calm, there will be sense talked fairly soon, but I must first go on for a bit longer about Mr McIntosh. I learn that the litigation over this business has been going on for five years (oh, mother, mother, why did you not apprentice me to a lawyer – by now I would have ruined hundreds and *hundreds* of perfectly inoffensive people, for huge, nay, gigantic fees?), and the end is by no means in sight. Obviously, the corporate finance business is crawling with corporate financiers, and one of them, *sotto voce*, gave his opinion that he would not, today, sign that which he would yesterday have signed quite happily, because "the judgment did not take full account of what Mr McIntosh meant by his reply".

Now that, I have to say, takes the Levin breath away. Mr M's answer was, in its entirety, "Yes". You can read it backwards, you can translate it into any number of foreign words meaning yes, you can parse it, you can – if they will agree – get the monks of a Trappist monastery, line them up, and have them nod silently in chorus, but for you and me there is one meaning to the word "Yes".

But not in high finance. There – well, I'll quote again – ". . . other bankers argued that they would be wary about making such an unqualified verbal assurance in a minuted meeting. It would be more common to sign a letter with a number of disclaimers and conditions." Well, yes. Indeed, I should think that if business like that is being done, the participants would be wise to have an enormous sack of disclaimers and another one of conditions. Now, I have heard that there are tribes in remote countries who are willing to make monetary and other pledges with no documents involved, nor even verbal promises; indeed, it is said that these trusting folk rely on a handshake or a kiss; nor is that the end of their generous simplicity, because some of them are willing to lend money in this world to be paid back in the next.

But not, I repeat, in the world of high finance. And here a mystery raises its corporate head. Come back for a moment to Mr McIntosh and the five years of litigation that followed his somewhat romantic reply which caused all the trouble. Come back also to the high-finance experts who interpreted the word "Yes" to mean ". . . that an assurance that a client has funds usually means there is a credit facility in place from banks. However, such credit facilities will usually contain provisions that mean that they can be withdrawn in some circumstances . . ." Come back, if your nerves will stand it, to the original Fayed *v* Lonrho match, which had – no, I shall not take sides. And having come to all those enticing circles of high finance, turn to my question.

Here it is. If it fell to you, would you allow any of these people – "Yes men", "However men", "Perhaps men" and all the other categories involved in this enormous ball of wool – would you allow any one of them to go to the corner supermarket to buy you a pint of milk and a Mars Bar, with any hope at all that they might come back with something roughly like what was ordered (say, two dozen sausages and a packet of frozen peas)? You wouldn't? No, nor would I.

Are we hypnotised when we contemplate the people who direct the world of high finance? For consider: if you engaged a man to replace a broken slate on the roof of your house, and then went out for the day, only to find, when you returned, that instead of dealing with the slate the workman had painted the entire outside of your house, including all the windows, a particularly nasty shade of green, would you not think that the workman in the case was – how shall I put it? – not quite up to the job?

There is no suggestion in this business that anyone was breaking, or trying to break, any law; I am tempted to say that it would have been better if someone had been, though I suppose the outfits concerned would fetch up with a bunch of incompetent crooks. For look at BCCI – now they *were* crooked; but where were the scrupulously honest guardians and watchdogs and sniffers-out-of-rip-offs? Again, I ask, are we on Cloud Nine when billions are being discussed? It cannot be just that we do not understand high finance, though we don't, because that would be true of any complex matter; I am sure I would not understand the intricacies of nuclear fission, but then I wouldn't press the button. In the world of high finance the place is deafening with the pressing of buttons – buttons, mind you, that are pressed largely at random.

Here is a comment from one in the world we are discussing; asked what would be the outcome of this apparently eternal merry-go-lawyer, he said:

I suppose it will make some sloppy operators tighten up a bit . . . But it is bog standard to be asked to give this sort of assurance. Not many people will give it without being positive that they are telling the truth.

Perhaps we have been looking in the wrong direction; have I not heard of a remote language in which Yes means No? If I am wrong, how about inventing such a language; why, Mr McIntosh could be our first teacher of it.

I shall never be enormously rich – rich enough to join the club where Yes means Perhaps. But couldn't I be allowed to sit in on the doings of those who really understand how high finance works, and indeed who make huge fortunes in the business before losing it all and more? The awful truth, I fear, is that if, in such a session, I were to cough gently, and they politely paused in their labours and asked what I wanted to say, and I pointed out that – contrary to the words of the document they had just signed – twice two make four, not thirty-nine and a bit, they would smile charmingly and murmur that I do not understand high finance. And I'would have to say that indeed I do not, and say under my breath that I don't want to, either.

The Times, 21 December 1993

I heard it somewhere

IF, SAID VOLTAIRE, I was accused of stealing the towers of Notre Dame, I would make a bolt for it at once. Wise man, for my story today (the details are from *The New York Times*) reinforces his wisdom. It begins in Calais, Maine, a month or two ago. One day, a child came home from school and said that a man had been taking photographs in the vicinity. That was true; a municipal surveyor had been taking visual notes for a proposed alteration to the buildings in the area. That, I say, was true; in what followed there was not the slightest element of truth to be found, in any form, by any person, at any time. Which is comforting, because what was *believed* was that scores of children from the local school had been pornographically photographed and abducted, and had thereafter been variously raped, beheaded or eviscerated, or even suffered two or more of these uncomfortable fates.

From the innocent local council employee on a job with a camera, there was an almost immediate quantum leap to the belief that a sinister dark-skinned figure had been enticing children and taking lewd photographs of them. On the same day, the headmaster of the school was called to the door of it, to find an angry crowd of 20 parents, who had taken another and greater quantum leap, saying that throat-cutting, too, was now rife. No evidence of any kind was offered, though the conviction of the now raging parents was absolute.

*

A few hours and some slit throats later the next quantum was reached: a culprit, Christophe Beddeleem. He was indeed dark-skinned and even pock-marked; he had a record of drugtaking and petty crime, though he had been cured of the drug-habit and had come to the area from elsewhere to live with his mother and put all that behind him. No matter; a culprit had been found, and the next stop was clearly a lynching; he fled the neighbourhood and went into hiding.

In an attempt to stem the tide of madness, the local paper pointed out that the police had found no evidence of any wrong-doing, whether by the scapegoat or anyone else. No child was missing; none had been abused; no pornographic pictures had been seen by anyone. Nevertheless, when the headmaster of the school arrived next day, he found a crowd not of 20 but of 200, some of them equipped with megaphones, and to the substantial variety of infanticidal practices already logged, burning alive had been added.

Gradually, this *folie en masse* died down; presumably the slit throats had been stitched up, the stomachs of the eviscerated victims carefully put back, the missing heads replaced from the local hospital's headbank, and all was peace again – except for the chosen scapegoat, M Beddeleem, who is still in hiding.

And that is where I come in.

For I, when I read about the massacre of the innocents, leaped back 23 years in my mind, and remembered a story that marches, step by step, beside the story of the Calais rumours.

In May 1969, in Orleans, a whisper began to run through the town; its substance was that there was white-slave traffic going on. The method used was simple: young women going into dress-shops were shepherded into the fitting-cubicles and there drugged by injections. They were kept, unconscious, in the shops' cellars till night came, when they were smuggled out and sent abroad to be captive prostitutes.

The rumour began with one, specified, dress-shop, called *Dorphée*. It was well known in the town, and had a high reputation for its wares; it had a fitting-room, at the back of the shop, and a basement. The first rumour was that two women had been found by the police, drugged, in the basement of *Dorphée*; they had been taken to hospital, where they regained consciousness.

The rumour ran through the town like a mad bull; within a few days *Dorphée* had been joined by *Boutique de Sheila, Alexandrine, Félix, Le Petit Bénefice*, and *D.D.*, all engaging in this dreadful trade. And all six of the shops were owned by Jews.

Unlike Calais, the local newspaper decided not to publish anything about the story, on the ground that publicity about it would spread it further and more rapidly; but like Calais, the police investigated the rumour and found no evidence of any such goings-on. Again like Calais, no one was reported missing, whether in sinister or explainable circumstances. The Public Prosecutor, too, looked into the story, and naturally found nothing amiss.

Nevertheless, just like Calais, the rumour went into full metastasis; it was claimed that the six shops running the terrible business were linked by underground tunnels (though some of the shops were several hundred yards away from any other), which ultimately ended in the Loire, where boats were waiting nightly to load their human cargo. The next wave was inevitable; since the police, the press, the town Prefect and all the authorities were saying and doing nothing, it was apparent that they had all been bribed. And who had bribed them? Why, obviously, the Jews.

Crowds gathered at the six shops; it was touch and go – one convincing shout, one brick, one crash of glass, and Orleans might have experienced a pogrom. But meanwhile, the forces of reason had at last begun the counterattack. The two provincial papers broke the story under, respectively, the headlines "An Odious Calumny" and "A Campaign of Defamation", and Paris woke up to what was happening, whereupon *Le Monde, L'Aurore, L'Express* and *Le Nouvel Observateur* gave the story appropriate coverage. The Bishop of Orleans demanded an end to this "odious cabal"; the political parties denounced the campaign; Jewish and inter-faith organisations took up the cudgels; and, as you would expect of a university, the university ran away and hid.

The greatest conviction of human beings is their belief that they guide themselves and their actions not by impulse, dreams, omens, hunches, guesswork and the ideas of other people, but by reason. This dreadful absurdity has ruined countless millions, and made many billions unhappy, without making even the slightest dent in the original belief. ("Depend upon it", said Shaw, "if Macbeth had killed Macduff, he would have gone back to the witches next day for advice on how to deal with Malcolm.")

The madnesses of Calais and Orleans demonstrate plainly that reason has no place in the human heart, and precious little in the human head; it is astonishing that, over the centuries, we have never shaken off the delusion. It was, after all, the human race which thought up the notion "No smoke without fire", and until the human race ceases to believe it we shall continue to see episodes like those in Calais and Orleans. It is happily true that neither in the Calais frenzy nor the Orleans *arc-en-ciel* was anyone hurt, let alone killed. But a very great number of people were killed in Auschwitz, their deaths having been ordered by a system based on the most thorough and logical premises, steeped in impeccable reason.

"Think it possible", said Cromwell, "you may be mistaken." Possible? *Possible?*

The bird has flown

YOU MUST AGREE, surely, that this is an amazing country, perhaps the most amazing the world has ever seen. At least, I cannot think of any other in which certain recent events could have taken place.

It began pictorially, and the picture was in itself sufficiently amazing to clinch my assertion. It was of an empty field. The picture ran right across an entire page of the *Telegraph*, and it showed a perfectly straight line of people, beginning in the immediate foreground and running off the other side into a kind of infinity, every one of them looking in the same direction. I took a powerful magnifying-glass to the picture, trying to count them, but it was impossible; they were certainly hundreds. And – if you have amazements, prepare to amaze them now – the entire line of spectators were looking, in the same direction, at *nothing at all*.

True, they were hoping to see something before darkness fell, and they kept their vigil loyally to the end, though fruitlessly. And what was it that they hoped to see? The Second Coming? Buried treasure, to be sought when the whistle went? A duel to the death between John Smith and Bryan Gould, the loser to accept the whole blame for Labour's election defeat? No. They were awaiting the arrival of a lesser short-toed lark. (Here, I pause to rebuke Mr Geoffrey Wheatcroft, who long ago announced that he was at work designing a typographical symbol which would mean "I am not making this up", but who has wholly failed to carry out his promise.)

The day before the gathering, this elusive bird had been spotted near Weymouth, and the word had immediately spread. The excitement was caused by the fact that the lesser short-toed lark has never been seen in this country, preferring less treacherous weather; hitherto it had ventured no closer than the south of Spain, though there had been a claim ("Mind you, I've said nothing") for Ireland.

But wait. The very next day, as recorded in *The Times*, a harmless couple, Mr and Mrs Shedden, living in Hamilton, Scotland, were invaded by 250 people, who went clumping up the stairs and bursting into the bedrooms. The reason for the sack of the Hamiltons was that there had been a sighting of another rare bird, this one the dark-eyed junco. (Wheatcroft, for shame!)

I made the obvious remark: how delicious must these birds be, that so many gourmets would take so much trouble to get it on to their plates, particularly since the sighting referred to two single birds, not flocks, and with two vast throngs all salivating for the culinary experience of a lifetime, the odds against landing it must have been pretty well hopeless.

To my astonishment, I learned that they had no intention of cooking and eating them, with – it was my suggestion – a couple of rashers of streaky bacon on their breasts and a veal forcemeat (what the French call a *godiveau*) inside. Why, then, were all these people either standing around from morning till night in a ploughed field or re-running *The Return of the Body-Snatchers* in the Sheddens' home? Merely, it seems, to *see* the creatures, although since they are both about the size of a sparrow, the bystanders might as well have changed their minds and raffled them for the oven.

But that is the birds' problem; my theme, as announced, is the amazingness of this country, and I think that the story of the lesser short-toed lark and its friend the dark-eyed junco, with the hundreds of people who turned out in vain to see them, proves my claim.

I understand the collecting instinct, and also the sub-instinct inside it, which is the longing to acquire every item of the species. A long time ago, small boys clustered on railway station platforms, clutching booklets in which they solemnly recorded each sighting of a locomotive, indistinguishable from a hundred others, except for its number; it was the numbers they were recording. For all I know, there is a grown man somewhere in this country (it *is* amazing, you remember) who managed to collect every locomotive in the land, and from time to time takes down the completed booklet and turns the pages.

But after all, he has pages to turn. A glimpse of a bird which might or might not be a lesser short-toed lark or a dark-eyed junco is hardly the stuff of dreams by the fireside in old age. Yet hundreds of people are content to get the glimpse and nothing else; why, they are apparently content *not* to get the glimpse, and on this occasion didn't, yet went happily on their way.

Suppose that on the way home, one of them met a sane friend. "Where have you been?"

"Looking for a lesser short-toed lark and a dark-eyed junco."

"Did you find one?"

"No."

"If you had, what would you have done with them?"

"Nothing."

"Er – here's my bus, I must fly."

Well. Is there, could there be, another country in which such shenanigans take place without the police arriving in the company of two doctors and a magistrate? Frenchmen may cluster in a field, but only to shoot the birds and eat them. Italians may likewise cluster, but only to spread a picnic. The Spaniards themselves, mindful of their Lesser Short-Toed visitor, may do their share of clustering, but in the end they will be found under a tree murmuring "mañana".

Do you know what Heine said about us? He said: "England is a country which the sea would have swallowed long ago, if the sea had not been afraid of getting indigestion." Is there anyone – the prime minister, Michael Heseltine, Paddy Ashdown, John Smith, Ted Heath – who, when alone, with the lights low and the curtains closed, really believes that Britain will stay in the EC?

Ask the 400 who sought the lesser short-toed lark all over Dorset, and the 250 who did likewise in Hamilton with the dark-eyed junco, and who, having failed to find either, went home not grumbling at fate but cheerfully intent on spotting their prey next time.

What do you think Shakespeare was referring to when he spoke of "This happy breed of men, this little world"? Obviously, it was the breed of those who were willing to stand all day in a ploughed field to welcome a lesser short-toed lark and a dark-eyed junco and then shoo them away. Moreover, we must not be bound by those figures – 400 or 250: if there had been time to round up *all* the devotees of these two elusive birds from all around the country, the field would have had to expand to the size of Yorkshire, and the Sheddens' semi would have been reduced to splinters. Well, are you still unconvinced that this is the most amazing country in the world?

P.S. There have also been recent sightings of the cattle egret, the alpine swift, the red-rumped swallow and the pie-billed grebe. If any experienced poulterer is reading this, I would be very grateful for some recipes.

The Times, 25 June 1992

Down under: 1

IT IS WELL known that New Zealand is many thousands of miles away from anything on one side, and similarly many thousands of miles from anything else on the other side (of course I don't count Australia); this isolation suggests that the Lord made a strange and deleterious mistake when He was sorting out the continents (see Genesis, Chapters 1 and 2). But we also know that the Lord does not make mistakes: if He put down New Zealand where it is now, He did so for a purpose. And it was that purpose which, a few weeks ago, I decided to seek out.

And that is why I found myself in New Zealand, having been told that when I had pushed my baggage-trolley past the immigration desks and the customs procedures (both manned by people of perfect courtesy) that I would find a man very tall and very bald who was to be my cicerone for something like a month. Tall he was, and bald he was; little did I then know that he was to look after me so carefully, so thoroughly, so generously, so knowledgeably and so amusingly, that no newborn baby could have asked for more in the way of being made happy and enlightened. But littler still did I know that my hero – his name is Phil O'Reilly – was to lead me to countless people of all New Zealand walks of life, all parts of their country, all courtesies, all welcomes, all generosities and all – all – for nothing but that New Zealanders are like that.

But I am going too fast. I did not alight on New Zealand unprepared; indeed, there had been for some time

messages back and forth (I still believe that the fax, infinitely useful as it is, must be an instrument of the devil, so
uncanny is its faraway whirring, and sooner or later we
shall all be burnt at the stake). I had been invited by
the Newspaper Publishers Association of New Zealand,
no less, to be taken to their country and shown round
it. Nor was there any obligation to concentrate on newspaper matters. I was told that the NPA had embarked
upon a series of such invitations from the other side of
the world, and I was to be the first to enjoy such hospi-
tality.

We drove into town, and I experienced my first New
Zealand shock. The sky – it was a warm and unclouded
day – was as clear and pure as though it had been scrubbed.
I was not then to know, though I soon discovered, that
New Zealand does not have polluted air, and when I say it
does not have polluted air, I do not mean that it has air less,
or even much less, polluted than that in countries like ours,
it means that New Zealand *does not have polluted air*. End of
first shock.

Five minutes later, I had my second shock. On either
side of the airport motorway, there was rolling beauty; no
debris, no factories, no noise *and no billboards*, only beautiful, immensely tall, poplars, and smiling fields. I commented that the leaves looked as though they had been
washed, and Phil smiled; it was the first of hundreds of
such smiles, and each of them denoted another wondrous
shock for me.

But again, I am going too fast. The first public encounter
with New Zealand was a barrage of newspaper, radio and
television interviews. To my astonishment, I found that
there is no national newspaper, only local ones. It is, of
course, a very long country, but surely, I thought, with
today's technology a national paper can hardly be impossible. But then a thought struck me: perhaps New
Zealand does not want a national newspaper. I had already
discovered that New Zealand is not like other places, and

this might be more evidence. If so, it is not for me to demand a national newspaper immediately I land. (And while I am on the subject, I have to add that their newspapers are rather strikingly different from ours, as witness *The Dominion*, a highly respected daily, which one day led its front page, beneath a banner headline to match, with "British firm wins sewerage contract", which I think one would be unlikely to find in our dear *Sun*.)

The interviewers had done their homework, but then came the next surprise; the interviewers, almost without exception, were amazingly gentle; I wouldn't be so rude as to call it pussy-footing, but there is surely enough in my millions of words to provoke them to stick into me at least a pin. That unterrible ordeal over, it was time for me to think about what came next.

My splendid jaunt had, naturally, a price – a tiny price, a very tiny price – but a price, for what was in store for me (and what was in store for me, I may say, was a seven-room suite for starters) included my giving a set of lectures. Now anyone who knows Levin knows also that far from his being dismayed when asked to talk, it is almost impossible to stop him talking once he has started. This, I said to myself, is going to be a doddle.

And a doddle it was, though a doddle that changed into one of the most profound and moving experiences of my life, an experience that is with me as I write, an experience that I savoured on the way home (and 25 hours in the air with only *one hour's* break would normally savour only a longing for death) – an experience that I am still far from encompassing and of which I may never fully take the measure.

Meanwhile, a drive round the suburbs revealed one-storey white clapboard houses, bursting with flowers meticulously and lovingly tended. A strange and horrible thought came unbidden: are there thugs and tearabouts in these parts, like those we know all too well back home, and who smash beauty just because it *is* beauty? I asked the question: my guide looked at me as though I had gone mad. We chattered on, but I could not stop asking for another peculiar look. "How bad is the drug problem in your country?" I asked, and this time there was a real answer. "There isn't one," he said. (Later, and with others, I asked the same question. I got the same answer.)

So we went to the park, via the sea and its harbours, with gigantic fleets of yachts – this is a seafaring country, and shows it. They told me the names of the trees and bushes in the park, but I was far too deeply enmeshed by beauty such as I have never seen before. I, urban man personified, who once said that the best thing that could befall the countryside would be its covering with an even layer of asphalt – that very man, as he wandered through every kind of greenery and every kind of beauty, found that his eyes were wet. What have I got into?

I begin to be genuinely afraid. This is a country that I have heard of (well, Kiri came from it) and dismissed as too distant to bother with, yet it is disturbing my sleep, and the beauty of its unspoilt landscape is matched by the depth of its people, who mean what they say when they embrace a newcomer. I was, again and again, that newcomer, and never on this earth and my wanderings on it, have I found so much truth in such smiles. It strikes me – and it should have struck me much earlier in this panegyric – that the Lord quite certainly *did* know what He was doing when He put New Zealand where it is.

Then I was taken to New Plymouth, a city of only some 140,000 inhabitants (but, after all, the whole country is not much more than three million), and was guided round New Plymouth by a man who not only knew every stone in his city, but loved every such stone. Hills, rivers, sundials, memorials, lakes and hills – I have to say that New Plymouth is a rather ordinary city, *if you are only thinking of outsides*. But its inside is filled with human beings who do not know or care who I am and why I was among them, but treated me and my entourage as they would treat any visitor from anywhere.

And it ran everywhere: my lectures were most warmly received, and considering that one of them had an audience of 600, and another one went on for 50 minutes without a break, I have nominated New Zealand as the most tolerant place in the world. But my nomination was superfluous; long before that, I had realised the truth about this astounding place. Meanwhile, I strolled down to the beach. The beach in question was two miles long, and I had it to myself. And as the water ran up across the sand, I could see that it was absolutely clear and absolutely pure.

The Times, 3 January 1995

Down under: 2

I HAVE PAINTED THE New Zealand portrait in the brightest of colours; but what else could I have done? Can it really be as amazing as I think? The surprising answer is yes. This is a country at ease with itself, but it is a crisp ease, not a soft one. They have, it is true, gone mad over their wine; wherever I went I had to inspect the cellar, but since the visit to the cellar was invariably followed by some serious tasting, I found it not much of a handicap. They are proud of their awesomely old glaciers; yes, but when I looked over those mighty frozen rivers, where countless visitors tread, I could find no sign of litter; perhaps more to the point, I could find no sign of a plea eschewing litter.

The cities – most of them named after their originals in Britain – flew by: Wellington, where Parliament sits and where I had half an hour with a remarkably untroubled Prime Minister (*o si sic omnes!*); Christchurch, which looks more like the one in Britain than the one in Britain: Queenstown, the Venice of New Zealand, not for its beauty but for its bustle and huge influx of visitors; Arrowtown, the very opposite, with its calm and shops selling only beautiful things; Greymouth, with its mighty breakwater wall (once, before the wall was built, the town was flooded); Dunedin, where they still revere the name of Stevenson; but, alas, not Levin – oh, yes there is a town called Levin, but a visit would have strained the crowded schedule, and I had to be content with seeing the name on a signpost pointing off the motorway. (And anyway, they pronounce it with the stress on the second syllable.)

There is one missing link in the perfection of New Zealand: although it is a long, narrow land, it is – very surprisingly – without a substantial railway network. The result is that everybody drives. No, that does not mean, as it would in almost all of the countries of the world, congestion and stinking exhausts, for I was driven for hundreds of miles in all, and very rarely indeed did I meet more than two cars coming the other way. But it means that sometimes a good many hours are needed to go from hither to thither, and when the winding hills are involved, even more hours are spent.

That, however, brings me to the winding hills themselves, and the description thereof. Easily said; almost impossible to describe. I have kept the best and the most moving to the end, because it is fitting that I should. Every time I close my eyes and think of what I saw among those hills, I am overwhelmed by beauty – beauty the like of which I have never seen before and will never see again, unless I go back to New Zealand. I am tempted to ask the Lord to describe it – after all, He made it. Anyway, I must try.

A lot of New Zealand stands on earthquake ground, and tremors are almost daily fare; moreover, much of what isn't troubled by the shaking of the earth can claim a footing on extinct volcanic matter (well, everybody hopes it is extinct), but I believe I am right when I say that this remarkable place can boast (although it doesn't boast – it is the least vain country in the world, though it has much to boast about) that the greatest part of the country is untouched by human hand. And that is why it is so difficult to describe those millions of square metres.

It is easy to say that New Zealand is made of hills and lakes; it is. But when you stand high on a hill and look down, and see the gigantic, rolling, infinitely mighty mountainsides, clad in a thousand shades of green, you can only think that some legendary giant has simply scraped with his fingernails the inhospitable sides where nothing would grow, and watched with a smile as the barren walls burst out in beauty – beauty that has endured (I am told that forest fires are few and trivial) to delight and stun with its mighty loveliness.

And that was only the hillsides. What of the water? Dear reader, how can I describe a mighty New Zealand lake nestling among hills? The first thought, when the twist in the path draws back the curtain below, is that the lake is frozen, so still, so perfectly still it is. But it cannot be frozen; very little can freeze in New Zealand, and that little – well, Shakespeare said it for me:

> Orpheus with his lute made trees,
> And the mountain-tops that freeze.
> Bow themselves when he did sing:
> To his music plants and flowers
> Ever sprung; as sun and showers
> There had made a lasting spring

And if the hidden lakes of New Zealand are not frozen, why do they look like that? It is because there is nothing to stir their water, other than an occasional leaping fish, and because the glitter of the water is so beautiful it is almost impossible to believe that it can ripple.

There are fish in those lakes, and deer in the hills; sheep and goats browse the hillsides, and sometimes it looks as though the hill that is being cropped is so steep that the browsers must be perpendicular. I learnt that there are no genuinely indigenous animals or – I thought they said – even birds. I am no bird expert, but I remembered looking up at the velvety sky one night in Australia, and feeling a touch of fear as I saw the wrong stars, and I felt something similar when birds I was sure I had never heard before began to serenade me.

As I write, I conjure up the friends who filled those weeks for me, and I warm myself on the memory of those who are now basking in their new year sunshine. Sometimes, I think I dreamt it. Did I really go all the way to New Zealand, a country that I had hardly heard of, and did I find there a place that is not like any place I had ever been to, and make friends, and feel yearnings, and make even more remarkable discoveries? My experience in New Zealand can only be categorised as the *coup de foudre*, love at first sight. Now love at first sight is notoriously precarious, but I am certain that this love will endure. At the moment, I am trying to think of ways of getting back there as soon as possible – to salute my friends, to see the glorious Milford Sound, said to be the most beautiful sight in all New Zealand (a very considerable claim), and which I missed because of the cruelty of the schedule.

But I conclude with something very different. My last lecture was to be my final word on Utopia. I was introduced by the chairman, most generously, and I walked to the podium. But before I launched on my Utopia lecture, I said that I had something more personal to say. And this is what I said:

"Ladies and gentlemen: At last, my magic carpet comes to rest. In a matter of hours. I shall be packing for the journey home to Britain. I am crammed to bursting with the people I have met, and with whom I have made instant friendships. I have seen your breathtaking and unspoilt landscapes, and revelled almost every day I have been here in beautiful weather. (I was *told* that your weather was by no means perfect; I don't believe a word of it.)

"I have learnt, in those few weeks, that there is a country, many thousands of miles away from mine, in which I have discovered things that I had no idea existed. I am flooded with happiness, with food and wine, music and words. But of course, all these put into one do not begin to take the measure of the greatest richness of your country: its people.

"Wherever I went, my eyes were opened in a way that allowed me to gain understanding and simultaneously deepen the regret that I must leave you. There is, in the New Zealand people, a combination, as I saw it, of warmth, of steadfastness, of courage, of innocence – of what Chesterton said of England a sadly long time ago: that she was made of 'faith, and green fields, and honour, and the sea'.

"It is hard to leave; so hard, that I have something to say so startling that I can hardly believe I am saying it; I beg you to believe that I mean every word of it.

"It is this. I am 66 years old, but if I were only 20 years younger – only 20 years – and had had such an experience as I have just had in New Zealand, I would without hesitation, and without regret, tear up my return ticket."

The Times, 6 January 1995

If you can get it

IT USED TO BE the fashion, one that may be returning in this election, that newspapers canvassed men and women prominent in fields other than politics, asking how they would vote, and why; it was deemed interesting to know how these apparently uncommitted figures would commit themselves on polling day. One reply has remained in my mind; it was from Evelyn Waugh, at his dottiest, and he replied (I quote from memory, but I am sure of the gist): "I would think it an impertinence to offer advice to my Sovereign in her choice of government."

That is rather like the situation I find myself in now. I am in most generous and comfortable hands (and beautiful surroundings), but in California, a place which does tend somewhat to distort reality; moreover, my host is seeking election to Congress, which distorts sanity, never mind reality. All things considered, I would be delighted to miss our election campaign entirely, and simultaneously to flee from the even greater lunacies of the American system. A compromise; I shall stay in California, comment on neither election, and come back in time to vote. Until then, if you want a rest from the parties and their nostrums, you may seek sanctuary in this space on Mondays and Thursdays, as of yore.

When I want to annoy Californians, I draw their attention to the fact that in the first edition of the *Encyclopaedia Britannica* California is clearly depicted as an island. When I want to increase the annoyance and widen its scope, I ask why American newspapers are all terrible. They don't, mostly, behave like our beastly tabloids, but even from those they could learn about layout, headlining, intelligible compression and what a newspaper is. (It is certainly not *The Los Angeles Times*, which appeared yesterday with a front-page headline reading Moths Threaten to Ravage Lands in North-West.)

Desperately short of humour, page after page doing nothing but roll out acres of grey columns, not one tenth of which does one tenth of the readership glance at – this is what lack of competition does for a press. Alas, it is unimaginably rare – perhaps unique – to find a town with more than one serious but sensible paper, and it is unimaginably common to find towns with a paper that is neither serious nor sensible.

But no newspaper, however poor, could miss the story of Clarence Chance and Benny Powell, which for some time convinced me that Lords Lane, Donaldson and Bridge had been visiting the United States at the relevant time and had been shown the courtesy of the American bench by their opposite numbers; what else, I mused, could explain the fact that Mr Chance and Mr Powell, having been fitted up by crooked policemen, who were then believed by the judges, had each spent 17 years in jail until somebody – right outside the legal system – noticed that they were both entirely innocent, and pointed out the fact to the authorities, who took the point and hastily let them out.

Now it is generally agreed that American law is not as other nations' law. For instance, if you think that our libel laws, which invite any crook to dive into the bran-tub and come out smelling of hundreds of thousands of pounds, are a little extravagant, you should see the American system of compensation; a twisted ankle can deliver a quarter of a million smackers, and a leer at a not very respectable woman twice that. But I think we would have to go very far indeed to match the story of Patrick Hinrichsen and what happened to him, together with Mr Hinrichsen's mother and sister.

Mr Hinrichsen lived for many years with another man, a Mr Robert Saari; as far as the information goes, it was a most respectable and devoted relationship. In the fullness of time, Mr Saari died, and Mr Hinrichsen arranged for his cremation, with the ashes to be scattered at sea. So far, so good; Mr Hinrichsen was doubtless heartbroken, but he did this last loving duty for his companion. But by some mistake or failure in communications (certainly it seems there was no malice or deliberate disrespect involved), the burial at sea was accompanied by a Christian service. Neither Mr Saari nor Mr Hinrichsen was a Christian, and neither wanted such ministrations at their obsequies.

Whereupon, and thereupon, Mr Hinrichsen, his mother and sister sued the burial society for "emotional distress", and collectively collected $242,500 for the said distress. The defendants took a curious line; they argued that because Mr Saari was not related to Mr Hinrichsen he was not entitled to damages for the dreadful experience of listening to some daft old geezer saying things like "I am the Resurrection and the Life . . ."

The court ruled (upheld on appeal) that Mr Hinrichsen's relationship, though it had not been solemnised in a formal and binding marriage (I think you can get such marriages in California, and I have no doubt at all that whoever does the splicing is careful – or now will be – to listen carefully for instructions as to the happy pair's denomination), was close enough for compensation. The defendants fell back on the quantum of damages, holding that a quarter of a million greenbacks, for being told that we brought nothing into this world and it is certain that we can carry nothing out, would be a trifle on the generous side. No dice; chap, mother and sister carved the joint, in what exact proportions history does not reveal, and were left alone with their emotional distress and their money.

"Emotional distress" has presumably existed since human beings became fond of each other and were bereaved, dismayed, shocked, pained and sympathised with;

the term is a fairly recent one, and its appearance in our courts much more recent. There are those – I am emphatically one of them – who think that to pay monetary awards for emotional distress is a shameful and even disgusting practice. Since the human race existed it has suffered, and much of that suffering has been through seeing loved ones suffer. But only when greed and the law joined hands was the concept created.

To see a loved one die assuredly gives rise to emotional distress; to watch the burial of a loved one can also cause truly painful feelings. We can argue at leisure as to whether those feelings should be paid for. But to demand – *and get* – a quarter of a million dollars for seeing a Christian burial over an agnostic testifies to nothing but the depths to which American jurisprudence has fallen.

The Times, 23 March 1992

Arms and the man

I AM NOT QUITE sure whether you should be reading this at breakfast; to be on the safe side you might perhaps have a stiff whisky beside your scrambled eggs. It concerns an 18-year-old youth who was working on his family's farm in North Dakota, when he got tangled in the agricultural machinery; he was near some kind of power system. However it happened, the effect was that the rogue machine tore off both his arms just below the shoulders. Drink the whisky.

Having lost his arms, he kept his head. He staggered to the farmhouse seeking help. Nobody was home and the door was shut. He opened the outer door by bending down, taking the handle in his mouth and turning it; he did the same to the living-room door-handle. Once in the room, he sought and found a pencil; he picked it up in his teeth (not an easy manoeuvre at any time, and positively fraught when the conjuror has no arms), and with it, laboriously tapped out the telephone number of the emergency services. Replenish your whisky.

The ambulancemen came quickly, and the surgeons were ready no less speedily; I have no details of who stumbled across the arms and what he said when he saw them. (Possibly it was, "Well, well, what have we here?") Anyway, the arms were re-attached to the body, which was presumably pleased to see its lost members again; no doubt the young man was even more pleased. Then everybody sat back to see what would happen.

What happened was that some six weeks later our hero left hospital; he had been warned that it was not clear whether the arms would eventually work, and in any case there would have to be more surgery. His *sang-froid* did not leave him; on the steps of the hospital, he made a speech thanking everybody, and concluded with the memorable words "I came here in three pieces and I'm going home in one." He politely refused the use of a wheelchair.

Arma virumque cano. It is no use trying to play the old game: how would *we* measure in such a situation? The game only works if the supposed events are within credibility, but if the question-master said "Bernard, what would you be thinking while you were chasing round a ploughed field looking for your arms?", I would pass, or more likely pass out.

The youth presumably did not himself know how he would behave in such an emergency; at the age of 18 one does not spend much time wondering how one would cope if one's arms went astray. But this is not a study in youthful psychiatry, nor even a lecture on orthopaedic surgery. It is a hymn to the indomitable human spirit, which this boy demonstrated in no uncertain manner.

Of course it helped that he was young. At that age the determination to survive is very powerful indeed; give someone four or five more decades and the life-force is not so easy to conjure up. But youth alone will not solve the gory problem; from what depths of will-power did he summon up such fortitude accompanied by such clear-headed ingenuity? Remember that throughout the experience blood was pouring out of his body; loss of blood weakens the injured party rapidly, and with every minute that passed his strength must have been waning.

Human beings can do the impossible, if the determination to do it is powerful enough. There is an organisation called the Mouth and Foot Artists, which is precisely what its name says it is: artists who have lost both arms, or were born without them, paint pictures with the brush held in the mouth or between the toes. (Be warned; they are proud. They will not let you give their organisation money except in return for their work.) For that matter, one of my very dearest and closest friends has had laid upon her so many bodily afflictions that Job himself would be ashamed to bemoan his comparatively trivial complaints; yet she lights up any company with her faith-grounded laughter.

We do not know what qualities we have or lack until we are tested to our limit. But surely that boy must have shown, among his family and friends and fellow-students, some kind of exceptional character. There is a rather repulsive procedure in American schools and even universities in which the student body vote one of their number as "Most likely to succeed". Did he receive such an accolade?

"Man, proud man . . . most ignorant of what he's most assured . . ." Perhaps our young man was better off not knowing what he was capable of. Perhaps, indeed, we should all be glad to have no inkling of what lies in us; after all, suppose we could tap the source of knowledge but discover that in a coming test we shall fail, and fail ignominiously. A benevolent providence has drawn the curtains close on hero and coward alike; better so.

Still, we have the testimony of a youth in North Dakota to show us that the impossible can be done. And although we are sure we could never emulate him, he gives us all fresh courage, hope and presence of mind; O brave new world, that has such creatures in't! For what is the essence of his achievement? It is one of the greatest of all qualities, and it is one that I believe is steadily dying out: self-reliance. Yes, we are all members one of another, but there are times, many times, when we have nothing but our own bodies, minds and souls with which to challenge and beat down the demons. This 18-year-old, when his moment came, took his mind, his body and his soul into the fiery furnace that is always ready to test us all, and in the assay he was not found wanting. He came out of his day of trial with his mind and soul intact; let us pray that the surgeons' skills will give him back his body, also intact.

The Times, 3 April 1992

Face to face

A YEAR OR SO ago, I wrote here of a very remarkable accident, and what happened after it. A youth in the United States, who lived and worked on his parents' farm, became entangled in some kind of agricultural machinery, which tore off both his arms at the shoulder. The boy staggered to the farmhouse to find no one at home; he opened the door by turning the handle with his mouth, and when inside, summoned help by picking up a pencil in his teeth and tapping out the emergency number on the telephone. The arms were collected where they had fallen, and united with the rest of him; when he was ready to leave the hospital, he thanked everyone concerned, and finished with the memorable words: "I came here in three pieces, and I'm going home in one."

The last I heard of him, he was steadfastly undergoing physiotherapy, in the hope that his arms would eventually work properly again. May he be successful; such courage, ingenuity and coolness under fire deserve no less.

In retailing the story, I warned my readers to have a stiff whisky at their side, particularly if they were reading it at breakfast. Today, I make the same request.

This story comes from the *Wall Street Journal*; more exactly, it comes from the hearts and feelings of a series of men and women, the chief of the band being a Scottish doctor, a craniofacial surgeon, Ian Jackson by name.

Ian Jackson has seen a pantheon of bizarre deformities. He has seen the horselike faces of hypertelorism, and midline clefts so severe they split the face in half. He has seen the misshapen heads of neurofibromatosis, the so-called elephant-man disease. But until Dr Jackson went on a charity mission from his native Scotland to Peru 15 years ago, he had never seen anything like David Lopez. The tiny Indian boy, just two years old, had virtually no face at all. A gaping hole covered the area where his mouth and nose should have been. There were no upper teeth or upper jaw. The most striking thing was that his lower teeth could actually touch his forehead . . . Craniofacial surgeons use power tools and chisels, as well as delicate scalpels and pins . . . But . . . with all his other patients, there had been bones to rearrange and skin to stretch. In David's case, the surgeon would have to build much of the face from scratch . . . Because David had no real mouth . . . he had developed a way of chewing or mashing his food with his tongue. To drink, he simply tilted back his head and poured the liquid straight down. One day . . . David came across a mirror and began screaming. Until then, the boy had never seen his face.

Drink the whisky, unless you have already done so.

Dr Jackson wondered whether it was possible to save the boy, partly because of the difficulties mentioned above, and partly because if he undertook the project it was going to cost a very great deal of money; this doubly heroic doctor would give his services, but the immense and pro-longed hospital facilities that would be needed were not easily come by. After months of seeking a sponsor, Dr Jackson found a Scottish Catholic bishop who promised to find the money, and did so. The work began.

David Lopez has so far gone through 85 major surgical operations, and the end is not yet. He has been taunted as a freak, but as his manufactured face has been built up from countless grafts, he now looks no worse than someone who has been in a severe car crash or fire.

So much for the medical profession. Now for the human race.

Doctors, and in particular surgeons, must always be detached from emotion when dealing with a patient, as witness the unwritten rule that no surgeon, except in a dire emergency, may operate on his own wife. The reason is too obvious to discuss, but Dr Jackson, as the face of the dreadfully deformed child slowly began to take shape – that is, a human shape – found his feelings growing ever stronger, until he realised that he had come to love the little boy as he loved his own four children. He and his wife discussed the possibility of adoption, but there was a threat over the whole enterprise, even including the surgery; by then, Dr Jackson and his family had emigrated to America, and because David had no documents he was, strictly, an illegal immigrant, liable to be deported at any minute.

Over to Mrs Jackson.

I don't know whether she felt that she was caught in a bad novel, the kind you see in the section of bookshops headed "Romance", but if she did, she must have thought that not only was she trapped in its pages, but that it was an even worse book than she had thought. For Mrs Jackson found herself flying to Peru, in a haystack-and-needle endeavour to find David's lawful parents, if any, and to discover whether they would agree to formally give up the ravaged boy. After a no doubt interesting journey into the interior, she found the mission from which David had been taken, to the chance of a real life.

The only means of following the meagre clues was by canoe; she stepped aboard, accompanied by a priest from the mission, and this extraordinary couple paddled off into the sunset – or, as it might be, the sunrise. (Are there crocodiles in Peruvian rivers? If so, their table-manners were perfect, for there was no sighting.)

The priest (I am by no means sure that it wasn't St Jude in disguise) followed the tracks and found David's parents.

Asked whether they would consent to adoption they agreed. In any case, David's father explained that the tribe to which they belonged would no longer take him in. (This, I understand, was not because of the child's appearance, but because he had been too long away from the tribe and its observances.)

Now the boy, nine years old, had a new name to go with his gradually appearing new face: David Jackson. Today, at 17, he has a girlfriend, as any 17-year-old would, whatever he looked like; Mrs Jackson, that very wise woman, says: "Even at that age, there are girls who can see beyond David's face."

So there are, as Simon Weston would testify, holding his wife's hand as he does so. For this is not an account of a unique surgical success; that will be recorded in due course, no doubt, in the specialist journals. The real story goes much deeper. It is a story about people, each one of them with the divine spark that we all possess, but in addition, in this case, all of them with the courage, insight, patience, wisdom and greatness of heart to bring the story to its triumphant conclusion.

The Prayer Book bids us ask to be delivered from all sorts of evils: sin, the crafts and assaults of the devil, blindness of heart, pride, vainglory, hypocrisy, envy, hatred, malice and all uncharitableness. On top of all that are fornication and all the deceits of the world, the flesh and the devil; not forgetting lightning and tempest, plague, pestilence, famine, battle, murder and sudden death. On the whole, I have no inclination to challenge the mournful catalogue; indeed, I could add a good few items to it – broccoli, for instance, and Gummer. But as any coin will tell you, there are two sides to every situation, and I have never allowed myself to see the darkness in mankind without seeing at the same time the brightness.

There is no point in saying that there are in the world hundreds of thousands of men and women and children who are deformed or diseased or dying in horrible ways, and that for them there has been no rescue by a genius of the scalpel and the genius of the human heart. Did not Abraham bargain with the Lord, and get a promise that He would not destroy Sodom if ten of the righteous could be found there, whereas at first the Most High was minded to do it unless there were more than 50?

The story of David Jackson, you will allow, is enough to make one think well of the human race, whatever its failings. The boy himself has said that if the miracle had not happened he "would have been a beggar, or dead". But it did happen, starting with the immense skill of Dr Jackson, together with a supporting cast who in their own ways deployed a joint skill without which this story might not have ended in such perfection.

It was indeed a miracle; partly from heaven and partly from earth, the best possible combination. And the knot that tied the two halves together to complete the miracle was those three words that speak more profoundly than many shelves of many books, the three words that tell us that goodness will always triumph in the end, if we are only sufficiently patient, and if our eyes are sufficiently clear: *Omnia vincit Amor.*

The Times, 2 April 1993

That's the way the money goes

COINCIDENCES CAN BE cruel. Here are the brothers Reichmann, of Olympia & York, with a debt of 19 billion dollars (Canadian dollars, to be sure, but that number of even those would strain most men's jacket pockets), awaiting a solution to their troubles, and just when the Reichmanns didn't want to be reminded of the truth that for every sky-rocket there is a stick, enormous headlines announce the end of the happy hours of Alan Bond, who was once so rich that he had a daily delivery of noughts, but is now officially bankrupt, and none so poor to do him reverence.

For many years, I used to harbour a secret wish that there would be a nuclear war, not out of a misanthropic rage against humanity but because it was likely to knock down the Trump Tower in New York. Similarly, I bear no illwill towards the Reichmanns, but it seems possible that the ultimate outcome of their plight may encompass the demolition of Canary Wharf. My old mum used to urge me to look on the bright side, and I would like to, but the trouble with Canary Wharf is that it has four identical sides, and your guess is as good as mine when it comes to saying which is the bright one.

I don't want to upset anybody, particularly on a bank holiday, but I was irresistibly reminded of Canary Wharf – many of you, I am sorry to say, will have had the same image spring to mind – when I read of a case of alleged sexual harassment; this turned upon an office in which there was a distribution, at Christmas, of chocolate penises.

(Would you please note that I do not make the news, I comment upon it. Some were accompanied by whipped cream, others not.) But the question is: did the Canary Wharf architect do it deliberately, or did he – er – miss the point?

I suppose most of us would like to be immensely rich, and although for most of us it remains a dream, I have always thought that although almost all newspapers put their financial pages at the back, or in a separate section, they are underestimating the interest in the *news* of money – who has made lots, who looks like going smash, how much Moonbeams Inc have paid for Cucumbers plc, which shares have risen and which have sagged.

I do not believe that the interest shown in money by so many people is a form of *Schadenfreude*. They do not, I am sure, lick their lips with pleasure when some great magnate is brought low, though the exception, of course, is the high street banks; whenever (it has been twice weekly as far back as I can remember) one of them announces another irretrievable loss of some hundreds of millions incurred by lending it to President Mobutu on note of hand alone, the very same high streets are soon filled from side to side with merrymakers. But nor do I believe that reading about monetary coups makes people think that they, too, could turn the magic key to Aladdin's cave.

To some extent, I think, it is akin to the excitement of gambling as a spectator, with all the fun and none of the danger. We all dream of winning the pools jackpot, but although of course we would like to have a couple of million pounds – to buy a bigger house, to take early retirement, to travel the world in luxury – it is the excitement, not the avarice, that is uppermost in most people's minds.

I go further; I think most people would like to see the Brothers Reichmann find a way out of their troubles, if only because the chutzpah of getting into 19 billion

Canadian greenbacks of debt is so breathtaking that it deserves applause. (I think it was Kean who played Shylock so powerfully that at the moment of the villain's fall a member of the audience cried out, "The poor man is wronged!")

The biggest mystery is the most obvious one: why do men who have hundreds of millions safely stowed go on stowing, even though the new money brings danger with it? You don't have to be as monomaniacal as Tiny Rowland to be classed as obsessive; but why incur the classification in the first place?

Gold is beautiful, valuable and does not tarnish; but I cannot believe that that is why it has been elevated to something almost godly. If you think I am coming it too strong, try to count the metaphors attached to that strange, passionately coveted metal, and see if anything else that can be dug out of the earth has been pressed into service so far beyond its literal borders.

The greatest double meaning to be found in money raises its head in *Timon of Athens*. It is Shakespeare's most terrible nightmare, and it is easy to see why it is so rarely revived; Timon's offer to accommodate on his favourite tree as many Athenians as wish to hang themselves must strike a chord (nay, a cord) in a good many members of the emerging audience. With *Timon*, Shakespeare comes closer than in any other of his plays to a real rejection of humanity; at the end even of *Lear* ("vex not his ghost") there is a resolution that cannot be missed, despite the horrors that have gone before, but the chill that *Timon* spreads takes days to shake off.

The figure of the miser is a fascinating one, and one that I think bears out what I am saying. For the miser has taken his hoard to the ultimate limits; he has the money, but does nothing with it, except – it is the familiar scene – to open his strongboxes and run the gold through his fingers.

The actual mechanics that were used to arrive at 19 billion dollars in the hole are, of course, beyond me; beyond all of us, I imagine. Do they do it in the gambler's way – one more throw and I shall recoup all my losses? Some do, I suppose, but it is inconceivable that the Reichmanns did; there was nothing flamboyant or risky in their lives, their business or even their dismay. Incidentally, the photographs of Brother Paul puzzle me; does he brush his hair in an odd style, or is he wearing a *yarmulka*? Well, the latter would be appropriate for a nice Jewish boy like that, and he would always be ready for a prayer when the next billion goes astray.

There is another, very different, aspect of money: the crime to which it leads. I have a memory that illustrates that connection – but let me tell the story in full. The office in which I then worked was just off a main road which was replete with shops of all kinds. But this was before late-night shopping and even before supermarkets. Mindful of those who worked late, sensible entrepreneurs had installed, here and there, machines which dispensed cartons of milk. From time to time, when I had forgotten to visit the grocer ("grocer", forsooth; that dates me!), I would get some milk from the machine and take it home.

The machine was about the size of a fairly large refrigerator, and held, I suppose, something like 120 or 150 half-pints of milk. One evening, after I had finished my work and left my desk, I went round the corner for some milk and to my surprise found that the machine had gone. There was a newspaper seller nearby, and I asked him if he knew why the machine had been removed. He told me that it had been stolen.

Just think. The thieves would have needed a crane or similar device, together with instruments for prising the thing out of its niche. In addition, they would have needed a substantial van or lorry for their getaway. And for what? A few gallons of milk and at most a few pounds in sixpences. Surely the thieves' enterprise could have been channelled into a legitimate course, where such cool heads (remember, it was a main road) would have been sure to prosper. Yet they not only preferred to break the law than keep it; they broke the law for a wretched pittance.

Extrapolate from that story. Our prisons must contain hundreds of men whose lives alternate between being behind bars and living high on the hog, and who, if they put their minds and strengths to it, could live just as high on the hog without the intervals of prison. Again and again we are struck by the ingenuity of criminals when the charge is read out, and feel that, with all that cleverness, why not go straight? The work could not be harder, indeed it would most likely be a genuinely cushy number compared with another year's porridge, and more remunerative as well. But the criminal mind is something too alien for me to offer any opinion on it.

Remember Robert Maxwell? Towards the end, when the sand was running out, reality broke in; but remember that for very many years he had been thieving, swindling, forging, lying *and enjoying himself enormously*. Did he think, through those years, that he would never be found out? Or did he bank on the thought that he would die in criminal harness and let the world find out when he was gone? And his timing, you must admit, was almost good enough; another few years and he would not have needed to step off the yacht. Mind you, there is another riddle to unravel: did he *need* to be a crook? Could he not have made his millions honestly? Or – as I think – do he and those like him live in an imaginary world, refusing to recognise the real one, so that the things he did were not to him in any way strange?

And now for the national lottery; be ready with pitchforks, ducking-stools and blunderbusses, for as sure as day follows night the government will, if we let it, declare a top prize of, say, £75, on the ground that a larger sum might unsettle the winner. No; let it be millions, many millions, lots and *lots* of millions, so that some lucky devil will be rich beyond any reasonable doubt, and the rest of us can murmur *O si sic omnes*, or at least "me next week".

Come; we mustn't finish on so greedy a note. Once upon a time, there was a mighty king, the richest in all history. He mounted his golden throne, with his golden crown on his head and his golden sceptre in his hand, his very garments made of the same precious metal. Then he turned to his holy man, and said, "See – here I sit amid more gold than has ever been heaped up anywhere; how much am I worth thus?"

The holy man bowed low and spoke. "Sire," he said, "the saviour of the world was bought and sold for thirty pieces of silver. Shall we say twenty-nine?"

The Times, 20 April 1992

As time goes by

AGE SIGNALS ITSELF in a thousand ways, almost all of them accompanied by a sneer. On the other hand, wise men learn to dispense with the impossible. I, for instance, have long ago faced the fact that I cannot run a mile in under four minutes, or for that matter in an hour and a half, and the knowledge does not dismay me.

Death, of course, is less trifling. Two of my dearest and oldest friends have been among those who have tiptoed away in the year gone by, and the toll inevitably grows longer all the time, and the years steadily shorter:

> Then many a lad I liked is dead,
> And many a lass grown old;
> And as the lesson strikes my head
> My weary heart grows old . . .

Happily, the years also bring in their merry recollections as well as their gloomy ones, and the further away is the past they emerge from, the merrier they are, however startling the realisation of their antiquity.

Will a quarter of a century do? I think it will.

In 1967, I was seeking the ideal pocket diary, and I was failing to find it. They were all either too thick and heavy to be easily accommodated in a breast pocket (I had long been a snappy dresser, the glass of fashion and the mould of form, for whom an unsightly bulge was tantamount to unpolished shoes), or, if sufficiently slim, they provided too little space for appointments, notes and other entries.

There was no problem with my desk diary, but I could hardly lug around something getting on for the size of a telephone directory. Letts were useless in the search, and the Filofax had not yet been born (though I would not have sported the horrible thing if it had – I chortled long and loud when it fell out of favour as rapidly as it had fell in); what was I to do?

I can no longer remember what or who guided my steps to a firm called Day-Timers. I don't think they advertised at all, let alone widely; their telephone number, as I recall, was not even in the phone book then, though I am glad to say it is now. (I might as well give it to you all; they are in course of moving, because their present premises are once again too small, but only up the street – Kentish Town Road. Try 0171-485 5252.)

Anyway, I wandered into a neat office-cum-shop, and ten seconds later let out a scream; actually it was two screams – the first because I had found exactly what I was looking for, and the second because I hadn't invented it.

The place was run (at least I could not see or hear anyone else on the premises) by a couple, whom I subsequently discovered were husband and wife, a Mr and Mrs Elliot, Americans. Friendship soon exchanged formality for first names: the Elliots are Mervyn and Edna. But the friendship has lasted for 25 years almost exactly to the day on which I write here.

Before I continue with the friendship, let me explain the trick that solved my problem. The Day-Timer has expanded over the years: you can get desk diaries and all sorts of office helpfulnesses. But what I was looking for took the form of a beautifully neat, spiral-bound pocket diary which gave (and gives) two full pages a day, 6 1/2 in by 3 1/2. But how then is the breast-pocket bulge-problem solved? Simple: the thing comes in a box, wherein are found not one pocket diary but 12; there is a separate one for every month of the year. (Yes, yes; they *have* solved the subsequent problem of diary-entries for more than a month ahead; at the back of each book there are pages of summarised space for forward planning, months ahead.) Moreover, the whole caboodle comes with an exceptionally handsome leather holder, into which the current month's diary fits; but that's only the beginning – the holder is not just a holder but a wallet and notepad as well: everything a breast pocket will ever need (and there are even smaller, shirt-pocket size ones) comes to the modern man's or woman's hand.

I can still recall in the greatest detail my first time on the Elliots' premises, because their American helpfulness was so much greater than the surliness and ignorance that so many indigenous sales-people offered, and still do. Every question I asked was at once answered; every explanation was clear; the array of items I might be interested in was spread out before me, whereupon the Elliots moved to the back of the store to leave me alone with the choices.

I made my choices and bought the Day-Timer style C21; I paid by credit card. Shortly after I got home, I discovered that I had carelessly left the credit card on their premises; the place was by then shut. The phone rang: it was Mervyn, telling me that the card was safe and sound; he had traced my address and had already sent on the card by registered post. The following morning he rang to make sure that it had arrived.

I was then writing a column for the *Daily Mail*; I told the story and its background to my readers; what I didn't know was that the Elliots had only just set up in business in Britain (they were acting as subsidiaries for the company that had produced the Day-Timer), and my encomium gave them a hearty push.

Twenty-five years have passed since that day; their business flourishes still – they have separated from their parent company to go it alone – and their son now largely runs the business. I send them, each year, my new book, and they send me my annual Day-Timer; this time, when I dropped in, I apologised for the fact that for the first time in 11 consecutive years there wasn't going to be a book in 1991. "OK," said Mervyn instantly, "you'll have to write one twice as long in 1992."

"We brought nothing into this world," wrote St Paul to Timothy, "and it is certain we can carry nothing out." I agree, not least because in the very same letter Paul urges his correspondent to abandon his habit of drinking water and try wine instead. But although of course the saint is right as to material things, surely his stern admonition was not intended to stretch as far as the words of friendship?

I hope not. It would be horrid to think that some kind of celestial customs officer, after clearing out the pockets of the prospective candidate for Heaven, and confiscating the money and the earthly treasures, went on to demand also my shakehand with Mervyn, and the kiss bestowed on me by Edna. And if he can unbend that far, would it be too presumptuous for me to bring my Day-Timer, too?

The Times, 10 February 1992

The art of friendship: one

THERE ARE VERY many ways in which a profound, intimate and lifelong friendship can come into being, but I think I can produce a rather novel one: the friend in question, Sidney Bernstein, who died last week, had threatened to sue me for libel. The details are hazy in my mind, though I recall that I was then the television critic of the *Manchester Guardian*, and he was the head of the newly formed Granada TV. I think I implied that he had somehow interfered in the programming; on looking again at what I had written, I felt that, writs or no writs, I had maligned him, so I wrote to say so, and promised a retraction.

As soon as he got my letter, he rang me and said "No, no, forget all that nonsense – just come and see me," and I did; I realised at once that this was no ordinary tycoon, when, instead of sitting down behind his desk and directing me to one of the two armchairs, he gestured to me to make the choice, and then took the other; a trivial thing, no doubt, but significant. A few minutes after we began to talk, the phone rang, and he picked it up; "Excuse me," he said, and turned back to the phone, where he proceeded to talk for five minutes, quite unconcerned at the presence of a stranger, in the most extravagantly absurd baby-gibberish. When he finished, still unconcerned, he explained that he had been talking to his then two-year-old son.

He proceeded to offer his traducer a job in Granada TV, and a well-paid one at that. I did not take it; his parting words were to the effect that if I ever changed my mind there would be a place for me. A few weeks later, I was dining on my own at one of my favourite restaurants (a habit of mine in those days when I wanted a good meal and no conversation), when Sidney and his wife, Sandra, came in from the theatre. I had only just started, but his tact was faultless; only towards the end of the meal did he come over to my table (not, you note, a message brought by a waiter): would I join them for coffee? I did; they then invited me back to their flat for a nightcap. (Entering the drawing-room, I was struck silent by a magnificent Modigliani and a tiny Klee; they had a fine, eclectic collection.)

The evening ended with an invitation to a weekend at their home in Sussex; I went, and was royally entertained. We were near the end of the year, and with more quiet tact they asked whether I had plans for Christmas, and if not, whether I might wish to spend the holiday with them. I had had no plans, and did so. On the evening of Boxing day, Sidney broached a bottle of his finest champagne (his cellar was as rich as his art gallery) and announced that Sandra was pregnant; we drank to the new life. When the girl was born, they asked me to be her godfather; Jane is now in her thirties, and has two children of her own. *Eheu fugaces.*

The friendship ripened, became deeper, deeper still. Sidney's generosity was marvellous to behold; to partake of it was even more marvellous. Yet he was nothing like the Hearst cartoon-tycoon, scattering buckets of $100 bills just because he had an enormous number of them. The Bernstein gifts were chosen with love and care; I have never known people with such unerring, perfect taste in everything he and Sandra owned, indeed everything they touched. (Another bubble of memory floats to the surface; the delicacy and beauty with which Sandra wrapped a present was an art in itself.)

The way Sidney ordered his munificence was entirely characteristic of the man: his public benefactions were invariably in the name of Granada; his personal ones came with an iron seal on the recipients' lips. As in all he did, his helping hand was stretched out in the form in which it would be most useful, and he despised many of the larger charities for their amateurishness and waste.

His own charity took a variety of forms. He once hired a house on the sea for the summer; it was near his beloved brother's country house. There was a proposal for a large house in the vicinity to be converted into a convalescent home for people who had had breakdowns or other mental disturbances, and a pack of Nimbys had got up a petition against the use of the house for such a purpose. I was in Sidney's garden when the petitioners called on him to sign it, no doubt thinking that because Sidney was a millionaire he would join their wretched boycott. Without a single swearword, he chewed the mean-spirited visitors into shreds so small that they fled in disorder.

He had a vast range of interests, but one dominated his life: he was an architect *manqué*, and I believe would have made a great success if he had taken it up professionally. His knowledge of the subject (and, again, his taste) was not only wide; it was original. He had a house in Barbados, in which many of the happiest hours of my life were spent, the design and building of which he had supervised down to the finest detail.

Granada Television was his cherished offspring; he threw himself into it, and made himself intimately know-ledgeable in every aspect. As in everything, not just tele-vision, he backed his people fiercely and unambiguously; once a man or woman was tested as trustworthy and capable, he or she knew that Sidney would fight to the end to defend his colleague – he did indeed think of them as colleagues rather than employees, and for him the word "friend" was practically a religion.

He could rise very high indeed in integrity, even in the most recondite form; when Granada's licence came up for renewal, he was to be questioned by the board, the mem-bers of which had the power to decide whether Granada could go on for another five years. They questioned him, and agreed that Granada could indeed continue under his aegis. On the steps of the building he drew a sheet of paper from his pocket and read out an announcement to the effect that Granada was to go on, thanking the board for having trusted Granada to continue with its remit, and promising more good programmes. What the board did not know, and what nobody but I and a few other trusted friends knew, was that Sidney had another sheet of paper in the other pocket, just in case, on which he had written that he was sorry that Granada had lost the franchise, but that he had had great pleasure and happiness in it, and warmly hoped that his successors in running the station would be as happy and proud of it as he had been.

His friendships were many, and very varied indeed. The greatest sin in his decalogue was the betrayal of friendship; again, I was present once when he discovered that that crime had been committed. His response was exactly what I thought it would be (by then I knew him very well). There was no condemnation, let alone thoughts of revenge; the only emotion to touch him was sorrow for the sinner.

He was a huge man, and hugely he loved life. Music meant little to him, but the theatre much; he and I often saw a play together and then dined; I loved the relish with which he chose his meal and ate it. In trifling matters he was the most inquisitive man alive; I told him that if I wanted to conjure him up it always took the form of him beckoning a waiter, pointing to another table, and saying "What are those green things they are having?"

I was made a full member of the Bernstein family, *honoris causa*, which reminds me of another of Sidney's qualities. Both Sandra and Sidney had been married before; Sidney's first marriage was childless, but Sandra had a child from her previous marriage. But from the day he proposed to Sandra, the word "stepdaughter" was banished from their home as though it was an obscenity; Charlotte was invariably their *daughter*, to be in every way equal to the children who came after.

As I have said many times, and shall say many times again, I have been fortunate above most of mankind in my friends. This man, some 30 years my senior, towers over my life – not with a shadow, but with a triumphal arch. His friendships were absolute and lifelong, and the one he stretched out to me has enriched my life and will continue to enrich it till my own death. And his friendship was unfailing; when once he heard from a roundabout source that I was troubled and despairing, he telephoned me, and when I answered he said simply "Friends are for good times and for bad times; you know where we live," and rang off.

He was made of the finest and longest-lasting qualities: a fierce integrity, a gentle kindness, a deep understanding, a limitless courage, a ready laughter and a voracious appetite for life. I have known, and loved, no greater man.

The Times, 9 February 1993

The art of friendship: two

THERE WAS A man in the land of Uz, and that man was perfect and upright, and one that feared God, and eschewed evil. And now he is dead, and I, like all his friends (we were a vast and varied company) cannot believe it. And considering that he was 92 when he died, that feeling must say something significant about his quality. And so it does; it says that he was one of those rare spirits whom the world cannot spare, and who, when they do slip away, leave a wound that can never be healed.

Such a man was Cecil Rolph Hewitt, a.k.a. C.H. Rolph, who answered to the name of Bill. He started out in the world as a policeman, following in his father's bootsteps; Bill was a copper in the City of London police for exactly a quarter of a century, ending up as a chief inspector, and it was as a kind of chief inspector that he spent the rest of his life, chiefly inspecting an amazingly enormous variety of interests, causes, studies, themes and ideas. Bill was one of those who cannot pass an alleyway without going up it to see where it leads to; he wrote a couple of dozen books, and even in those with a very specific subject he could rarely refrain from digression. As for conversation, it could, and did, range from the reason that window-cleaners' ladders taper towards the top to the glories of Rachmaninov and the idiocy of those (me, for instance) who cannot appreciate those glories.

Bill was naturally, considering his background, much involved in matters criminal, forensic and rehabilitative, but it was impossible to classify him; his writings on these subjects were deeply rooted in the huge and comprehensive range of his knowledge, but there was nothing pat, nothing predictable, nothing ideological, above all nothing dogmatic, in any of his work. I had the feeling that when he was about to embark on a new project in his special field, he would wipe out from his memory all the arguments he had ever deployed, leaving only the facts and a blank page to fill with understanding and originality.

Nor did he fit any template when the matter of crime and punishment was to be examined. His career as a policeman endowed him with a hearty scepticism; he knew all the devices of old lags and all the corners cut by the police, and his balances, though they would turn in the estimation of a hair, were never loaded. Once, when I had written at length about a particular group of damnably corrupt and criminal police, he wrote me a letter of wonderful fairness and wisdom to point out, with infinite tact, that at one point I had come too close to implying – with insufficient evidence – that such behaviour was widespread.

His industry was prodigious. Apart from his substantial shelf of books, he wrote regularly and frequently for a wide variety of journals and newspapers, from the *New Law Journal* and the *TLS* to *Punch* and the *Author*, in addition to the job he did on the editorial staff of the *New Statesman*. (He wrote the biography of Kingsley Martin, and when I rebuked him for not being severe enough on the dreadful humbug that was one side of Martin, he said: "But I thought I had".) But his most amazing feat of continuity was to contribute a weekly *feuilleton* to the *Police Review* for some 60 years without any remission for good conduct.

The clue to Bill was his abhorrence of cruelty. That sounds like something hardly strange in a good man. But for Bill it was something so deep and tenacious that it plainly shaped his life. In his autobiography, he gives an account of an instance of unthinking brutality; it was when he was still in the force, and he and a colleague were faced – they were not the only policemen who ever met the problem – with a woman beginning to give birth before the ambulance arrived to take her to hospital. Bill's oppo took off his belt and with it bound the woman's legs firmly together, explaining that that was a useful trick in the circumstances, and one which he recommended Bill to remember when it happened next time. In Bill's account of the episode there is a note of such horror that I have always thought that he must then and there have taken some kind of vow never to do anything like that to any human being.

He lived simply, unostentatiously, feelingly. I once made the appalling mistake of taking him to lunch at the Savoy. I could practically hear him wince. Yet there was nothing posed or flaunted in his chosen lifestyle; he was exactly what he seemed, and I have rarely known anyone who was so completely one thing to all men.

Inevitably, and rightly, he sat on committees dealing with his special subjects. He was appointed a member of the Parole Board when it was set up, though he ended by declaring that it had failed. Yet Bill could never denounce anything or anybody, however culpable, without at least suggesting how things should instead have been arranged. He put forward the suggestion that parole should be based on the same principle as remission; that is, it should be automatic, after a fixed proportion of a sentence, in default of any offence against prison rules. (But the Moors murderers had by then served only ten years of their sentence, and even Merlyn Rees, who was the Home Secretary, and on occasion a bold one, could not nerve himself to institute so obviously sensible a rule.)

The longest and most anguished letter I ever had from Bill was in response to something I had written about anti-Semitism. He told of a woman friend of his who, very many years before, had been, or thought she had been, cheated by a Jew, and from then on condemned all Jews indiscriminately. At one point (this was before the Second World War), he tried to interest her in a private effort to help German Jews escape from Hitler, but she refused. Bill's point, however, was not that anti-Semitism is wrong and vile – it would be rather odd for anyone, let alone Bill, to feel that this needed pointing out; it was her irrationality, so intense that it had led her to turn her face away from such abominations as Nazism, that gave him pain.

That is not, incidentally, a metaphor. Bill really did feel sick and hurt when he came up against the wrongs done by human beings to other human beings. Yet his natural disposition was a sunny one. He had a curious mien, which made him look gloomy, but his appearance belied his character, and he laughed freely and often.

He did much work for charitable and other worthy causes (he was of course a stalwart of the Howard League), and in one of his concerns I have myself been indirectly involved. The enterprise, named Calibre (nobody seems to know why), was founded with a very large library of books on audio-tape, lent free to blind people or those who for any other reason cannot read. My relevance to the story of Calibre is that Bill recorded all my books (Calibre's first rule was that there should be no abridgement) for the organisation. I have always found it a strange and touching feeling to hear such a friend's voice coming out of the cassette player speaking my own words. I treasure the memory of the day he rang me up shouting in triumphant tones, "I've done it, I've done it, I've done it at last!" When he had calmed down a bit, I asked him what he had done. "The sentence, the sentence!", he shouted even more loudly, and this time I understood; there is a sentence in my book *Enthusiasms* which is 1,667 words long, with nothing but commas until, six words from the end, a semi-colon limps into sight. He had been wrestling with it for weeks, and had at last had a perfect run through the monstrous thing.

He did more than that for me, and I guess for others. Once, when I had just finished a book, he volunteted to proof-read it; that surely is friendship, for anyone who has done it knows that proof-reading is a miserably grinding task; and what is more, when I finished yet another book, he asked again to proof-read it. (His proof-reading, incidentally, was meticulous; he missed nothing.)

Abou Ben Adhem (may his tribe increase!) had a word for my dear departed friend. "Write me", he said to the angel, "as one who loves his fellow-men".

> The angel wrote, and vanished. The next night
> It came again with a great wakening light,
> And showed the names whom love of God had blest,
> And lo! Bill Hewitt's name led all the rest.

The Times, 15 March 1994

Capital punishment

How many times have I told you that Lord Acton did *not* say "All power corrupts", and he would have been a prize nana if he had said such a silly thing. Mother Teresa, by the force of her character and what she did with it, achieved much power: who will be so daft as to imagine that corruption ever touched her? Good King Wenceslas had power over an entire kingdom, but do you suppose he was having a bit on the side as well? When the wind of freedom blew down the gates of communism, did Alexander Dubcek and Vaclav Havel, at last free to speak and act, make a rush for the treasure-chest?

Acton said "Power corrupts", and it does; but so obvious was it to him that there were people who could never be corrupted by power that he did not bother to emphasise the point. But even he failed to spot that there was one more aspect of this thing called power, an aspect that it would be perhaps too harsh to call anything like real corruption, which yet must be struck down whenever it raises its head. It is the kind that adheres to those who have only one tiny fragment of power, one almost invisible crumb of power, one ridiculous and pathetic spot of power, and who know, deep inside them, that they will never get more power than they have now, and must be satisfied (but are *not* satisfied) with that.

I have never wanted power, in any form; I would shun it if it were to be offered to me free, on a silver salver, and with a promise that I would be allowed to use it for none but benevolent actions. Power must exist, I suppose, but it should come with a stamped warning on it in Day-Glo. But if I could abolish all power, or take it from the hands that now clutch it, I would start not with the tyrants and the bullies and those incapable of pity, but with the little, the very little, the microscopically little wielders of their little, their very little, microscopically little measures of power.

And I would not have to go further than Berkshire.

There, a public-house, built in the 14th century, has been feeling the weight of one of those figures who have to make do with the shadow of power. The publican, Ian Macaulay, who will shortly be celebrating the 20th year of his tenure, looks like a man who is at peace with his soul, the world, his pub and his lady wife. Or rather, he *was* such a man until a few weeks ago, when the tiny patter of power was heard, and entered to disturb the placid, happy and well-ordered lives of all the people in and around The Bell at Aldworth.

Mr Macaulay smokes a pipe, and has done for half a century. He smokes it in his own pub (and why should he not?), but of course he puts it down away from the beer when he pulls a pint. A careful and scrupulous man, then, Mr Macaulay, though I may say that even if he didn't put the pipe down as he poured the drink, he is clearly capable of making sure that no ashes or smoke would flutter into the glass. Anyway, no such pollution takes place; there is no contact between pipe and glass, and no problem of hygiene can arise.

No, but it can be conjured up in the most ingenious way, so idiotic are the laws concerning such things.

I begin to believe that the greatest step forward for this country, the most urgent and needed reform, the thing that would produce the most harmonious and pacifying state of affairs throughout the land, is a measure that would forbid – on pain of the severest punishment – any public official who needed to make clear what was his or her position to use capital letters in doing so.

I am not joking. The threats to publican Macaulay (who, it is right to record, is the holder of awards that would make any publican proud – such as ones from the Campaign for Real Ale, and the Consumers' Association) come, for the moment – I dare say that reinforcements are already on the way – from the Environmental Health Manager for Newbury District Council, and from members of the Local Authorities Co-Ordinating Body on Food and Trading Standards; these suffocating capitalists are said to be acting under the Food Hygiene (General) Regulations 1970.

But what are these threats that I mentioned a paragraph or two ago? They are no joke; although our host is, as I say, most scrupulous in seeing that his pipe and anyone else's pint never in any circumstances come together, the capitalised weasels have worked out a very fine wheeze. Although Mr Macaulay is infringing no law because of the gap between tobacco and beer, they can claim that the jolly publican is "engaged as a food handler" and propose to catch him on that preposterous hook. If they manage to get such an impudent case on its feet, (and I suppose that somewhere there is a magistrate so monumentally stupid as to take the complaint seriously), Mr Macaulay can be fined anything up to £5,000 and/or put in prison for three months, and I dare say that many an Environmental Health Manager for Newbury District Council, and many a member of the Local Authorities Co-Ordinating Body on Food and Trading Standards, all sheltering under the umbrella of the Food Hygiene (General) Regulations 1970, would not be wholly displeased to see Mr Macaulay, his head shaved, broad arrows on his jacket and trousers and gyves on his wrists, being flogged at the cart's tail and then thrown into a dungeon, not, of course, for anything amiss in his pub, but for showing too little respect to all enormously important offices, and in particular the Environmental Health Manager for Newbury District Council and members of the

Local Authorities Co-Ordinating Body on Food and Trading Standards.

Try my suggestion: what would happen if a publican were to be threatened not by the Environmental Health Manager for Newbury District Council, but by the environmental health manager for newbury district council, and at the same time by members of the local authorities co-ordinating body on food and trading standards, both transgressors having been disrespectful to the food hygiene (general) regulations 1970? Where then is the bubble of power that these weasels clutch to their chests to persuade themselves (they can persuade no one else) that they are, as they really believe, very important persons? This thing could spread. What about gummer, mp? What about mr justice gotitwrongagain? What about the bishop of muchpomposity? What about – ooh, but *what* about – the duchess of york and mr bryan? What – but this one is really dangerous – about the director-general of the bbc?

I jest, I suppose. But those creepy-crawlies who want to creepy-crawl all over an honourable man pursuing an honourable trade in perfectly hygienic premises – they do not jest. Somehow, someone gave them a sniff, a sprinkle, just a tiny morsel, of power, and when they got their hands on it, they bathed those hands, like the stage miser of melodrama running his golden pieces through his hands, and said to themselves, "We have power, but what is the point of having power if it lies unused? We must seek a use for our power, lest the very passers-by fail to notice that we have it?"

And then spake one of their number, and he said as follows: "In that placid place, Aldworth, there is an honourable publican, who does not water his beer, nor does he give short measure, and he is at peace with all men, and also, as far as I can see, with God. So now let us go to there and make his life a misery, by using the power that we have."

And at those words there was a tremendous shout of joy, and from all over the land there came a host of Environmental Health Officers, and – not to be surpassed – another host, this one composed of members of the Local Authorities Co-Ordinating Body on Food and Trading Standards. The last I saw of them they were on the way to Aldworth, and although I have poor sight, I am almost certain that as they set out on their hunt they were smiling, and I am quite sure that some of them were singing.

And that is what power does to many a perfectly respectable Environmental Health Officer, and does also to many a perfectly respectable member of a Local Authorities Co-Ordinating Body on Food and Trading Standards.

But do you know what Montaigne said on the subject? He said "However high the chair you sit in, you still sit only upon your own arse."

The Times, 14 May 1993

It will have blood

THE APPREHENSION, TRIAL, conviction and sentence of Nicholas Vernage is, I think, something more than the imprisonment of an exceptionally savage triple murderer and the feelings of the bereaved. The widow of the policeman killed by Vernage, when asked whether she favoured capital punishment, understandably said yes, and it would be difficult for even the most committed abolitionists (I was one) not to have more than a moment's unease at what he did, though in this case it would be absurd to think that such a man might be deterred by the thought of the hangman.

We can also say that such a creature is – must be – mad, though that will not get us much further, apart from the fact that he did not plead insanity at his trial; but assuredly, what he did (and did it laughing) is so far out of ordinary human understanding that we are reduced to falling back on the nearest explanation, which is that he was deranged. The trouble with that argument is that it immediately begins to grow in several directions; is it mad – literally mad – for a criminal to hate policemen so much that he vows to kill one and carries out his vow (Vernage nearly killed two more) and if it is, does the almost unbelievable violence with which he carried out his threat make it more or less likely that he is mad? And then, what is madness, if not that which most people do not do and would never do in any circumstances? That is an inadequate definition, but I have never come across a better one.

The next, inevitable, word comes to the surface: Vernage is an animal. But no animal would behave like that. His impulses have no directing control in his make-up; hate and violence, neither of which he can restrain when in frenzy (not that he wants to be restrained), act as a creature which has no understanding at all would. What, for instance, are we to make of his murder of his former girlfriend; certainly the world has often found love turning into hate, and many rejected partners have killed the thing they loved. But Vernage, after accusing her of failing to visit him in prison, stabbed her 16 times. In what part of the spectrum from wholly sane to entirely mad are we to put that?

Or: when Sergeant King approached Vernage on suspicion of having stolen goods, Vernage stabbed him four times in the front and four times in the back, and was running away, as any murdering criminal naturally would, when he ran back to the officer and stabbed him again, which any murdering criminal naturally would *not* do.

But we cannot shrug off Vernage, even after that, as a subhuman figure; witness what he wrote on the wall of the cell in which he was being temporarily held after his arrest for Sergeant King's murder: "Sergeant King was killed, stabbed to death in red, boiling and unbearable blood." The mystery deepens, because that is not the language of an illiterate or someone mentally defective. It *is*, however, the language of a man with an unquenchable fire of rage burning inside him.

> It will have blood, they say; blood will have blood;
> Stones have been known to move and trees to speak;
> Augurs and understood relations have
> By maggot-pies and choughs and rooks brought forth
> The secret'st man of blood. What is the night?

In normal circumstances, whatever they might be, we can find an equation; a petty thief, a wife-batterer, a confidence trickster, a killer caught in the act of breaking and entering – we can measure the degree of criminality and, with our very rough and ready system of punishment, decide what to do with the criminal in the dock, from letting him off with a caution, to sentencing him to a double-digit stretch in prison. But what can we do that has any meaning with a man like Vernage? Where is the magic yardstick that can measure such a figure? With what instrument can we get into his head, to understand him or – even more unlikely – to make him understand what he has done?

There will be, there have already been, arguments to the effect that such a man has no right to live after what he has done – an eye for a dozen eyes; other arguments, from more practical sources, leave out the morality of the decision but say that it is a counter-productive waste to leave him alive; the costs of keeping him, watching him, feeding him, could be spent a thousand better ways.

But what does such a creature represent? What have we allowed into the world that it turns out to be Vernage? Long, long ago, there was a photograph – it became a kind of icon, and I am sure many people reading this will remember it – of a gorilla that had gone mad. It had rushed into the sea; the photographer shot it standing up to its waist in the water. The eyes, the stance, the immobility made an unforgettable scene, but it made something else as well; the rage and the pain intertwined. But we are not animals, and probably we are not mad, either.

"Heat me these irons hot"; some would say that Shakespeare need not have bothered; such pseudomen are born with the irons sizzling inside them. Not so, I think. Still, I do not know how such a man becomes what Vernage became, so we must ask the impossible question: how does such wickedness and hate get into such men? It is no use, none at all, to say that Vernage was born like that; nobody is born like that, because nobody is born like anything – we grow into what we become, and while we are growing into it we have choices, and we take some of these and reject others. Why did Vernage take the wrong ones? The usual fools will say that it is all the fault of society; he stabbed, and went on stabbing, because of our capitalist system — it meant that he had had a deprived childhood, poor fellow. But *I* had a deprived childhood, too, yet I have never stabbed anyone.

We *are* responsible for our actions, and if we go on saying that we are not, we shall sooner or later find ourselves in a society in which Vernages can be found in every street.

> *Blood hath been shed ere now, i'the olden time,*
> *Ere human statute purg'd the gentle weal;*
> *And since too, murders have been perform'd*
> *Too terrible for the ear: the times have been,*
> *When the brains were out, the man would die,*
> *And there an end; but now they rise again,*
> *With twenty mortal murders on their crowns,*
> *And push us from our stools: this is more strange*
> *Than such a murder is.*

The Times, 17 December 1992

In the beginning was the word

*L*ITERA SCRIPTA MANET, *verbum imbelle perit*. But the Clarendon Press was taking no chances, and lo! here is the New Shorter Oxford Dictionary, of which the first thing that can be said with confidence is that if you drop it on your foot you will never walk unaided again. The second thing to be said is that Dr Johnson took eight years over his dictionary, and the sluggards of Oxford took 13; moreover, he did it all himself, whereas they were 24 in all. (However, it is most unlikely that on this occasion there will be any such contretemps as followed the completion of Johnson's edition of Shakespeare, when one who had put up part of the original funds asked for his dividend, and got the immortal reply "Sir, I have two very cogent reasons for not printing any list of subscribers; – one, that I have lost all the names; – the other, that I have spent all the money.") The third thing to be said of the New Shorter is that the clarity of the print is astonishing. The Plantin in its tiniest is here hardly bigger than the two-volume micrographic version of the Oxford English Dictionary, and that comes with a magnifying-glass; in the New Shorter you can read with ease anything but the tilde and the umlaut and other such unnecessary baggage.

Would that I had shut the book on that compliment, and turned to something important, such as staring out of the window, or scratching my head. For I had forgotten – everybody does, though that is no consolation – what happens when a new dictionary bursts upon the world.

The pattern is always the same, and I followed it to the grim end – oh that it *would* be the end! But let me explain.

When I used the word "contretemps" in my reference to Johnson, I casually turned to the word in this dictionary, to see whether it had been fully naturalised, or remained, like other foreign words, in italics. I learnt that it had indeed crossed the bridge to Roman type, but that did not stir me. What did, was that I discovered that contretemps also means, in fencing of all things, "a thrust made at an inopportune moment or at the same time as one's opponent makes one", and in addition "a feint made with the intention of inducing a counter-thrust", and as if that wasn't enough I discovered that it also means, in ballet (everybody knows I detest the ballet) "a step danced on the off-beat", and finally, to complete my discomfiture, I learnt that contretemps, may it rot, *also* means "an academic ballet step involving a partial crossing of the feet and a small jump from a kneesbent position".

I cannot summon up sufficient noise to do justice to what I felt at the end of that. But it was *not* because I do not wish to read about fencing or ballet; it signalled that I was trapped in yet another dictionary, and from this one I would be lucky to get out alive, it being the kind that makes certain that the seeker, after three pages, forgets what he was looking for.

I love reference books of all kinds; at home, I can count, on only one of the shelves full of them and in no particular order, the *Dictionary of Archaic and Provincial Words*, the *BBC Pronouncing Dictionary* (well, they must have torn that up a long time ago), the *Oxford Dictionary of Nursery Rhymes*, a *Dictionary of World Literary Terms* (one of the entries is headed just "Meaning"), a *Dictionary of English Phrases*, the *Concise Cambridge Bibliography of English Literature*, a *Dictionary of Clichés*, which I should have sent to Gummer, and nearly a yard of the great Partridge, including his rare *Dictionary of the Underworld*, "being the vocabularies of Crooks Criminals Racketeers Beggars Tramps

Convicts The Commercial Underworld The Drug Traffic The White Slave Traffic and Spivs", and a very great many more, including the *Encyclopaedia of Typefaces* and seven volumes of the Dictionary of National Biography.

I mentioned the micrographic reduction to two of the many volumes of the great OED; I have it, together with Dr Burchfield's splendid four-volume Supplement, marred only by that same frightful Dr Burchfield, who will not let me have "*au quais*" for OK, and insists it must be "Orl Korrect". (Ha! I have just spotted something! Our Shorter, bless it, gives the Burchfield version of OK but prefaces it with the wonderful word "apparently"!)

To the problem. With any really comprehensive dictionary, but particularly a new one, and one many years in the making, we instantly subside on to the carpet and begin to turn the pages, seeking, say, fucoid ("of the nature of or resembling a seaweed"). We *find* fucoid, and our lives are the richer for it. We close the book; but no, we do not close the book, because just as we are about to do so, our eye slides down an inch and a quarter, and we find fucoxanthin: "a brown cartenoid pigment occurring in and generally characteristic of the brown algae". *But we did not wish to know that.* Or take bournonite, of which we are eager to learn more ("an orthorhombic sulphide of lead, copper and antimony, usually occurring as steel-grey prisms"), and we feel well pleased with ourselves, until, again, we propose to shut the book on our thus extended knowledge, whereupon we bump into boustrophedon ("written from right to left and to left from right in alternate lines"), and then we are stuck with bouse ("to haul with tackle"), and from that we cannot resist brachistochrone ("a curve joining two points such that a body travelling along it 'e.g. under gravity' takes a shorter time than is possible along any other curve between the points"), but – hell and damnation – *we did not want to know that either*, and it is now well after midnight.

This tremendous enterprise has one crucial difference from the previous Shorter; the earlier one simply looted the OED, but added scarcely anything that the OED did not already have. This Shorter has taken cognisance of the inevitably huge number of words and usages that have entered the language since its predecessor was published, and I take it that the four-volume Supplement would also have opened their coffers to our Shorter. (Though the fourth and last volume of the Supplement was published in 1982, and this Shorter only 11 years later, there can be no doubt that there were many words unknown to the former but familiar to the latter, so fast does a language grow.)

Oddly, the unavoidable newer slang words that climb aboard when the bus of language pauses for a moment, stick out as (to my eye and ear) feeble and without roots. Take "fab", short for fabulous, and "brill", short for brilliant; I am sure that they will only gather dust in the New Shorter's pages, whereas "Uganda" (in full "Ugandan practices"), coined in *Private Eye* to mean illicit sexual goings-on, seems already settled in. Incidentally, why is "fab" labelled colloq., though "brill" is dubbed slang? (Alas, that nasty "to liaise" is now immovable.)

Inevitably, such a work will find itself encumbered with useless stuff; don't tell me that anyone calls himself a frequenter, and is rewarded by doing so with the accolade of "a person who frequents (a place, meetings, etc)". No matter; the rule must be, and it was surely followed here, that if there is a doubt about whether it should be in or out, then in it goes.

Inevitably, also, such a work must startle. Who will claim to have known that the word "jape", in addition to its familiar meaning, can mean "seduce or have sexual intercourse", and that that meaning was known in England in the 14th century? And who, knowing perfectly well that a ream is a measure of a quantity of paper, is not brought up short to find that it means, in Middle Low German, scum and froth, and in the 15th century in England "to stretch oneself after sleep or rising"?

The late Marghanita Laski, a self-taught but highly professional lexicographer, did sterling work on the OED Supplement, bringing countless references and words. When the work was over, she confessed that a few of them, now embedded for ever in the mighty volumes, were her invention, and as far as I know, they lie there still, for she never let on. I do hope there was such a prankster, in this work, again without attribution; it would be nice for her or him to know that somewhere in the three and three-quarter thousand pages of these mighty volumes, there is a word or a reference that does not exist.

But of course it does, for that is what lexicography means. One day, that buried word will come to the surface; someone will have used it, and then others will use it, and it will gather references, and in time, perhaps – no, not perhaps but certainly – it will find its place, legitimately, in the even Newer New Shorter.

The Times, 7 September 1993

On the villains' side

WHEN I WAS young – still young enough to be wondering what I might do for a living, and not a guess in my head – I toyed with a variety of improbable jobs. I used to chant the "Tinker, Tailor . . ." jingle, possibly because it might give me the answer, but the only answer that I remember, I remember with horror to this day. I have written elsewhere and at length of that first career genuinely looming before me – and loom was the right word. For I was to be, at the age of five, a world-renowned violin soloist, this being my mother's choice and longing, despite the fact that after only a few dozen lessons it was all too obvious, not least to the neighbours, that I had no aptitude whatever for the fiddle.

Tinker (I never discovered what that was, and I am by no means entirely clear what it is even now), tailor (well, my forebears were tailors, so it wasn't all that unlikely), soldier (only on the backs of cigarette-cards), sailor (somehow, the Regent's Park child's pool did not stir any latent nautical ideas), beggarman, thief.

Allow me a diversion; it was the word "beggarman" that stirred me to think aloud now. When did begging for a living begin in earnest in this country? I stretch my childhood eyes, but stretch them as far as they go I cannot summon up such a figure. With one exception, which actually strengthens my belief: it was the blind man, who stood on the pavement rattling his tin cup, but he *wasn't* begging, because he always had a tray of matchboxes for sale – the fact that only a few took a box when dropping coins in his cup was nothing to do with begging. Come to think of it, there is a black blind man in New York who takes up his stand on the busiest stretch of Fifth Avenue; he exactly mirrors my childhood memory: metal cup, tray, matchboxes, dog and all. (Did my blind man have a dog? That I can't remember, but presumably he would have needed one.)

Now then; I am speaking only of Britain, and I say that in my childhood there was poverty far more profound than anything – even the worst – that we see now. Homelessness there must have been, though as a young child I wouldn't have understood it, but in the place of today's "benefits" (I swear that if I discover who it was who began that use of the word I shall pour porridge all over him) there was almost literally nothing.

"It's the poor who help the poor," went the song, and by Heaven it was true; I can never recite without tears coming to my eyes that terrible notice – we saw it in shops, particularly food shops – "Please do not ask for credit, because a refusal can often offend".

But we didn't beg, and now we do – everywhere, and without shame, and in many cases as a straightforward lucrative business.

End of diversion. But I was diverted only because I was going through the tinker, tailor routine and I had got to "beggarman". What I was actually looking for was the last profession in the jingle. Tinker, tailor, soldier, sailor, rich man, poor man, beggarman – ahem – *thief*.

I was at breakfast with the newspapers, and one item was sufficiently startling to stop my second cup of coffee halfway towards my mouth. I put down the coffee-cup and began to savour the story of Mr and Mrs Guba-Pecher and what they did for a living. And *what* they did for a living!

Usually, I eschew making fun with stories that involve crime; obviously, when the crime is of violence, but also when somebody who cannot easily afford being robbed has been the sufferer. But in this case, I was happy to learn that the only people who were or might have been stripped of their assets (the better to sit on them, I imagine) only momentarily went pale beneath their tans and shrugged when they learnt that only three million pounds was involved, particularly as they got the three million back when the case had finished.

But now for the story. And I might as well start somewhere in the middle, because the story of Mr and Mrs Guba-Pecher is so improbable that you might as well call me a liar right now instead of trying to break it to me slowly.

Very well; the Guba-Pechers, in furtherance of their scam, bribed the then Panamanian Ambassador to Egypt to the tune of £64,000, for a fraudulent death certificate which would assert that Mr Guba-Pecher (I keep trying not to call him Gutta-Percha) died by a heart-attack when on a cruise, and was buried at sea; his grieving widow donned black throughout the rest of the voyage, and when she returned to Britain, she did not fail to organise a Requiem Mass for the peace of his soul.

Very well, I'm a liar. But if I'm a liar, I might as well go on being one. Here goes.

The Gutta-Perchas (I've given in) were German, but they had got wind of good British pickings, so they came here to pick. And they picked thoroughly, their particular practice being to buy gigantic mortgages with no less gigantic life-insurance policies. These (they must have had a substantial briefcase to hold them) were then realised, because Mr Gutta-Percha, you recall, had died at sea, Requiem Mass and all. History does not reveal whether, when she was trotting about claiming the policies, Mrs G-P was still in her widow's weeds.

Unfortunately, even Lloyd's were not sufficiently stupid to pay out on policies that were manifestly crooked, so Madame Gutta-Percha started to sue the insurance companies. Meanwhile, the dead Mr Gutta-Percha was living in Portugal, awaiting, if not the Resurrection, at least a word from Mrs G-P to say that the coast was clear. It never came; some spoilsport got wind of the scam, and both the Gutta-Perchas were fingered at last.

And that is where my discussion of my infant future came in. Because when I read about the Gutta-Perchas and their depredations (I forgot to say that the frightfully clever people who run the life-policy business forked out £150,000 to Mrs G-P when she had already been tagged as an obvious crook), a great sadness enveloped me as soon as I had stopped laughing. For, however shocking you may think it, there was something in me that wanted those two crooks to win, to go away together to some sunny strand and there live out their comfortable lives. (Comfortable, because lined with other people's money.)

And – now I make it worse – every time such a tremendous theft hits the news pages, I am secretly cheering on the crooks. Of course, and I repeat my mantra – no violence, no taking the money of those who cannot replenish their coffers immediately – it is only the immensely well-heeled whom I want to see done up proper. I would put the high street banks foremost in the list of those who ought to be robbed, were it not for the fact that the high street banks are run by people so hopeless that they lose hundreds of millions of pounds without a criminal in sight. But give me British Airways, or best of all the Body Shop, and I shall be rolling on the carpet with a handkerchief stuffed in my mouth.

I do not admire this feeling, but I cannot shake it off. And then – going back to where this started – another question is asked. Would I, could I, in the appropriate circumstances, be a crook myself? Well, that one I can answer with absolute certainty; those of you who have read the saga of my mother, her right hand, Woolworths and the sugary sweet will be able to answer for me: no, in no circumstances could I have turned to crime, not even the crime that makes me laugh, like the Gutta-Perchas.

I suppose that my admiration for a certain kind of villain is akin to my admiration for anything else that someone can do with ease but that I cannot do at all. If so, it is then only a step, surely, to admiring a cat-burglar as he swings from a frail window-sill, knowing all the time that not only is he in danger of being put in prison, but also that one careless step could break his neck.

The Gutta-Perchas have given me a good deal of mirth. I had no idea that they would also give me a great deal of serious thought. The least I can do in return is to reveal that they are now out of prison. I hope they stay out; but if they don't, I want a seat in the front stalls.

The Times, 2 December 1994

The Balun Declaration

RATS! BEFORE I start on the matter in hand, can somebody tell me why that word, with an exclamation mark, is used for anything that the user of it finds annoying? It's no use looking up Brewer, the frightful fellow, because all he says is "Nonsense! etc.; or an exclamation of annoyance", though he ventures to claim that "I smell a rat" is an allusion to a cat *smelling* a rat, while unable to *see* it. A likely story!

Anyway, this column today is devoted to rats, but as the theme unfolds, you will find that much more than rats and their habits is to be discussed. (At one point, a man, red in the face and hardly able to speak for rage, will be heard spluttering about his brand of rat-poison, which I have regularly jeered at for reasons I have forgotten, but when he is finished spluttering we can get down to the subject under discussion.)

Experts in these matters say that there are now more rats than people in Britain, which would be alarming enough, but it is much worse than alarming, because the same experts tell us that there is now a new and rather frightful strain of rat; the common or garden rat would fall dead at a whiff of the old poison, but the new rat is said to breakfast on the new poison and come out with its eyes gleaming, its fur sleek, and its form plump. Clearly, a stronger strain of poison is needed, but that is where the problem rears its head; there *is* no stronger poison, and it is that that had prompted the experts to seek out a new name for the new rat. That, at least, has been done, and the new furry menace has been gloomily nicknamed Son of Super-Rat, because he is. So first, there was Rat, just plain Rat, and then (when the rat-poison failed to kill Rat), there was Super-Rat, who was to wipe out every rat for thousands of miles around, but unfortunately didn't (I think this is the point at which the spluttering man takes down his splutter, ready to use it), and now we have Son of Super-Rat; just stay where you are, and sooner or later you will meet Grandson of Super-Rat.

So much for the rats; now for the rat catchers. To meet them, we must hie ourselves to Hillside, New Jersey, where we shall find Mr Frank Balun, in a considerable temper. Mr Balun is what I believe is called the backbone of a country; he fought in the Second World War as an air-gunner, survived, lives peaceably with his neighbours, sired two children and now has two grandchildren, and presumably looks forward to many more happy years. But one day Mr Balun found that someone or something had been raiding his tomato patch, and he traced the raids to a rat, which he caught and killed.

Whereupon, all hell broke out.

A Mr Lee Bernstein, Executive Director of the Associated Humane Society in Newark and Animal-Rights Enforcement Officer (there's glory for you!), announced that Mr Balun, in killing the rat, was liable to prosecution and could be fined $1,250 (£830) and/or imprisoned for up to six months. Mr Bernstein then laid two criminal charges against Mr Balun in the form of "needlessly abusing and killing a rat".

Whereupon, much more hell broke out.

The general public was, virtually to a man and woman, on Mr Balun's side. But so were the officials in these matters, who, you might think, would feel obliged to go by the book. Not a bit of it; they, too, lined up behind Mr Balun. Then it gets better still; the head of the local health board, Mr Angelo Bonano, gave three cheers, or at least said that "Mr Balun should have a medal", adding, almost unnecessarily by now, "We encourage people to kill rats because they carry disease".

Then a state senator (Ah! the voice of the people, and what it can do when its representative would very much like to be re-elected next time round!) announced that he was immediately going to table an amendment to the state law, which would make it clear that a killer of rats, mice and any other animals that carry diseases, would not be *hostis humani generis* (if you see what I mean). Next, the law had its say; the county prosecutor made clear that if any charges had been laid they were null and void. And in Hillside, New Jersey, we take it that all is now calm, happy and satisfied, yes?

No.

For Mr Balun is a fighter, and it is clear that he is the kind of fighter who

> . . . like so many Alexanders,
> Have in these parts from morn till even fought,
> And sheath'd their swords for lack of argument.

And he wants – well, let him tell us what he wants:

> I want to have my day in court. I want people to know this man abuses authority and should be curbed. What I did was with innocence, not with hatred or anger. If this doesn't go to court, what's to keep this man from doing this again to anybody? Let him squirm a little.

No, you are too kind Mr Balun; make him squirm not just a little but a lot. Because, whether you know it or not, you could have begun the counter-revolution; the counter-revolution that may in time destroy the entire fabric of political correctness. Of course, it won't happen immediately just because of The Balun Declaration (as it will go down in history), but we have to start now, and this is as good as any time and place for it.

And apart from the Declaration, we have a clue to our future success. Mr Bernstein, the pest who started this odious ball rolling, is running away as fast as his politically correct little legs will take him; listen to his endeavour to get out from under: "I think it's time we laid the matter to rest; it's gotten out of proportion. They're making him the hero and me the bad guy." But you *are* the bad guy, and Mr Balun *is* the hero, you politically correct twit! Because to kill a rat, which is indeed a harbinger of disease, is a sensible and useful thing to do, whereas to protect rats (which breed, incidentally, very fast and very fecundly) is folly, and worse than folly. And Mr Bernstein cannot fall back on the argument that the rat was ill-treated before being killed, because our hero, the progenitor of The Balun Declaration, even went to the lengths of saying "What I did was with innocence, not with hatred or anger", and a man who can say such words *in the course of killing a rat*, is not a man who tortures anything.

How did the poison of political correctness and its off-spring come into the world? And to come in so quickly? Why, only a few days ago, in Britain, there was a municipal booby who was tying himself in politically correct knots by calling men men and women women; he got so twisted that he found himself calling one of the dazed hearers by the sobriquet "theirself", because, he said, he would otherwise be constrained to call a group of both sexes "theirselves", *and that would not do, because it might offend*.

Such absurdities are no more than irritants, but any driver of the PC train knows that one thing leads to another. This has gone much further in the United States than Britain; the internal cowardice of that country is such that whole vocabularies have been suppressed, and even – when I heard this I truly could not believe it until it was shoved under my nose – dictionaries are being examined for correctness, and words that do not pass political standards will be thrust into outer politically correct darkness.

The Balun Declaration may in the end turn the tide. Mr Bernstein is, as we saw, on the run, not least because he has now retreated into saying of the dead rat: "The key is not what he did but how he did it; the rat was caught in a trap and deserved a humane method of euthanasia."

Mr Balun, I beg you not to laugh just yet. True, you have played your hand superbly, and if Bernstein dares to come into court against you, I trust you will eat him, together with a very large steak (I presume he is a vegetarian). But although all criminal charges have been thrown out, remember that the crazy law is still unrepealed, and the PC brigade will fight every inch to keep it that way. I don't know if you are a devotee of the palindrome – the sentence that reads the same forwards and backwards – but there is a famous one that is perhaps most appropriate today: "Rats live on no evil star."

The Times, 6 October 1994

The end is nigh

I AM FRIGHTFULLY SORRY, but I am going to write about Wagner today, and don't say I didn't give you warning. Moreover, I have just written about Mozart, so you can't really complain, though I am sure you will, and I don't blame you.

When a new Bayreuth *Ring* is seen over the horizon, the first thing that happens as far as I am concerned is that I get letters, telephone calls and even street accostings from strangers, all demanding to know how they can get tickets. In vain do I tell them that if I answered that question I wouldn't get tickets myself; in vain do I reveal that there is a waiting-list fully 7,000 long; in vain do I tell them to join the hopefuls who are to be found wandering round the *Festspielhaus* holding up sheets of paper saying "*Suche Karten*" ("I am seeking tickets"). Hopeless, I can hear you saying: not so, for this invariably works *for a few*. With an opera house holding 2,000 it is inconceivable that *nobody's* mother has broken her leg, that *nobody's* brother has been called away on unavoidable business, that *nobody's* uncle has been arrested for saying nasty things about Hitler. So every time a car draws up alongside the *Festspielhaus* it is instantly surrounded by the hopefuls, and this time one of the hopefuls truly deserved to win; he had made and coloured a beautiful wooden sandwich-board on which he had painted his plea – a most striking and ingenious way to catch the eye and claim the prize. (He must have succeeded, because I saw him marching up and down, two or three days before the *Ring* started, and I did not see him again.)

Ah, but at Bayreuth nothing changes, and definitely not the programme-book; as always, it is beautifully made, handsomely printed, the pictures and photographs immaculately chosen and placed, everything generously in three languages – and the articles that fill the book the most dreadful pseudo-esoteric bilge you can imagine.

Never mind that; even before the doors swing open, there is a terrible fear to face for those who have kept an eye on not only Bayreuth but other leading opera houses. Look at the Bayreuth cast: John Tomlinson for Wotan, Poul Elming for Siegmund, Deborah Polaski for Brünnhilde. And whom did New York find singing in the *Ring?* Poul Elming for one and therefore no doubt Deborah Polaski and John Tomlinson for the others. And who is singing in the Berlin *Ring* under Barenboim? Yes, it consists of Deborah Polaski, John Tomlinson and Poul Elming. And when Covent Garden's new *Ring* is finished, who will be the leading singers? Covent Garden has told us already: Deborah Polaski, John Tomlinson and Poul Elming. The truth is that the days of the great Wagner singers are no more, *and Wagner knew it would happen, the bastard*; what does Loge say at the end of *Das Rheingold?* He says "*Ihrem Ende eilen sie zu*"; "They are hurrying to their end". And so they are. But that is only one of three dangers that Bayreuth faces, as you shall hear.

Very many years ago. I am happy to say, I found on my way to Bayreuth the good Herr Pflaum and his restaurant-hotel in Pegnitz, some 20 or 30 minutes from Bayreuth (Herr Pflaum's comfortable bus takes us to the music and brings us back), and since then I rarely visit the town, though it has spruced itself up a good deal over the years. But, yes, the Parsifal Chemist is still there, and so is that most wonderful 18th-century masterpiece, the most beautiful building for hundreds of miles around – the old opera house, the one that Wagner first thought to use for his own works, until he realised that, although it was huge, it was not huge enough for what he was about to give to the world. And it is what he gave to the world that enthralled me almost 50 years ago and enthralled me yet again this time, and will go on enthralling me until I die.

There are, alas, obstacles in the way of being entirely enthralled at Bayreuth. The brothers Wagner (Wieland and Wolfgang were the grandsons) first worked in harmony; later, a deadly hatred sprang up between them, and Wieland was lucky to die early, leaving Wolfgang in single charge, as he is still. But no one with the name of Wagner sleeps soundly o'nights; before Richard himself was cold in his grave the entire family and everybody for miles around were *and still are* involved in conspiracies, banishments, sackings, traducings, cursings (well, those have always been easy to come by, because the texts themselves are full of them) cheatings, lyings, spites, calumnies – enormous quantities of anything just short of murder was and still is to be found strewn in the tainted air of Bayreuth. Wolfgang is in his mid-seventies, but when he came before the curtain he looked not more than half of that, and I have no doubt that he will live to at least 97. Ah, but then, then! He has made clear that his (second) wife will inherit the whole caboodle, but gigantic heaps of writs, summonses, affidavits, garnishees and the like have been piling up for years, ready for anything as soon as Wolfgang is heard sneezing.

I said that there are three dangers in the path of Bayreuth and its glories. I have discussed the alarming shortage of Wagner singers; the second danger, which I have also discussed, is the quarrelling that goes on behind the scenes and what will happen to Bayreuth when Wolfgang is no more. But the third danger is in some ways the worst.

The first time I came to Bayreuth for the *Ring* was for the first production after the war, in 1951. The brothers had understood that they could not go back to what the prewar audiences saw; with an astounding leap into the future, Wolfgang and Wieland made the first non-representative *Ring*, and the audience was too stunned to boo. But the brothers, in taking such a step, had done so with unstained integrity.

Eheu fugaces.

For when did we last see – in Bayreuth, at Covent Garden, in Vienna, in Paris, in Salzburg, in Berlin – a *Ring* that Richard Wagner would recognise as his work? Mind, I am not advocating the return of pseudo-realistic staging, with long beards and longer robes, and helmets invariably askew. But if there was one thing that Wagner understood, it was the difference between artistic honesty and cheapjack vanity. And with a single exception – the tragically aborted Peter Hall/George Solti *Ring* – Bayreuth has not for scandalously many years staged a *Ring* that its creator would claim as his own.

I have seen worse; oh yes, I have, much worse and frequently. But I have not seen sillier, or lazier, and I have certainly not seen more bloated vanity. Let me give you a few illustrations. The Rhinemaidens, when the curtain went up, were sitting in something like a cheesemonger's scales, and their feet were clad in Doc Martens. Freia was clad in an overall basket. Brünnhilde, and others, were enveloped in gigantic crinolines. In the passage nicknamed "Forest murmurs", there dangled huge meaningless metal contraptions looking like enormous air-conditioning machines.

And so on. The ridiculous woman who had done it did not dare to take a bow – one thing Bayreuth can do *en masse* is boo, and another thing Bayreuth can do is to sniff out the poodlefakers. As for the director, I have never seen anything more effete; in *Rheingold* he couldn't bother to mock up a dragon, let alone the hopping toad which Wagner delightfully set to music. Moreover, for once there was a credible sword and a credible anvil, which he reduced to a knocking on a wooden box. And so on, and on and on. He took one very brief single bow, to a colossal blast of booing, and scuttled back behind the curtains.

Which brings me back to Wolfgang. Wagner's grandson has a great treasure; a treasure much greater than the one Fafner hoards in his cave. Has Wolfgang not also a duty to see that his grandfather's genius is not to be stained, much less spat upon?

Of course, nothing in Wagner's work stands still; when Cosima, after his death, insisted that everything *must* stand still, it did, and Wagner's work was nearly destroyed in the suffocation that ensued. It is right, indeed necessary, that Bayreuth should try everything once, and some things more than once. But it is not very difficult to see the difference between insubstantial stuff and the real thing. Should not Richard Wagner have the real thing? I say he should. The only man who can fully and truly answer that question is his grandson.

But I cannot finish on such a note. As dusk fell, so did silence on the great terrace; once, twice, thrice, the brass called us to our seats and to the end of the great work, and I saw again, as I fought back the tears, that magical moment in which two thousand people were bound into one, bound into the genius of Richard Wagner.

The Times, 26 August 1994

Blind eye to murder

WE ARE URGED not to speak ill of the dead, and *a fortiori* of the recently dead. This morning I propose to break that unwritten rule, and my excuse is that the deceased himself broke it, and broke it several million times.

His name was Andrew Rothstein, and he died at the age of 95; a good long life for a scoundrel. Scoundrel, do I say? I do assure you that there are no words to encompass what he did in the way of wickedness, so scoundrel will have to do.

Born just before the turn of the century, Rothstein served in the First World War; he had a first-rate mind and was a remarkable linguist; he could have flourished in many a discipline. He did flourish, but the discipline he chose was stuffed full of evil, and for the rest of his immensely long life evil was his star.

For Andrew Rothstein was one of those whose gods were Lenin and Stalin (and for a time Trotsky) and Yezhov and Vyshinsky and Beria and Yagoda and Brezhnev, and whose enemies were the millions – *millions* – who died not for crimes committed but because, and only because, the Soviet state demanded millions of innocent men, women and children to be taken and murdered. And Andrew Rothstein looked upon it and saw that it was good, and so did many, many thousands more.

I have always thought that between the two great murderers, Hitler and Stalin, there was one difference. Hitler's evil stemmed from something, Stalin's from nothing. That is to say, Hitler, in his mad brain, decided that the Jews had to be exterminated because they were wicked people who were poisoning the pure blood of Germany; thus the Holocaust. And if someone had asked Hitler why all these people were being killed, Hitler would have an answer – a mad answer, but an answer. But if someone had similarly asked Stalin why so many people were being killed, he would be unable to give such an answer; there was no specific enemy.

That makes the Soviet slaughter no less evil, but more mysterious. But that is where I start; I sometimes truly think that it was the very meaninglessness of Stalin that attracted rather than repelled the camp-followers. To slaughter millions – ah, what courage to dare the lightning, what delicious shudders facing the numbers, what markers for posterity! I don't know whether Andrew Rothstein took such a sanguinary attitude, but if he didn't, the mystery becomes even more mysterious.

Enough of such grandiose speculation. Let us get on to an even more puzzling question. Andrew Rothstein had a brilliant brain; why did he switch it off when the Soviet Union was under discussion? He knew, of course, over the decades, that millions were being slaughtered, and millions more were dying in the camps; he knew that there was no meaning for the deaths; he knew that all the citizens of the Soviet Union – from the highest in the land to the least – went in terror of their lives, every minute of those lives; and he acquiesced. No – he did *not* acquiesce, that is the whole point. To acquiesce in this context meant not that terrible things were happening but he could do nothing about it; it meant that he knew that terrible things were happening and he was happy that they were. Now do you know why I said that there were no words to describe such a man?

Of course he was not alone. That wonderful and indispensable book *Political Pilgrims*, by Paul Hollander, catalogues literally hundreds of wicked fools. Try this now; it is from John Dewey, the great American philosopher and educator:

> I had the notion that socialistic communism was essen-
> tially a purely economic scheme . . . That the movement
> in Russia is intrinsically religious was something I had
> often heard and that I supposed I understood and be-
> lieved. But when face to face with actual conditions, I
> was forced to see that I had not understood it at all . . .
> for this failure there were two causes . . . One was that,
> never having previously witnessed a widespread and
> moving religious reality, I had no way of knowing what
> it actually would be like. The other was that I associated
> the idea of Soviet Communism, as a religion, too much
> with intellectual theology, the body of Marxian dogmas,
> with its professed economic materialism, and too little
> with a moving human aspiration and devotion. As it is,
> I feel as if for the first time I might have some inkling of
> what may have been the moving spirit and force of
> primitive Christianity.

Well? But the mystery deepens. Only a handful of fools, dupes and savages applauded Hitler and his actions. Long before the Final Solution, the Nazis were branded as dreadful terrorists. Yet the Soviet Union remained un-touched by reality from those who went there and pro-nounced it Heaven at last.

Let me come back to Andrew Rothstein, the knowing spectator. He had been decorated with the Order of the Red Banner and the Order of the October Revolution, the second of these in 1983 from the hands of Andropov, 1983! And still he trotted behind evil, loyal to the last.

Of course, some of those who followed evil repented. I don't mean the kind of repentance that, for instance, Arthur Koestler felt, together with the other writers who made up that remarkable book *The God that Failed*; these saw sense and light and decency very early on. But there was a test, devised by Anthony Hartley, and it was created when Stalin swallowed Czechoslovakia: Hartley said that from then on, anyone continuing to follow the Soviet trail had "failed as a human being".

When did Andrew Rothstein fail as a human being? More to the point, why did he never wish to be a full human being? I have met many who repented, and when asking that question I found that for many of them it was a kind of inertia, but a very singular kind. Again and again, when I have asked the question "why did you not break away, but continue living a lie and knowing it to be a lie?", and the answer is profoundly painful for the repentant, and indeed for me. The answer is: "We had gone on so far, we realised that if we stopped now, our lives would have been worthless."

A dreadful fate that I would wish on no man. But what of those who went the whole mile, and went another mile, and another, and another . . . Did any of them touch the fire and vow never to touch it again, lest it burn them fatally? Surely, Andrew Rothstein must have had *some* inkling of the way he was ceasing to be a human being? I rule out those few – I hope they were few – who actually *wanted* to be unhuman, those who cheered all the louder when the next contingent of Stalin's victims went to their deaths. But the Harry Pollitts and the Palme Dutts, the Hewlett Johnsons and their like – and pray God we shall never again meet their like – lived without a true word passing their lips, and manifestly thought nothing of it.

There were, of course, the ranks of *Sancta Simplicitas*, who would believe anything they were told. But even they cannot be entirely excused; what about the terrible blindness they displayed when they actually went to the Soviet Union and saw the misery, the poverty, the fear – all plain as the noses on their faces. What did they do then? Why, they turned the mirror to the wall lest it tell the truth, and to make quite sure, they stuffed cotton-wool into their ears.

*

Andrew Rothstein must have made the manufacturers of cotton-wool millionaires a dozen times over. There is a tiny vignette which makes the head swim. It happened at one of the annual Communist Party conferences. Remember, the hall was filled with the faithful, no infidel was to be seen. One member of the party dared to criticise the Soviet Union: it was hardly a criticism – no attack on the murderers of course – but the complainer had said that there was too much bureaucracy in the Soviet Union. Rothstein was so steeped in bootlicking that he could not bear even the thought of anything in the Soviet Union not being perfect, and denounced the member who had spoken. That, happily, was too much for one of the delegates, who shouted at Rothstein "You lying old swine!"

That should be on his tombstone, for assuredly a lying old swine he was. And now I think you will understand why I thought fit to condemn a man who was hardly in his grave. For Andrew Rothstein at least died in his bed, whereas many, many millions in the Soviet Union died in agony, the victims of the terrible evil that Andrew Rothstein believed in, gloried in, wallowed in, and, still unrepentant, finally died in.

The Times, 30 September 1994

Come let us kiss and part

L OOK HERE UPON this picture, and on this. Two stories
from far away, yet all too hideously recognisable; they
are crammed into the brief space in which the details are
recorded, but still find room for hate. Different kinds of
hate, though I have always held that hate, like love, is
indivisible.

First, then, the details of the first story, which comes
from the United States. (But, alas, where else *would* it
come from?) Burt Reynolds, the American film actor,
has parted from his wife, Loni Anderson, or to put it
the other way – and it will have to be put the other way
as well – Loni Anderson has parted from her husband.
(She too acts, perhaps somewhat less star-studdedly, but
their mutual profession does not figure in the estrange-
ment.)

Each of the partners, or perhaps I should say combatants,
has charged the other with infidelity, but infidelity of a
particularly lurid kind. I cannot improve upon the words
in which Mr Reynolds delineates his position, vis-à-vis his
estranged spouse, so I shall quote them verbatim; after all,
he spoke them on American television, so presumably he
was not looking for secrecy, much less reticence. I should
say, to avoid bewilderment, that he believes there is a
"truth drug", the mere ingesting of which will infallibly
show whether the taker is telling the truth or lying. This
absurdity, happily, has not gained credence in Britain, but
it seems that no respectable citizen of New York and all
points west would ever leave home without it. Anyway, it

is called Sodium Pentothal. Now let Mr Reynolds speak for himself:

I will give her everything I own, including the $13 million she is asking for, if she will take a Sodium Pentothal test, and I will take one right beside her. We'll ask how many extra-marital affairs she's had since we got married and she'll ask me how many I had, and ask the dates of hers and the dates of mine.

There is something of a PS in the story: Mr Reynolds says that Ms Anderson refuses to take such a test, and he obviously claims that her refusal denotes guilt. But he adds that the dollars are not the important thing: what he wants is Quinton, the four-year-old adopted son of their marriage, and he says that that is *all* he wants.

That suggests a tug of war over the child; sometimes I wonder how any of the children of American celebrities can ever grow up without dreadful neuroses to accompany them through life. Following the Woody Allen and Mia Farrow story as it unrolled day by day for months, I found, as I am sure many others did, that it was exceptionally difficult to decide which of the two protagonists was the more dreadful a human being. What the children will become I dare not think.

A charming vignette of life in Hollywood, don't you think? For remember once upon a time Mr Reynolds presumably loved his wife, and she him. That they have parted is one thing; that they have parted in a state of mutual hatred is another, and rather terrible, thing; but what condition can describe two people who once loved each other and can now contemplate millions of television watchers guessing which of these two erstwhile lovers could have clocked up the greater number of adulteries?

Now let us go far away from both Britain and the United States; to South Africa. But however far we go, we cannot shake off love and hate, for these Siamese twins are not only indivisible in their own bodies, but by some alchemy cling to practically all mankind.

One would think that South Africa, which is walking on razor blades as it struggles towards the light of colour-blindness, and may yet collapse into hideous triple civil war, would have not enough breath to tell the story I offer as a counter for the Hollywood marriage scene. But that would be to forget what human beings can do.

There is a magazine in South Africa, run by blacks, which recently made of its front cover a photograph of a woman breast-feeding an infant. The censors (censorship has not yet entirely vanished from South Africa) took umbrage and banned the issue. They gave as a reason that the picture was "an intrusion on the privacy of the nude female body", which would not have deceived even the infant who was being suckled, so they tried again with a second shot, saying that the picture would "exceed the average tolerance" of the public. But you and I, clever-dicks that we are, had solved the mystery before it was propounded; the picture was of a black woman breast-feeding a white child.

I hesitate to criticise the Almighty, but I do sometimes wonder what He thought He was doing when He coloured certain peoples much darker than others: He must weep as He sees what terrible things have been done in the name of colour since He gave us the freedom to choose good and evil, hate and love.

Love first; can you believe that well over half way through the 20th century there could be a country that sought out and imprisoned people who had sexual connections with a person of a different skin colour and were punished for nothing else? (Even Saudi Arabia, one of the most brutal and barbaric satrapies in the world, one which makes apostasy a capital offence, does so in the name of religion, not of colour.) With that background, and the stir over the photograph, it is not surprising – though it is lamentable – that a black South African writer should be impelled to pour out so much hatred as he did, when he heard of the banned picture:

My own feeling is that myopic Calvinism, bolstered by inbred racism, is responsible for this action . . . I'm very angry. Racism, bigotry, prejudice and downright hatred have once more come to the fore. I am personally beginning to feel that there may be no point at all in continuing to preach understanding and reconciliation.

He will, I trust, calm down; but let us come back to the picture. What thing could there be, in any civilised or uncivilised land, more innocent than a baby at suck? Come, don't be rhetorical; answer the question straight out. What could there be? Nothing, you say? Yet it unleashed unbridled hatred in the heart of a man, the writer I quoted, who may soon be urgently needed to extinguish some very terrible fires: did he *have* to say that "there may be no point at all in continuing to preach understanding and reconciliation"?

Whose baby is it? We don't know; to ask might exceed the average tolerance of the public, or even be an intrusion on the privacy of the nude female body. Not so the Burt Reynoldses and their marital differences; there is little intrusion on privacy involved in his going on television, in the sight of many millions, to claim that his wife's amours were more numerous than his own.

I have been told by experts, and believe it, that the human race, of all creatures on earth, is the only one which hates, indeed which understands what hate is. There can be no doubt that some animals love, which in itself is enormously significant, but if only mankind can hate, what does that say about us? To question God twice in the space of one column is certainly rash, but I am still bewildered in the matter of skin colour, so much terrible trouble has it caused and is still causing.

*

I am unable to believe that the whole thing is a tautology, that we have been given hatred the better to stop loving. In the first place, real love *cannot* turn to hate; that is how you know it is real. In the second place, of what possible value for the world could hatred be? Of course, we use the word lightly, and I rather feel we shouldn't, just as we shouldn't invoke the devil, though we do. But take me: I have much more anger in me than most men, and certainly more than is good for my arteries, but I truly don't think I have ever hated any individual, and I will go further and say that I am not at all sure that I can understand what hate is. I am glad I can't; it helps me to understand the amazing truth that there are heroes so remarkable that they do not know what is meant by the word fear.

If anyone reading this is contemplating marriage to either Mr Reynolds or his former wife, I would counsel a pause for thought. If, also, anyone begins to believe that South Africa will never be rid of the curse of colour, I will plead the opposite on my knees. One day, there will be no hatred, neither in South Africa nor Hollywood. Let there be light.

The Times, 5 October 1993

The longest journey

I THINK IT IS time to make the writing of biography a criminal offence. Perhaps it should not be completely abolished, but certainly there must be no more about the lately dead; let us say nobody more recent than the Venerable Bede or, at a pinch, Charles the Bald. Would any MP, lucky in the ballot for private members' bills, care to put forward such a measure?

I speak with some impatience, and I speak it with the new biography of E.M. Forster before me. Its very title gives the game away: *Morgan*, it is called, presumably to give an air of chumminess, an air that might make people think that the author (Nicola Beauman) knew him, which she didn't. The magisterial two-volume Life by P.N. Furbank (who did) was published in 1978, a model of scrupulous and comprehensive understanding – understanding, that is, of the man and his writing. Mrs Beauman has not written a bad book, and has found out several things that Furbank did not know; moreover, a good many of her speculations are not ridiculous. But apart from her book's superfluity, the Furbank biography having been written, she seems to think that in a biography of Forster, the number of his homosexual lovers is more important than a thorough examination of the novels. This task she decides to avoid, and announces as much in one of the most ghastly excuses for not working harder I have ever been sick over:

But do I know where I'm going, the biographer asks herself, the moment having come when somehow – but how? – she must convey, not merely precis, the plot, and at the same time try and convey why, to her, this is one of the most perfect novels of the twentieth century, aware that if she uses hyperboles like these her ever-vigilant husband will write 'truly wonderful' in the margin and she will realise that, yes, she has gone over the top. But then what vocabulary will do? Quoting would do. But that great slab of prose centred on the page might repel.

I dare say it would.

If my readers, not least Mrs Beauman, detect a rare disturbance in my normal equanimity, it is because Forster has a place in my life that no other modern author even comes near to filling. Because Forster completed only six novels, and one of these he would not allow to be published until he was dead, it is thought that his *oeuvre* was limited to that handful of books and an occasional *feuilleton* in the *Listener*. Well, I have 18 volumes of his work on my shelves. (One of these is the first edition of *Pharos and Pharillon*; I dare say it might bring me a tidy sum, considering that it was first published in an impression of only 900 copies.)

Biography, essays, short stories, bits and pieces of fiction, travel, even a guidebook (to Alexandria) – these belie the picture of a lazy author. Yet, of course, it is the novels that made his reputation, a reputation that no attack, no denigration, no misunderstanding, no envy (there's a lot of that), no patronising, no nit-picking (there's a lot of *that*) can diminish. And the reason he survives, and will survive indefinitely, is that he says, and even more implies, things that no other novelist does. If Forster had not written that handful of novels, there would be a hole in our literature, and we would be indefinitely puzzled as to what was missing.

First, let us examine the quietness of Forster, that seeming unwillingness to raise his voice because he can make his point without doing so. It is an illusion, a huge illusion, and I shall illustrate it first from one of his book reviews. The book was R. W. Chapman's scholarly edition of Jane Austen's *Letters*, in one of which Austen is writing to her sister Cassandra, giving her all the local news, one item being this:

> Mrs Hall, of Sherborne, was brought to bed yesterday of a dead child, some weeks before she expected, owing to a fright. I suppose she happened unawares to look at her husband.

Forster raises his voice instantly: "Did Cassandra laugh? Probably, but all we catch at this distance is the whinnying of harpies."

We have struck the Forsterean tone at once; it is the human voice in its most humanist form. Austen's joke, to anyone with enough imagination to understand Mrs Hall's feelings, is disgusting, and *inexcusably* disgusting. And I picked the right adverb; throughout Forster's novels, there are things that cannot be excused. The great confrontation scene in *The Longest Journey* (flawed, but his masterpiece) is almost a definition of the inexcusable, as is the confrontation scene in *A Passage to India* in the courtroom, prepared for by the scene in the club with the "Turtons and Burtons".

Nor is that steady, gently ruthless voice stilled merely because the two slighter novels – *A Room with a View* and *Where Angels Fear to Tread* – do not encompass such dramatic scenes. Again and again in both books, which in any case have their own dramas (what about the scene in which Gino, in *Angels*, tortures Philip with his broken arm?), the quiet voice, ready at a moment's notice to be raised, is there, watchful and never despairing.

But Forster is no martinet; how could he be, when the other half of his philosophy is based upon what he calls "the unawakened heart"? Like Dickens, he strews his stage

with villains, but – again like Dickens – a closer inspection
reveals that the real, irredeemable villains are astonishingly
few. There are horrible people in those books: Herbert, in
The Longest Journey, Cecil Vyse in *A Room with a View*,
Henry in *Howards End*, but all of these, ghastly as they are,
are suffering from the same affliction: the unawakened
heart. Stephen, in *The Longest Journey*, is practically illiterate and absurdly childish, yet

> . . . Stephen is a bully; he drinks; he knocks one down;
> but he would sooner die than take money from people
> he did not love . . . Why did he come here? Because he
> thought you would love him, and was ready to love you.

That is the awakened heart speaking, as it speaks in Mrs
Moore, less simply but more deeply, and with Forster
there is no possibility of confusing the unawakened with
the enlightened.

I have read these books over and over again, and I
cannot tire of them. After his death in 1970, his repute
went down, a very frequent occurrence among writers of
every kind. But Forster could not stay down; they are in
Penguin now, a good sign. Of course, for those who loved
his work, he never disappeared.

Forster's milieus have all changed utterly; imagine,
today, the Italian boarding-house in *A Room with a View*,
the moral code in *Howards End*, the terror of being homosexual in *Maurice*, above all, the change in India, which
Forster would not recognise. Yet there is no sense of
jarring, of puzzlement, of quaintness; so powerful was
Forster's deceptively deep-rooted planting that the fruit is
still there to be plucked. More than any books I know, I
can come back to these any number of times and still find
them fresh; and more than fresh – true.

Good wine needs no bush. Though I began in tetchiness
today, with the news of an otiose new biography of

Forster, by the time I had gone through the books in writing this, I realised that even the best as well as the worst of books about him (I have at least a dozen, not counting the two biographies) cannot touch him. Nor do we need to touch him, by which I mean that no exegesis, biography, interpretation, "Write short notes on", or even our old friend "Discuss" can improve or spoil the novels themselves.

Yet I still think that biography should be abolished. Biography dismantles an artist, examines him, and puts the bits together again, not invariably in the right places. Of all people, Forster defies such examination. How does biography help us to understand Ansell or Mr Beebe or Aziz or Margaret Schlegel, let alone understand what Forster himself meant by them, if indeed he knew himself? We interpret, consciously or unconsciously, his words, but who will be so certain as to interpret the artist's soul? Not I; I may find myself identifying with Ansell, but that doesn't mean that Forster had ever heard of me. (Actually, he had; I have a charming letter from him which I treasure.)

It doesn't matter. There are six novels by a man of undoubted though elusive genius, and we can go on reading them indefinitely. No, I don't know why he stopped writing novels; perhaps he was sick of people asking him what they meant.

The Times, 11 June 1993

The worst thing since

THE OTHER DAY, browsing through the *FT*, I came upon some words that would harrow up thy soul, freeze thy young blood, make thy two eyes, like stars, start from their spheres, thy knotted and combined locks to part, and each particular hair to stand on end, like quills upon the fretful porpentine. And those words were ". . . a loaf of pre-packed sliced white bread in Sainsbury supermarkets . . ."

Well? The remit of the pink'un, of course, can go no further than matters concerning the price of bread, loss-leading practices, the strength of grocery retailers in the UK, and similar grave subjects. But I have no such restraints, and I can say, as forcibly as possible, that the men – they are, of course, the Lords Sainsbury themselves – who sell loaves of pre-packed sliced white bread should suffer condignly, and my curse, therefore, falls upon each of them, viz.:

> Sleep shall neither night nor day
> Hang upon his pent-house lid.
> He shall live a man forbid,
> Weary se'nnights nine times nine
> Shall he dwindle, peak and pine.

To my shame, I did not previously know that there is an organisation with the sonorous, indeed noble, name of the National Association of Master Bakers, because if I *had* known I would have joined it long ago – not, of course, to barge in and start giving lessons to the experts, but to be proud to be a non-baking member. (After all, I am a *Chevalier du taste – Fromage de France*, and I have a handsome thingie on a beautiful green velvet ribbon to prove it.)

Now not for nothing is bread called the staff of life; just try saying "the staff of life" about carrots or sausages or fruit-cake, let alone – ugh – broccoli. A mere glance at the Scriptures will find them crammed with bread, as this list, a mere fragment of the full catalogue, will show:

"And the ravens brought him bread and flesh in the morning, and bread and flesh in the evening"; "Stolen waters are sweet, and bread eaten in secret is pleasant"; "How many hired servants of my father's have bread enough and to spare, and I perish from hunger!"; "Feed him with bread of affliction"; "Cast thy bread upon the waters"; "In the sweat of thy face shalt thou eat bread"; "Go thy way, eat thy bread with joy, and drink thy wine with a merry heart [one in the eye for the Rechabite]'; "Jesus took bread, and blessed it, and brake it"; "Man doth not live by bread alone"; "Wherefore do ye spend money for that which is not bread? [Clearly a reference to Sainsbury's]", "He was known of them in breaking of bread"; "And they shall eat flesh in that night, roast with fire, and unleavened bread"; "Our father . . ." but I cannot insult my readers by telling them where the most familiar use of the word is to be found; "Or what man is there of you, whom if his son ask bread, will give him a stone?"

And if I added the Shakespeare items we would be up all night.

Meanwhile, the fightback is coming, and the members of the National Association of Master Bakers, led by their president, Mr Roy Flint, can count on me. And *someone* has to be counted on, if only because – well, spit this bit out:

Mr Flint said: "We are the true fresh food manufacturers, not exponents of the process of pre-formed bread – a double-baked loaf however you disguise it."

He was referring to the trend among retailers towards buying in par-baked bread and then giving it a final baking in the store, and did you ever hear anything as nasty?

Some years ago, when I was doing one of my television series – *Hannibal's Footsteps* – I had to get up very early for several days in a row, and as I trotted the same route, towards where the cameras would be, very few of the inhabitants were stirring. But one was hard at work; I never saw him, but I knew he was the baker, and I knew that because as I passed his premises I was engulfed in the glorious scent that poured out into the street every day at the same time. (It made me drool; more to the point, it made me hungry.)

But it also reminded me of the mystery of the British Loaf; part cardboard, part warm water, part rags from the neighbourhood clothiers, part straw, part dust, part contents of the neighbourhood rubbish-bins. Why? Why, when it is no less difficult to make good bread than to make bad bread, do the British plump for the latter? Now I am a lifelong devotee of Marks & Spencer, but when I walk (rather rapidly) past the "bread" section and see all the pre-sliced, waxed-paper-wrapped stuff that my dog wouldn't touch, if I had a dog, and that my cat wouldn't go near, if I had a cat, I shake my head in wonder. (A tip; if you shop in the Marble Arch M & S, as I do, all you have to do is to hop across the road to Selfridges, where a wide variety of excellent, crusty bread is to be found.)

That scourge of all wickednesses that deserve to be scourged, Frank Field, MP, has taken up the cause of the bakers, but even he can do no more than help them in their struggle against the under-cutters; the British Loaf must be as much a mystery to him as it is to me. Even the Germans, who know nothing about food other than to stuff themselves to bursting, can beat the British Loaf with that black, very slightly damp bread of theirs. (The Italians don't even try to make bread, but that is not because they don't care, it is that their pasta, which is the best in the world, takes the place of bread in that country.)

Oh, yes, no doubt some of the bakers in the Association are backsliders, upholding the cause while dragging it down by going in for the British Loaf, but there are always worms in the crust.

I like the ceremony of taking bread and salt to make a bargain or a promise; is it still done in the Middle East (where it started)? I ask, because so many ancient rituals have crumbled away into the dust; a pity. The Jews have it both ways; their most solemn rituals are accompanied by *matzo*, their unleavened bread, but for the rest of the year they succumb. (The most Orthodox don't succumb; they eat kosher bread.) In my childhood, which was only very faintly religious, I acquired a taste for *matzo*, and I have never lost it: there is always a packet in my larder. Rakusen, to me, means my very oldest memories; it must have been one of the first words I could say, though it is only – only! – the name of the greatest purveyor of *matzo* and of all Jewish eating, right down to the pickled cucumbers.

I fear I have strayed; Master Bakers are surely not interested in something entirely flat. (You never know; they may be making *matzo* under the supervision of the Beth Din, which is the body that governs Orthodox Jews in many things, including food, and which, if you ask me, is a pestilent nuisance.) Was it not the peasants of Russia who marched as the Revolution began under the banner cry of "Bread, Peace and Land"? If so, they were shrewd; there was to be no peace for many years, and the land still eludes them; but at least they could ask for bread without getting a stone.

The supermarket has been a boon to many. But there was a catch. Not only am I old enough to have watched the butcher cut the meat and the baker hand over the loaf still warm, but I can even remember when the grocer wrapped the goods and tied the parcel with string. The question is obvious: who knows the name of the lady who puts the goods into the bag in a supermarket? Nobody. Who now stops for a chat across the counter about the new baby? (The answer is that there isn't a counter.) But I am not just remembering things past; the supermarket has dulled the edge of shopping in making everything the same, while the corner shop distilled not only conversation and the products, but something new and untried.

So hurrah for the National Association of Master Bakers, and down with the Sainsburys and their ilk! I wouldn't half laugh if they cut their thumbs off, but unfortunately that is most unlikely, because (and this is where we came in) it is impossible to cut a thumb off with a loaf of pre-packed sliced white bread. Oh, well; they might choke on it.

The Times, 2 June 1995

Battered masonry

O H DEAR, IT'S the Masons again. I suppose you know
that they get together to grab all the best jobs and
houses, and take over businesses by underhand methods,
and do down anyone who criticises them, and indulge in
sinister rituals which involve them rolling their trousers up
even when they are not going paddling. But did you know
that they are plotting to take over the world, starting next
Wednesday? Oh, yes, it's true; a man I met in a pub had
heard it from his neighbour, who had been told it by a
woman he sat next to on a bus, and she had found out
about it from her postman, who knew because he had met
a man in a filling-station who knew all about it. Ooh,
there's nothing the Masons wouldn't get up to if they felt
like it, mark my words.

Every two or three years, this spavined nag is trotted out,
and it is the very devil to get it back into its stall. And I
should know, because more than once I have been enlisted
in the defence, much against my wishes (I have better
things to busy myself with), when the sea of imaginary
allegations was rising. And that sea was no little municipal
baths; at one time, when the fit was on them, the leaders
of some of the London boroughs started dismissing known
Freemasons from their employ, not for any misbehaviour
or incompetence but solely because they were Freemasons.

Freemasonry hysteria is a disease that has had too little
serious medical examination; it is parallel to the same
principles as those of anti-Semitism, and indeed it has often
been, to a very considerable extent, a stalking-horse for the

more ancient vileness. It could hardly be otherwise; attacks on suspect Jewry have almost always been inextricably entwined with anti-Freemasonry. Hitler lumped them together without distinction of any kind – I recall, from a book about the Third Reich, a photograph of a huge banner, swastika-adorned, strung over a central thorough-fare in Berlin, reading "*Gegen Juden und Freimauer!*" ("Down with Jews and Freemasons!"). The reason that Jews and Freemasons are easy targets for this odious prejudice is that just as Jews can be accused of keeping together, a trait which can be instantly dubbed sinister, so equally can the Masons' privacy be similarly categorised. (If you don't mind me saying so, what the gentiles have done to Jews over the centuries suggests that they would be very wise indeed to keep together, and for extra safety to do the keeping behind locked doors, letting in only Freemasons, and even then only if they can remember the password.)

The hysteria that can be summoned up about Free-masonry comes close to genuine lunacy. There was a man called Stephen Knight, now dead, who was the author of a number of more or less demented books about the evils of Freemasonry; one of his tales (charmingly subtitled *The Final Solution*) proved, at least to his own satisfaction, that "Jack the Ripper" was a group of Masons who did the murders to hush up a royal scandal, that the conspiracy was led by Freemasons in the very highest quarters of the land, and that the bodies of the people they killed were muti-lated by having Masonic insignia carved into their flesh.

In another of his crazy books, this one subtitled *The Secret World of the Masons*, he told the world that he had written to the then Lord Chief Justice, the Master of the Rolls, the president of the Family division of the High Court and the vice-chancellor of the Chancery division, demanding to know whether they were Freemasons, and when three of the four ignored his missive and the fourth said it had no relevance to his post, he was plainly convinced that there was a Masonic conspiracy among the land's highest judges.

But why do I rake over these embers today? Because the bellows are once again being plied, and plied this time in the House of Commons. Christopher ("call me Chris") Mullin, MP, along with half a dozen other MPs of all parties, is promoting a private member's bill, *to be debated today*, which would compel Freemasons to declare their sinister connection if they fell into certain categories which, under Mr Mullin's proposals, they may not enter unannounced. To be on the safe side, Mr Mullin has dressed his odious campaign in a measure called the Secret Societies (Declaration) Bill, and the word Freemason does not figure in its text; but it is clear that the Masons will bear the brunt if the bill is passed; I have never come across any denunciation of comparable privacy.

Now pause for a moment and imagine a Jewish organisation, its members gathering regularly for, say, eleemosynary purposes which they reasonably wished confidential; what would you think of a law which compelled any member of the group to state, under penalty, that he *was* a Jew, if he was also – and these are the categories that are listed in Mr Mullin's bill – "the occupant of, or candidate to, a public office or a post in a public service"?

That was not a rhetorical question, and I would be obliged if you would stop what you are doing for a moment and think of your answer. Just what would you think of such a law? Surely such a custom will seem a little odd when Mr Mullin gets his legislation, will it not? No, Mr Mullin is *not* anti-Semitic; the worst that can be said of him is that he doesn't think very clearly. (None of this detracts from his tenacious campaigning for the release of innocent men from prison, which is wholly to his credit.)

But there is worse to come. Mr Mullin recently asked the prime minister at question time whether he, the PM, was still of the opinion that he had publicly held in 1986 (by filling in a questionnaire on the matter); the opinion "that police officers, magistrates, Members of Parliament, councillors and other public officials who were Masons should disclose that fact". Only Masons, you note; Mr Mullin later tried to tie the PM to his secret societies bill, as indeed he is trying to tie the Masons to anything secret that he can lay his hands on, to disguise the fact that the thrust is, and is manifestly intended to be, against the Masons. What John Major thought he was doing in the first place in committing himself to conduct so shameful I cannot imagine, but at least he could now have repudiated his folly, made a full apology and declared that Mr Mullin's measure stains both our democracy and the land it encompasses, which indeed it does. Our PM did no such thing, but said "It remains my personal view."

Right, then; a special question for the prime minister. If he really holds the view he has expressed concerning Masons, would he equally countenance a measure requiring Catholics in, say, a private trust, as above, holding such public offices, to be obliged to state that they *were* Catholics, *and if not, why not?* As far as I can see, he can either say that Masons, and the Catholics in my example, are in the same boat, and must be treated equally by the measures of the Mullin bill, or he can repudiate the Catholic half of the argument and say that Freemasons alone must pass the test, though the Mullin bill would catch both. And if he wriggles, saying that there is no suggestion in his mind that Freemasons cannot be trusted, he will have to answer a supplementary: if that is so, why does he personally endorse the principles of the bill?

Do you know how he will answer that one? I do, I am sorry to say. He will, after he has stopped spluttering, say that of course Freemasons are as honest and reputable as anyone else, but, you see, unfortunately a lot of people, quite erroneously, nay, altogether absurdly if not indeed ludicrously, preposterously and ridiculously, *do* think that Freemasons are dishonest, and just to be on the safe side –

because we wouldn't want the public to remain uneasy, would we? – we shall make them pass an extra test. And surely the Freemasons themselves would welcome such a test to clear the air? So everyone will go home happy, particularly the Masons, who will continue with their plan to take over the world, until, that is, Mr Mullin gets around to them. (Actually, the PM will do nothing of the kind; he will not be in the Commons when the bill is being discussed.).

I trust, though, that there will be enough sensible and honourable MPs in the house today to ensure that this rancid bill, and its even more rancid purpose, is thrown out. If they waver, I ask them this question: "Do you know that there is not one word in Mr Mullin's bill which explains why it is being introduced, let alone what evil it is supposed to cure?"

By the way; have you heard that 90 per cent of drug-dealers are Freemansons? Oh, yes, it's well known.

The Times, 29 January 1993

Death and self-delusion

As I write, it is not clear whether the deaths of Petra Kelly and Gert Bastian constituted a murder followed by a suicide, or a mutual suicide pact. (Third person murder, it seems, has been ruled out.) Whatever happened, and why, it is sad for more than one reason, and it is the more than one reason that I wish to discuss today.

I turn first to the extensive obituary in this newspaper.

> She was brought up in the American civil rights movement . . . she took a degree in political science, worked for two years in Hubert Humphrey's office and joined political demonstrations – notably against the Vietnam war . . . Later she worked in Brussels in the EEC Commission . . . Kelly was attracted into the West German Social Democrat party by Willy Brandt's idealism, but later left in disgust at the hard pragmatism of his successors . . . she went on demos and sit-ins everywhere, including Berlin, the Nato HQ, Frankfurt Airport . . . "We are the anti-party party," said Kelly . . . she was not convinced of the value of parliamentary action . . . she . . . became a media idol, being featured on the covers of both *Stern* and *Der Spiegel*. This angered many other leading Greens . . . she was once deported from East Berlin for trying to demonstrate there against the nuclear arms policies of West *and* East. In a party deeply split . . . Kelly stood in the middle . . . She campaigned incessantly for Turkish workers, homosexuals and other minorities, for feminist causes, and against pollution and

nuclear energy . . . She spoke very fast, non-stop with a manic urgency.

I have to say, however tragic her end, that there is something appallingly comic in her life. Every one of the stages of her career, from working for Hubert Humphrey, the one man absolutely certain not to succeed in his bid for the presidency, to abandoning Willy Brandt's party because it had a chance of winning power, to her reluctance to get involved in parliamentary action in case it might get something done, to the incessant chanting of her immense list of mantras ("Nato out, Nato out, Nato out, out, out!"), to Turkish workers and homosexuals and pollution and nuclear energy (imagine her joy if she found a Turkish homosexual who was against pollution and nuclear energy) – every one of the staging-posts of her *via dolorosa* marked yet another lost cause, to say nothing of those causes which had been lost before she could get close enough to lose them. *De mortuis*, of course, but no one, certainly not I, would want to speak *ill* of her; it is the absurdity that leaps to the mind, until her curriculum vitae reads like some of the characters conjured up by Peter Simple – she combined the silliness of Giselle de Frabazon with the "earnest, bearded, grenade-draped Ken Flabb". Reality, it is clear, never even came close enough to touch her.

Which was a pity, because all that energy and passion was worthy of a better home. Only a few weeks ago I was commenting on the collapse of the British Green party – a feeble, scattered bunch compared with the intensity of their German counterparts even in decline. I touched upon some of the reasons that such bodies, however clamorously launched, always wither, crumble and eventually disappear. I omitted one other cause, perhaps the most important; it is the way that such bodies put about claims which have no substance and which indeed are manifestly bogus.

There was, very recently, just such a ridiculous episode; we were told that because of the nature and toxicity of the pollution we breathe, half the population will shortly be suffering respiratory problems. (No doubt there is at this moment a group working on a claim that the other half will shortly be following suit.)

True, the Greens and their like have a problem; to keep themselves in the public eye, they must bid high in the auction, by announcing that, say, raspberry jam kills 17 million people a year in Britain alone. But the more gross and unbelievable are the claims, the less the public takes notice of them, and quite rightly.

When I am Imperial Censor of the Written Word, my first action will be to forbid anyone to use *breakthrough* on pain of being sentenced to read the whole of Proust, backwards. What the *groupuscules* will do then, I do not know, but I doubt if it will be to shut up. Whatever were the reasons for Petra Kelly's death, disillusion must surely have had a part in it, and probably a great part. It is bad enough to be compelled to slog on, year after year, towards a goal that gets no nearer, watching the faithful, one by one, slip away (are there *any* members of Vanessa's Loonies left, apart from the lady and her brother, if he?); it is much worse to have to fight incessantly against members of your own side.

That was the fate of the German Greens – who, it must be remembered, started the whole green movement. But so fanatically, implacably, unwaveringly determined to be defeated were the rank and file, that when Petra Kelly became known not only in Germany but in many other countries, her party in the Bundestag (where it had 28 seats), voted her off the executive of the party and off the parliamentary front bench, and even tried to get her thrown out of parliament itself. (Shortly after that episode, the Greens lost all their Bundestag MPs, and have never got any more.)

And the tragedy is that she herself was steeped in the culture of defeat, that defeat which is invited because of the danger of victory. For in victory, compromises must be made, proposals must be dropped, alliances must be forged, retreats must be considered – in other words, reality must be called in. In the end, these people, for all their oratory and beliefs and pamphlets on recycled paper, are only playing a game, and a childish one at that. What could she find to live for?

Not the hole in the ozone layer, even if there is one; nor global warming, particularly since there isn't any and it would be beneficial if there were; nor nuclear disarmament, which no one can get indignant about now; nor the heady feeling of being thrown out of East Berlin, because there is no such thing any more. All that remains is Turkish workers and homosexuals, and no one could make a life out of those.

But what a waste! It is summed up, perhaps, in an item in the obituary which puzzles me. She loved sit-ins, evidently, and one can see why, when the target was, say, Nato headquarters. But the list includes Frankfurt Airport, and for the life of me I cannot understand what Frankfurt Airport had done to deserve a sit-in. Perhaps she did not know herself; living so hectic a life, dashing from sit-in to sit-in, it would have been easy to get the schedule confused, and find herself sitting-in on a harmless airport instead of the cholesterol manufacturer who was intended. May she rest in peace; it would be for the first time.

The Times, 26 October 1992

The longest hatred

So THE DOWAGER Lady Birdwood has been in the news again, not to say in the hands of the police and the courts. (You *must* put the "Dowager" bit in, because there is another Lady Birdwood who has a burden to bear whenever she gets mixed up with this one, and a considerable burden it is, too. Anyway, I am discussing the Dowager one.)

Well, if she has been in the news again, it has behoved me to follow her progress, because I knew *why* she was in the news again. It was, of course, that she was being prosecuted, not for the first time, and I will bet a considerable sum not for the last time, either. And the offences for which she was taken to court were the same, *mutatis mutandis*, as they previously were, and will be the next time.

If you missed the proceedings (they were sparsely published – no doubt news editors are sick of the old baggage, and well they might be) I should tell you what exactly she was pulled in for. I have to say, in all justice, that the tenacity with which she holds her beliefs is worthy of a better cause, and indeed the courage with which she repeatedly breaks the law is also something to admire. Unfortunately, her tenacity does not match her cause, because it is an abominable one, and the courage with which she fights is a particularly foul kind. For her criminal penchant is the distribution of leaflets and pamphlets which on the face of them would be likely to incite anti-Semitic hatred – a criminal offence in Britain.

The last time she was being charged was a couple of years ago, at the Old Bailey. Then, there were ten offences; she was found guilty on all of them, but a wise judge conditionally discharged her, saying: "If you commit another offence in the next two years, you are liable to go to prison." Well, the two years are up, and she is at it again.

For nearly 20 years now, she has been distributing, almost or entirely by herself, tens of thousands of leaflets and pamphlets – the offence on which she is always arraigned. She complains in these documents that the purity of the white race is being mongrelised by the flood of immigrants with skins darker than hers, but there is not much on that subject; her real and passionately held belief is that the world has been taken over, or at least is in great danger of being taken over, by the Jews. The Dowager Lady Birdwood, it is safe to say, has got a *thing* about the Jews.

Most of the leaflets are about the terrible tribe; some of them merely claim that the English race is being mongrelised, but the Dowager Lady B can't get away for any length of time from the Jews. The leaflet that has this time got her into trouble is called *The Longest Hatred*, but she has an entire armoury of such things, called *The Ultimate Blasphemy, Revelations from the Talmud, Jewish Tributes to our Child Martyrs, The Holohoax, The Snides of March.* (And before I forget, she has proof that Jack the Ripper was Jewish. Well, of course.)

But the last of these lurid tales is the one that sums up her obsession; she believes, as certainly as she believes that the sun will rise tomorrow, that the Jews are in the habit of kidnapping gentile children, cutting their throats, collecting the blood in a bowl, and using it for Jewish ritual observances.

It is that last charming touch that convinces me that she should not have been prosecuted at all the first time – and indeed, I recall berating the then Attorney-General for letting the prosecution go on. One mad – very mad indeed – old woman is not going to lead to a rush of ritual murder by the Jews, and although she is certainly not a quaint old biddie who means no harm (she means a very great deal of harm, though happily she hasn't got the means to do it), she is some 80 years old, and even fuelled with the hatred of Jews she can hardly hope for many more years of hating them.

This time, she was convicted of possessing and distributing "threatening, abusive and insulting materials", in the form of booklets classified as "likely to stir up racial hatred". This time, too, a wise judge rightly dealt out mercy to her; she was given a three-month prison sentence, suspended for two years, and the judge took account of her age and poor health. (He rather spoilt the love-in by saying: "I accept that you didn't intend to stir up racial hatred; you are not a wicked old woman in that sense . . ." What he thought she was doing if not intending to stir up racial hatred, and what kind of woman she would be if not a wicked one is difficult to deduce. But to find a judge doing sensible things twice in one morning is to ask for a great deal.)

But that brings me to the whole world of obstinacy, and a huge and alarming world it is; some of the crazies I have come across would make Birdwood look like a sissy, with not a Jew in sight.

The courts, of course, are awash with such wobblies; very rarely is there a week in which no-one has sent me a bundle of legal papers proving that the sender has been done down and that I must do something about it. The tragedy of these stories is not that the world is full of crazy people (though it certainly is) but that some – not many – of those bundles of papers do genuinely reveal some monstrous wrong-doing, with the wronged person pleading for me to put it right. And so I would, if I had a staff of ten. (Even as it is, I am treated as though I am some kind of all-purpose global ombudsman.)

The one-track mind has a long history. Did you know that Hans Andersen was one of the greatest recorded sufferers from what is called *folie de doute?* He would leave his home, lock the door, and go off down the street. But when he had gone only a hundred yards or so, he would think "Did I lock the door?", and return to see whether he had. He had; and went down the street, only to wonder again whether he had locked the door, and would return to see if he had. He had; but when he had gone only a hundred yards . . .

Few of us are without any kind of obstinacy; few of us, indeed, are without any kind of *idée fixe.* I confess to a dozen of them, the most powerful and persistent being symmetry. You should see me packing a suitcase – if there are four pairs of socks on one side of the case, there *must* be four pairs on the other side, and you should see my agony when packing books, because they are – blast them – irregular in size and shape. But I think I have given too many hostages to fortune now, and the men may be coming to take me away. (If so, could they please come in twos?)

I don't want them to take the Dowager Lady Birdwood away. Unlike some crazies, she is not amusing at all, and the kind of people who come to court to cheer her on would cause a shudder to run down the spine of anyone not already imbued with the Birdwood-beliefs. But what real harm can she do? The pamphlets are of the crudest and maddest kind; I doubt whether anybody picking one up and reading it would instantly be converted to Jew-hatred, if only that anyone so susceptible to such rubbish would probably not be able to read anyway.

If you are by now wondering how and where do these poor, twisted, muddle-headed creatures get their poor, twisted, muddle-headed ideas, stop wondering. There is nothing in the world so strange that someone will find it perfectly ordinary. To Lady Birdwood, the idea that the Jews kill gentile children and drink the blood does not

seem strange. For that matter, there are people who believe that two plus two make five. Yes, Hitler was one of
these people, and Stalin another, but that kind of extrapo-
lating is meaningless; there were Hitler-lovers and Stalin-
worshippers in Britain, but they hardly made a nuisance,
let alone a threat.

So let it be – a nuisance – with the Dowager Lady
Birdwood. Punishment, even imprisonment, will not stop
her; nothing will stop her until she is dead. And I wouldn't
be surprised if she was ordered to come to life once a year
to make repentance and reparation, and instead took the
opportunity to denounce the Jews for their peculiar tastes
in blood.

The Times, 6 May 1994

The men who did their duty

L ET US NOW praise famous men, and our fathers that begat us. Well, let us; Ecclesiasticus is a very wise old bird, and if he says we should, I think we are bound to go along with his notion. What follows?

What follows is a detailed description of what makes the famous men famous, and a pretty formidable picture it makes. For instance, "they were such as did bear rule in their kingdoms, men renowned for their power, giving counsel by their understanding." Moreover, "they were wise and eloquent in their instructions"; some of them, indeed, "found out musical tunes, and recited verses in writing." "All these were honoured in their generations"; well, I should think so. At any rate, "they have left a name behind them."

So what's the problem? Just this: ". . . some there be, which have no memorial"; these poor devils "are perished, as though they had never been". Ah, but wait, because "these were merciful men, whose righteousness hath not been forgotten," and that's a mercy, you must agree. Oh, to be sure, "their bodies are buried in peace, but their name liveth for evermore," and to top it all off, "the people will tell of their wisdom, and the congregation will show forth their praise," which is pretty good work if you can get it, eh?

And today I shall record the life and work of two men, one from each of the two categories. They died on the same day, a week or so ago; it is possible that each of them knew of the existence of the other. Not that it matters;

they did their deeds – and what deeds! – and although both of them ultimately failed in their endeavours, Ecclesiasticus was right when he said "their name liveth for evermore". And so it should.

One was German, the other Dutch. The German was one of the famous men, the Dutchman one of those whose seed shall continually remain a good inheritance. I turn first to the German.

His name was Axel von dem Bussche; the "von" marked him as of good German blood. Born in 1919, he became a regular army officer as soon as he finished school, and when war came in 1939, though by then he despised Hitler and the Third Reich, he did his duty as a man fighting for his country.

His eyes were not quickly opened, but when they were, he was a man fighting evil to the end. His turning point was to see a queue of 2,000 Jews – men, women, children, babies, greybeards – waiting to be shot into the graves they had been made to dig. So unprepared for such dreadfulness, von dem Bussche ran back from the impending massacre and pleaded with his Commanding Officer to stop it; the CO did not, and must have been amazed at von dem Bussche's naivety. (There should be, in all fairness, a tiny extra memorial, to the regimental clerk who alerted von dem Bussche to what was about to happen.)

From that day, von dem Bussche knew that Hitler must be killed, and he offered himself to do the noble deed. He got into contact with the Stauffenberg group, and devised an assassination plot of heroic proportions; on a pretext, he temporarily left his regiment to go to a gathering at which Hitler, Himmler and Goering would be present. The hero went with a hand-grenade in his pocket; he was going to fling himself on the Führer and clutch him long enough to blow up the Nazis – and, of course, himself. But Hitler cancelled the ceremony.

Von dem Bussche was very seriously wounded in action, but remained ready to help Stauffenberg and the plot; in hospital, he heard the news of the failed assassination. So he did not kill Hitler; nobody did, till he did it himself in the bunker. Yet is not that patrician German officer – *sans peur et sans reproche* – worthy of the words of Ecclesiasticus, "There be of them, that have left a name behind them"? He failed in his great endeavour, but before the throne failure and success are one, and the only question that must be answered is: were you true to the end? Of a certainty, he was true to the end, and assuredly regretted only that his bravery had not born fruit.

And now for one of those who have no "von" in their names, who were not born of a long line of aristocrats, and who, had it not been for the Second World War, might well have figured in the list of those who "have no memorial", and "are perished, as though they had never been". But they, too, in the end, were saluted for their own endeavours, "and the congregation will shew forth their praise".

His name was Jan Gies; he was 87 when he died, 14 years older than von dem Bussche. He was Dutch; he had no particular reason to help Jews; for that matter, I don't suppose he would have allowed anyone to call him a hero. But a hero he was, for all that. During the German occupation of the Netherlands, Jan Gies, with his equally heroic wife, worked with the underground, finding them safe hiding-places, getting them ration cards, ferrying food to the members of the resistance who were undercover.

But that was not all. He and his wife hid a Jew in their own home throughout the occupation, at the peril of their lives. Yet this heroic couple (". . . merciful men, whose righteousness hath not been forgotten . . .") did even more than that.

I have seen the Anne Frank house in Amsterdam more than once; no truly human beings could stop the tears when, going round that little room, they come to the horizontal pencil-marks on the wall. Such lines signify, in many homes all over the world, that a child is growing up, and marking, half-inch by half-inch, the progress towards adulthood. In Anne Frank's secret home, that tradition was followed; it takes a moment to understand why for Anne the lines stop, though the child was still growing. But I have never stopped to think how the family lived, boarded up in their tragic prison-hospice. Only now, at the news of Gies's death, did I take in the fact that, since the family could not leave their hiding-place, others, gentiles, must have brought them food, drink, soap, handkerchiefs, news, hope. Jan Gies was the man who did it, together with his wife.

They had no call to do it, other than God's. They were not Jews, they did not know the Frank family, they could have lived quietly and undisturbed throughout the rest of the war and occupation, and have had no cause to reproach themselves. But "their bodies are buried in peace, but their name liveth for evermore", for what they did without any compulsion, any prompting.

I recall an account of the exploits of another such man, this one in Nazi Germany itself. He, too, was an ordinary citizen with no reason to risk his life, but he ended up hiding, in his own home, no fewer than eight Jews; his wonderful mantra, repeated every time he took in the next tainted wether of the flock, was "We have said A, now we must say B."

Sometimes, when I contemplate men like von dem Bussche and Gies, I begin to think that the world should not, after all, be consumed by fire from heaven; certainly, if heaven stays its hand, we shall have only them to thank. Do people like that even guess at what they have in them, until it is brought out by terrible necessity? When Axel von dem Bussche put the handgrenades into his capacious pockets, when Jan Gies whistled low at the boarded-up door of the Franks, signalling that a loaf or two was at hand, did they think of the potential consequences, did their hands tremble a little, were their mouths unusually dry? Or did they all chant the same mantra and proclaim

"We have said A, now we must say B," and get on with the job?

Who can say? Not they themselves, I'll be bound; Ecclesiasticus really did know what he was talking about. The blue-blooded German and the innocent Dutchman are, in the end, birds of a feather, and demonstrated it anew by dying on the same day. "And the people will tell of their wisdom, and the congregation will shew forth their praise." May they rest in peace. Oh, they will, they will.

The Times, 2 March 1993

The poisoned well

DREYFUS AGAIN! Will that tap never stop dripping? There are scores and scores of books on the subject, doctoral theses counted in thousands, ignorance of the facts by millions, and the end is not yet in sight, nor will it be until no scrap of injustice remains in the world, indeed until the word "injustice" itself is clean of it and it can be found only in the very biggest dictionaries. But assuredly, until that dawn rises, the name of Dreyfus will not be forgotten.

My introduction was not made at random; the name has surfaced once more, in France – where, after all, it started. The head of the French army's history office, one Colonel Paul Gaujac, was summarily dismissed by the Balladur government's Minister of Defence, M François Léotard; it seems that the minister was alerted by an article in *Libéra-tion*. And to what was he alerted, whoever heard the first bell?

That shall be my theme today, because *l'Affaire Dreyfus* is marking its centenary – the centenary, that is, of Drey-fus's arrest, and still the story bleeds afresh. I cannot believe that many of you do not know what the Dreyfus affair comprised, but it is so remarkable a story, and I have been so fascinated by it all my life, that I must once again linger over the things that happened in those days, though I shall conclude with the things that can happen now, some of which will surprise you.

Alfred Dreyfus was a French army officer, perfectly honourable, loyal and patriotic. Ferdinand Esterhazy was another army officer, but this one was by no means honourable, loyal or patriotic. In fact, he was in touch with German espionage forces, and was passing secret information to them, solely for money. Documents were found, making clear that there was a spy in the ranks. There was no evidence of any kind to tie Dreyfus to the crime, but *somebody* had to be guilty, and Dreyfus was a Jew, so the authorities put him on trial, *in camera*, found him guilty of high treason and sentenced him to be banished for life in French Guiana – nicknamed Devil's Island. Off he went, though not before, on the parade ground, his epaulettes had been torn from his shoulders and his sword broken across. (I have always wondered about that ceremony, not just in the Dreyfus case but in the considerable number of books, fictional or real, in which such degradation is carried out. What I want to know is *how* you break a sword in pieces? Surely you can't break steel across your knee, whatever the provocation?)

Enter Lieutenant-Colonel Georges Picquart, the first and greatest Dreyfusard. He had found the real culprit, Esterhazy, and the evidence, and told his superiors. They were horrified. They hastened to ensure that Esterhazy was not arrested and that Dreyfus remained on Devil's Island, and to be sure that nothing went wrong, they removed Picquart from his post. Then they made their first but critical mistake; Esterhazy, the criminal, had an accomplice, Major Henry, and both had been busy forging documents to put truth on false trails. The authorities staged a trial of Esterhazy, making sure that he was acquitted, but Esterhazy acquittal or no Esterhazy acquittal, Picquart went on pointing out that they had got the wrong man, so the authorities arrested *him*. From then on, a routine story about an unknown officer who had been wrongly convicted had split France in two.

And that is no exaggeration, for during *l'Affaire*, so many fights and even duels had broken out between Dreyfusards and anti-Dreyfusards, that hostesses, sending out their invitation cards, had them engraved not only with, as usual, the date, time and address, but also with the ominous rubric *Prière de ne parler de l'Affaire*. And before the seas climbed higher, came the news that Esterhazy's accomplice, Major Henry, had shot himself. (Not that the authorities took any notice; Esterhazy, now obviously the criminal, fled to Britain, but Dreyfus remained on his island, and the cover-up went on gaily.)

Now the heroes march past: Zola, with that wonderful, echoing, immortal headline; Picquart, cashiered for telling the truth (and thus – clouds and silver linings – able to devote all his time to the cause); Anatole France, with *Penguin Island* (the book, his masterpiece, still stands as fresh as when it was written, and the chapter on the Dreyfus case is masterpiece piled on masterpiece): Clemenceau, no doubt with an eye to the main chance, but unwavering in his certainty of Dreyfus's innocence; even Proust got out of bed long enough to sign a Dreyfusard petition.

Bliss was it in that dawn, as the see-saw began to tilt the Dreyfusard way; Dreyfus, however, was still on his island. The authorities brought him home, tried him again, convicted him again and sentenced him to ten years, hastily suspended. The conviction was by five votes to two, and a Dreyfusard caricaturist in a Dreyfusard newspaper drew a memorable cartoon. It showed the five who voted for another conviction, walking round and round, each writing *Dreyfus est culpable* on the back of the one in front, when *la vérité* steps into the circle and draws on the nearest back *Dreyfus est innocent, et vous êtes cinq menteurs*.

It *is* an extraordinary story, is it not? There is no jurisdiction that does not include errors – errors that put innocent men and women in prison, or indeed execute them. That is not an indictment of the systems; it is, alas, a demonstration of the fact that human beings make mistakes.

*

No one likes admitting a mistake, even a mistake that harms others, but in civilised countries there is always someone to draw attention to the errors. Look at our judges, sitting in a democratic land; they couldn't be more diligent in getting things right, but how they hate to admit it when they have made terrible mistakes, paid for by years of imprisonment – paid for, that is, not by them. And when the rescuers succeed, how the judges hate to be asked to apologise, which they never do!

But the Dreyfus affair was not made out of mistakes. The highest judicial figures in the French legal system connived and lied and cheated, to get an innocent man condemned and to see that he remained condemned; perhaps at first some of them might have believed the evidence, though it would have been difficult to do so considering that there wasn't any, but even allowing them an infinite amount of honest doubt, they were a bunch of blackguards. (Anti-Semitic blackguards, though that had run through the whole story – the two camps were separated by that alone.)

Prière de ne parler de l'Affaire; what years have passed, and revolutions in everything concluded, since those words were printed on invitation cards! And yet, there is a stir in Paris, a stir so amazing that it needs two looks to be believed. I started today with the dismissal of Colonel Paul Gaujac from his position as head of the French forces' history department; what I did not tell you is *why* he was dismissed. He was dismissed because, when writing about the Dreyfus affair, he could not bring himself to admit that Dreyfus was manifestly innocent, nor could he with any decency write that he was guilty. So he said that "Dreyfus's innocence is the thesis now generally accepted by historians".

Well, clearly not in the office of the French forces' history department.

How deep do poisoned wells run, and how much blotting-paper is required to mop them up? Leave the good colonel and his diffidence in admitting that Dreyfus was innocent; there are people much more senior than he in this story. For did you know that the French army has never reversed the findings of the two courts-martial that condemned Dreyfus? And did you know that when it was at last suggested that a statue of Dreyfus should be erected in the *Ecole Militaire*, the French army blocked the proposal so vigorously that it was dropped? Why, how shameful and cowardly must be the French Army Command that it feels obliged to pretend to this day that Dreyfus was other than innocent! And for that matter, how wretched a thing must be President Mitterrand, and how feeble a thing must be Prime Minister Balladur, that either or both of them cannot summon up the bottle to defy the army and do justice a mere hundred years late.

In the Second World War, Charles Maurras, the evil genius of modern French literature (but a genius none the less), threw in his lot with the Nazis during the Occupation. He was tried as a collaborator and convicted by a court more honest than any Dreyfus saw. But as he was led from the courtroom, he cried: "*C'est la revanche de Dreyfus!*"

The Times, 18 February 1994

Bombs away

I THOUGHT I SHOULD have nothing more to say on the subject of "animal rights" after I had expended some 1,500 words on the matter, but to my own surprise I find myself going back to the story only a few weeks later. My first article was devoted to the organisations whose members threaten violence against anyone who takes a contrary view of this complex subject. Let me quote something from my previous article, to set the scene. From an anonymous source (no martyrdom for them!) I read this:

> We are capable of dealing with anyone. No one has died yet, but that time will come. For now we have to make their disgusting lives hell so they won't want to live.

I digested that charming *billet-doux*, and continued:

> When I read those words, my mind flashed back – I would guess many people's would – to Jews being rounded up in the earlier days of Nazism, when it did not need much perspicacity to know that those using such language would not stop at making their victims' disgusting lives hell, but would in time extinguish those disgusting lives altogether.

So far, their wishes have not come true, but it is surely only a matter of time. Only a few months ago, bombs were planted in Harrogate and York; their intended targets were charity shops for the Cancer Research Fund. Only a few weeks ago, William Waldegrave (the minister dealing with the veal problem) was sent razor-blades in his post. Alasdair Palmer of the *Spectator* has counted, over a period of two years, 29 incendiary bombs and 42 letter bombs; in addition, there have been 61 packages containing razor blades, packed to injure anyone opening them. (There must have been tremendous joy among them on the day that one of their bombs went off and seriously injured a child of 13 months, a joy somewhat dampened when they found that the child had not actually been killed.)

As I have pointed out several thousand times, the animal rights gangs have no interest in the well-being of animals; who has ever seen an animal righter taking a dog to the vet, or binding up the paw of an injured cat? (When, for instance, they broke into a fur-farm and released all the animals, they knew, but did not care, that the animals would all suffer a fate much worse than that they would have had from the furriers.)

Very well; these things happen. But why am I coming back to the subject so soon? It is because there is another layer to this argument, and a layer very much more important than the one concerning the well-being of the animals. When the original row broke out, concerning the condition of the animals that were destined for the French and Belgian plates, it was impossible to distinguish those kind-hearted people who were truly horrified at the animals' fate from the thugs whose only wish was to cause as much havoc as possible. Indeed, after a time, many of the kind-hearts withdrew, rightly thinking that their cause was being stained.

But in the mêlée, something happened − something much more important than whether the calves were treated well or badly. The law was broken.

And it was broken by people − hundreds, if not thousands of people − who would not take a single penny from a millionaire unless the millionaire said that they could, and by people who would not drive six inches at 31 miles an hour if the traffic sign said 30, and by people who would in no circumstances drop a sweet-wrapper on the pavement, and by people who would run away immediately if anyone suggested that it would be fun to tap a tambourine (very gently) after, say, half-past-eight in the evening.

Yes, the law was broken, but if these people, law-abiding from their heads to their heels, feel it right to break the law (only the special law, mind, not the laws which forbid us to rob banks, to get drunk in the streets or to smash the windscreens of parked cars), because animals may somewhere be suffering, well, then, it is obvious that they are right in their beliefs. And, therefore, armed with genuine righteousness, they broke the law. And who shall say that that is wrong?

Me.

I cannot put it better than did Robert Bolt in his play *A Man for all Seasons*, so I won't try to, and instead I quote. The play is about St Thomas More, and Roper, his son-in-law, is urging More to actions that might save More from the scaffold. Here is the exchange:

More: The law, Roper, the law. I know what's legal, not what's right. And I'll stick to what's legal . . . What would you do? Cut a great road through the law to get after the Devil?
Roper: I'd cut down every law in England to do that!
More: Oh? And when the last law was down and the Devil turned round on you – where would you hide, Roper, the laws all being flat? This country's planted thick with laws from coast to coast – Man's laws, not God's – and if you cut them down – and you're just the man to do it – d'you really think you could stand upright in the winds that would blow then?

Now look at a few results of the contemporary Ropers and what they have done with their immovable certainty that they are right and everybody who disagrees with them is wrong. What about Mr Ernest Oliver, who is 73?

> The wharf-owner at the centre of demonstrations against live animal exports . . . was . . . under police guard after he fired warning shots over the heads of militant demonstrators who tried to tear down the gates of his country home and hurled lumps of concrete at the house . . . "A hundred of them turned up, screaming and shouting . . . They terrified my wife and me, smashed the house gates and broke down two security gates . . . The next day the local council had the cheek to tell a public meeting there had been peaceful protest outside the house."

The clue is not the shouting and throwing lumps of concrete: it is the words of the councillor. He condemned the violence, as those in charge of these things must, but he did not condemn the annoyance and trouble that those who want to go about their own business are suffering. And, much worse, the peaceful crowds have ruined businesses altogether and been proud of doing so. Hear the headlines (oh, yes, you can *hear* the headlines in this business): "Protesters claim victory in battle over animal exports." And underneath the sinister – yes, sinister – words, we read: "The owner of Brightlingsea wharf in Essex is putting his dock business up for sale . . ."

And I tell you that unless this trend is reversed we are on the slide to the destruction of our laws, and ultimately our entire world. *Why* must the owner of Brightlingsea dock sell it, when his business there is perfectly legal? Why? Because the peaceful mob will not let him, and I say again that unless the peaceful mob is dispersed, we are done for.

The excuses for breaking the law pour out: the animals are being ill-treated; ordinary people, having nothing to do with the thugs, are joining the marches in tens of thousands, so they must be right; if the owners of docks and wharfs are using them for transporting the animals, then they have only themselves to blame if they are ruined; yes, we are breaking the law, but we claim a higher law.

Amid the noise, a Mr Bene't Steinberg reminded us, in a letter to *The Times*, of what we should not have forgotten:

> . . . The defence of mass picketing which puts fear into those legitimately going about their business, and can lead to mob violence, reminds me of the weasel words used at the time of the mass pickets at the Grunwick plant and the Orgreave coking plant. If it was right for the country and Government to support the police in those two conflicts, it is right for us to give our support to the police now. Or is it the fact that it is largely middle-class people, not striking miners, who are causing the trouble which deprives the chief constables of vociferous public and political support?

For all its trappings and majesty, the law is a fragile instrument, and if it is broken – *in whatever cause* – something very much more important than the trappings and majesty is lost. Our law is the lifeblood of our democracy, and we live under the law's shadow. Through the centuries, our law has been, however imperfect, the one thing that has stood the test of time. Shall we break it now? I tell you that if you do so, you will never be able to put it together again.

The Times, 7 February 1995

Because it was there

ATINY PARAGRAPH, no more than 15 lines long, catches my eye: there has been a discovery at the hut in which Scott of the Antarctic and his companions died. The hut has been kept as something like a museum, and when, recently, an inventory was taken there, supplies of cocaine and opium were found. (These, of course, were for medicinal use; remember that we are in 1912. There have been one or two letters in *The Times* discussing the matter, but I am intent upon the greater mystery.)

And a great mystery it is, enough to make me stop and wonder. Why does the story of Scott of the Antarctic go on reverberating through the years – some 80 of them – without fading under the light of modern times? It was, to be sure, a noble endeavour and a pitiful fate, but there have been countless endeavours and fates in this ragged, unjust world. When Scott and his companions died, the First World War was only two years away; there were pitiful fates galore in that encounter, and if Scott's team had lived they would certainly have fought in the war, and perhaps died in it, but in either case bravely. Would we, though, have made such icons of that heroic band?

For icons they are. Getting on for 10 years ago there was a television series, based on a book, which sought to debunk Scott, and proving to the author's satisfaction, though not history's, that the hero was in truth a frightful fraud; if I remember rightly he was supposed to have virtually driven Captain Oates out of the hut, thus destroying the unforgettable picture of the hero's self-sacrifice, and those equally unforgettable words: "I am just going outside, and I may be some time."

The debunkers got short shrift; I even have a faint recollection that I joined in the uproar. If I had been strolling by when the noise was at its height I should certainly have broken a lance for Scott, or at the least cheered on the defenders, because the script-writer for the TV series was Trevor Griffiths, as usual burbling and glaring and muttering, all ings couched in the kind of suffocating pseudo-ideology he favoured, and no doubt favours still. Well, try some:

". . . revealed what British Imperial mythography had suppressed, namely what the Norwegians did and how they achieved their triumph . . . gives the lie to the official version, the heroized version . . . the case against Scott is devastating, but . . . I don't think you see him as a black-guard [why shucks, how kind BL] . . . One sees him as a victim of the values and structures of that age . . . the series looks at the characteristics of the age, at the class differen-ces and at nationalism . . . At a time when news manage-ment has reached such appalling levels as in the reporting of the Falklands, the Korean Airlines disaster and the invasion of Grenada . . . it seems important to look at how a myth of glorious and heroic failure was constructed in that way . . ."

I suppose it's a mercy that Mr Griffiths didn't know about the cocaine and opium the expedition carried when he was writing the script: he might have portrayed Scott and his team as a band of drug-crazed moon-heads, perma-nently smashed out of their minds.

Anyway, Scott remains, and always will; can the same be said of the television series, the book which started the trouble (I confess that I cannot even recall the name of the author, let alone the title of it) and even Trevor Griffiths?

The irony embedded in the tragedy is almost impossible to bear; when the team could go no farther, they were only 11 miles from provisions, help and safety, yet their illness, their months of suffering, their weakness and the weather made it impossible for them to trudge those miles. That weakness, incidentally, must have played a double part; true, it prevented them trudging on, but it surely must also have helped to break their spirit (they would have been inhuman otherwise) when, just as they reached their goal and renewed their resolve, they saw the traces left by Amundsen, and realised that he had got there before them.

Why doesn't the human race keep still and stay where it is? (That it can reject a plea to shut up as well is understandable, though only just.) The question, for all its apparent simplicity, is one of the most extraordinary puzzles in the universe, and the Scott expedition is one of the most vivid examples of our inability to answer it. For what were they doing? They were experiencing physical conditions, for months on end, which were no better than those experiencing the most fiendish and relentless torture by implacable enemies. And why were they willing to suffer so? To be the first human beings (the penguins had been there for centuries) to get to the South Pole.

There was no buried treasure for them to seek; there was no fortune awaiting them on their return; there was no mysterious ice-clad guru from whom they hoped to acquire wisdom. They did it for exactly the same reason that Mallory and Irvine (who also perished in their attempt) put forward when asked why they wanted to climb Everest: "because it's there".

Shakespeare's words are appallingly apposite: "Truly to speak, and with no addition,/ We go to gain a little patch of ground/ That hath in it no profit but the name./ To pay five ducats, five, I would not farm it;/ Nor will it yield to Norway or the Pole/ A ranker rate, should it be sold in fee."

Moreover, there is a catch in it even for the successful explorers of the seas, the deserts and the mountains, and a very cruel catch it is; a few instances will make the point.

When Everest was conquered by Edmund Hillary and Sherpa Tenzing there were, rightly, tremendous accolades for them: as I recall, the news came in the middle of the Coronation, and for a time looked as though it would put the royal pageant in the shade. Now: how many successful attempts on Everest have there been in the 40 years since the British flag was planted on the peak? I have no idea, but that is precisely the point; except for the few whose work includes following these matters, the names and nations of those who followed in the painfully planted footsteps of the first conquerors are utterly forgotten. Yet it is not at all likely that Everest has become easier to climb; the truth is that once something unique has been done we lose all interest in those who attempt to repeat it. Neil Armstrong was the first man to step upon the moon, and Buzz Aldrin followed him down the ladder; there were more landings later, but do you remember any of the names of those who followed?

It works in much less rarefied air. When Roger Bannister ran a mile in 3 minutes and 59.4 seconds he was, again rightly, applauded, fêted and made much of; it is said that he was offered a knighthood on the spot but declined, feeling that his record run was not enough to merit such an honour. (He took it some 20 years later, most rightfully, for services to medicine.) But his record has been broken again and again; I think the mile has even been done in something like 3.45, but if my life depended on it I could not tell you who holds the record now.

So we must recognise that of all things on this earth, fame is the most evanescent, not only for the latest dispensable pop-singer, hailed as immortal, but practically all of us. Nevertheless, from time to time — a very long time to time — something turns out to be indelible. There is no telling why this event is remembered and that forgotten, though perhaps a tragic death is more likely to catch the imagination of everybody, as witness Mallory and Irvine, and the unanswerable question: did they die before they reached the summit, or on the way down?

Thus it is too with the infinitely touching story of Scott of the Antarctic. If the British team had managed to get back safely, but nevertheless beaten by Amundsen, would they still be remembered throughout the years? And what about Amundsen himself? He behaved with perfect courtesy and humility, and truly grieved for his defeated rivals. But there is more irony here, for he too died tragically and heroically; he was seeking, from an aeroplane, any trace of a colleague and friend who had been in a dirigible which had crashed, and his own aircraft disappeared with him. I do not know whether he is revered in Norway or, if he is, whether someone has written a book and mounted a television series to say that he was a fraud.

One other thing; Scott's last words, in the journal he was keeping, are as haunting as those of Captain Oates: "For God's sake", Scott wrote, "look after our people." Did we?

The Times, 9 March 1993

More's the pity

WE ALL HAVE our obsessions. Some of us cannot step on the lines in the pavement, while others *must* do so; both parties are agreed that any variance from the law will bring down appalling retribution.

There are other, milder, unshakeable beliefs. We all want to win the pools; some of us, however, are regularly convinced that we are about to do so, and are genuinely bewildered and angry when the man from Littlewoods doesn't appear.

Then there is the even gentler *idée fixe*; the man who cannot pass an antiquarian bookshop or a seller of croissants.

Then there are – it is hardly a peculiarity – those who like a tidy home and get cross when the Sunday newspapers are strewn about the carpet. And then there is me. Why, when, and how did I get into my head the idea of a perfect world? I didn't mean that the world around me, the real world I lived in, was about to become perfect; I was not so obsessed as that. What seized me, three or four decades ago, was discovering the extraordinary unshakeable belief among millions of people throughout history, that the world *could* be made perfect, and at some time in the future would be. (To say nothing of those who believed it *had* been, once.)

That is much more remarkable than it looks and sounds. A glance out of any window, or for that matter a glance *in* at a window, will show that no such world exists or can exist. Nor, to give the human race its due, did anybody sane actually believe that it might. But the evidence belies the scepticism.

I read *Utopia* as a schoolboy, and found Thomas More's didactic (though not fanatically didactic) book very dull. I put it away, and forgot it. At least, I forgot the book, but I did not forget the title.

How splendid it must be to make up a word and find it, years or centuries later, in all the dictionaries of the world! True, the first title of More's book had been "Nusquam" [Latin for nowhere], a name that grew from More's discussions with his beloved friend Erasmus, and I have always wondered whether, if they had settled on that name, it might never have been found in any dictionary, let alone all of them. But as the discussions went on, "Utopia" took the stage, and became the word that in the end captured mankind. (Mind you, the word Utopia is Greek, and the book was written in Latin; how many people in 1516 could read English, let alone Latin and/or Greek?)

Anyway, Utopia won, and won so conclusively that it spawned more words; to call some project "utopian" condemns it to be a failure, based as it is on rickety foundations, and "Utopianly" "Utopianiser" and even "Utopianised" can be found in the dictionaries to this day. More was not a man to preen himself, but he would surely have smiled and even blushed to know that only 16 years after his death the words Utopia and Utopian were to be found in print elsewhere than in the book itself.

And where did I come in? I am astonished to have to say that I do not know. There was certainly no Damascus road for me, as there was for me in music; I would like to say that when I blew the dust off that old volume of *Utopia* the heavens opened for me, but it was not so. Certainly, when I began to assemble a bibliography of Utopian literature I had already been fascinated by the idea, but I did not at first know how extensive that bibliography was; I very soon began to think of the Hydra, and indeed I have never stopped thinking about the beast, because when I was too deep in to throw the thing up and abandon it, I realised that a hundred Utopias could be written, not one of them touching any other one anywhere. A hundred, did I say? It was not long before I discovered that I had plunged into a sea of thousands, and I have been swimming in that sea ever since, never once having the opportunity to write *Finis* and mean it.

But why? Why, that is, has the thing got me in its grip and refuses to let go (not that I want to let go – the drug-addict pretends to seek a cure, but he does not really want to get off the stuff)?

Could I not have submerged myself in exotic postage-stamps, examined South Sea manhood initiation rites, or compiled lists, in alphabetical order, of all the lawyers struck off between 1734 and 1990 for stealing the clients' money?

No; it was Utopia. It *had* to be Utopia. Sometimes I wonder why the whole world is not fascinated by the idea, and why most of the world have not written books on the subject. Sometimes, in my gloomier moods, I begin to think that most of the world *has*. At any rate, I have counted the items in great numbers of bibliographies (they all call themselves "*Select* Bibliographies" to make clear that they could have doubled the list of books without repeating themselves), and some of them run to 800 or more references. Where did they get the energy? Or the ink?

If my own feelings are in any way representative, the answer is the pity that lies beneath this whole story. We are, we remind ourselves, looking for the people who are looking for a perfect world. *Simpla simplicitas*! They are bound to be disappointed, and in their disappointment they come to believe, in one way or another, that they have been cheated. And so they have been, though not by the way of the confidence-trickster; those cheated out of their money are the lucky ones, but those who stretched out their hands to Utopia were – and are, for it has not yet finished – doomed to a disappointment far greater than robbery.

There are many layers of Utopian disappointment. Thomas More gave it the name, but the idea of a perfect world has been in the world for very much longer. And how could it be otherwise? Just think how many centuries have passed, in which the mass of all peoples lived lives of misery, pain, hunger, cold and fear; it was inevitable that such lives had to be somehow palliated, and the idea, whatever it was called, was needed. Troubled by wars, men dreamt of a world at peace; in want, of a land flowing with milk and honey; suffering exploitation, of a system in which no parasites could steal the honest toil of the honest man.

That was how it started; how it *must* have started. But as it moved through the centuries, the belief in a perfect world became more sophisticated. It was all very well to dream of wine and freedom, but in civilised lands today there is an abundance of wine and freedom, sold at very moderate prices, yet Utopia is there, still painting the way to perfection.

So why are we not perfect? That is the question built from Utopia's bricks, but no one has answered it to the world's satisfaction. True, there have been countless attempts, countless longings, countless fakes (oh, very many fakes), but still that perfection eludes us, and even eludes the first steps on the way. Do I have to remind you of the bibliography which points the way to 800 books on the subject, and the end not in sight?

It is not for me to jeer; I should really bury my face in my hands. Why? Because that book with 800 pointers to other books, when it comes out in its next edition, will do so not with 800 book references, but 801, and I confess that this eight hundred and first is called *A World Elsewhere*, is published by Jonathan Cape, and I wrote it.

The way we thieve now

WHEN I MOVED into the W1 area of London, very many years ago, my regular shopping street, just round the corner, was (it still is) Marylebone High Street, with its appendix, Thayer Street. In those days, the thoroughfare was not only a great shopping experience, but one of the most elegant and beautiful streets in central London. This was not simply a matter of "posh" – shops which were so expensive that only the rich could buy from them – because there were very many places in the street for people with modest means but who found that the goods they bought were of the finest quality, from the wonderful grocer to the wonderful fishmonger. (Strictly speaking, the latter was not on the High Street, but he was only two paces round the corner, and incidentally he is still there and still selling the finest fish in London.) The friendly grocer, of course, has long vanished; there are no such things anywhere now unless you want to go to Fortnum's – the supermarkets have done for the grocers, alas.

Eheu fugaces. Over the years, the street has deteriorated; the great map-seller rolled up his charts, the great butcher with his unforgettable name – "Wainwright and Daughter" – packed his carving knife, the great men's outfitters is still there, but half the size it used to be. Perhaps the finest place in the street was the glorious emporium (I can't call it a shop) which was run by a lady who surrounded herself with beautiful things made of silver and wood and pottery and everything that can be made by man's (and woman's) hand, and who sold that beauty for amazingly small sums. I remember – how could I have forgotten? – the day she told me that she would have to give up the shop, because the lease had run out and a new one would cost five times the old one. I still bathe in *schadenfreude* every time I pass the site. It has been derelict for some five years, I am happy to say.

From bad to worse, the High Street crumbled further. At one point, I counted 15 derelict shop premises, and some of the weirdest hopefuls took shops on the street, I remember one that sold nothing but nuts – nuts of every kind but only nuts; I think it lasted about three weeks. And then the street got even worse; some of the shopkeepers wouldn't have been allowed in the street in its glory days, and few there were to take a shop in a dying street. (One turned back the tide: Villandry – I suppose you could call him a grocer – is expensive, but sells the very finest stuffs, and nothing else.)

But lately, I have been sniffing a different breeze. One of the derelict shops has been taken for a display of what the High Street and its surrounds might become. And what might they become? The plan in the window is detailed; it looks like Arcadia, and if it ever came to fruition, it would be what the High Street was when I first moved in. (I had had a clue without realising it: the High Street Christmas decorations, slung across the street, were not only beautiful but singularly tasteful; unmatched by the vulgar, shoddy stuff that Regent Street provided, our High Street led the town.)

I peered more closely at that plan, and I regret to say that I murmured "I'll believe it when I see it". Yet even the pessimist in me cannot deny that one or two shops that might be harbingers of spring have been newly seen. Could it be that our High Street is going to have a new life? Ah, well, I'll believe it when I see it. (That may be when the harmless winos leave the High Street.)

But I have to tell you now that the above is not the matter in hand – my hand, anyway. And I regret to have to say that the real matter in hand shines no credit upon our street; indeed, for any ordinary person, it would be difficult to beat for baseness. Let me explain.

When those sadly derelict shops – as I said, sometimes they numbered by more than a dozen – were crumbling away, some sensible and valuable suggestions as to their use were made; these were, principally, that the empty shops should be leased (I presume at a peppercorn rent) to such noble causes as Oxfam, Sue Ryder, the Imperial Cancer Research Fund, and many more. These shoplets take in a wide variety of useful items from donors, which are then sold for their good – their very good – causes. There have been many such over the last few years in our High Street; at present we have Oxfam and the Cancer Research Fund. Sometimes, however, the shops are closed, and when that is so, donors have been in the sensible habit of leaving their gifts on the doorstep, for the good and generous souls to take in, when they open for business.

You get the picture? No, you don't. You *think* you do, but you don't. And when I tell you what the picture is, you won't even believe it. For not long ago, I was walking through the High Street and paused at the Oxfam shop; it was evening, and the Oxfam staff had long gone home. But some other people had not. I looked at the door of the Oxfam shop, and I saw, pasted on the inside of the glass door with the text outwards, a printed police leaflet, clearly for wide use, which ran: "Police Warning. Donations are being stolen from the doorways of this shop. Please take care of your property."

I strolled on, in what I think is correctly called a brown study, but I did stroll on. It was only a few paces further when I saw, again neatly printed and pasted on the inside of the glass – it was the Cancer Research Fund shop – this statement: "Due to the increased numbers of forged bank-notes in this area, we are checking all notes presented in this shop. We apologise to all our customers for any inconvenience."

I haven't finished. There was another police leaflet being distributed just before Christmas. This is how it ran: "Many of you will be flocking to the shopping areas of Marylebone to spend your hard earned money on 'prezzies'. However, you will not be the only ones shopping in the West-End. Extra 'shifts' of thieves will be drafted in to relieve you of a few items. They will come because some of you will be careless with your cheque books, leave your handbags unattended, leave your shopping on the back seat of the car and show off how much money you have in your wallet. Most of us will enjoy our Christmas – a few of us won't. Please take care and be aware."

Let us go back first to the doorways of the Oxfam and Cancer Research Fund. No one can be ignorant of what those organisations do and why they do it. Yet people will steal the donations (themselves hardly of much worth) from the thresholds of those shops, and other people will present forged notes wherewith they will pay for what they are in reality stealing. Then let us go back to the Christmas warning which tells us that "Extra 'shifts' of thieves will be drafted in to relieve you of a few items."

Auberon Waugh has said – it is practically a mantra – that only a few years ago he would leave his house in the country unattended and unlocked, without a thought or a care, and found it left as it was. He has just been burgled, in that very house, for the third time. And you could fill the Albert Hall from floor to ceiling with people telling the very same story, as they jangle their padlocks and compare floodlights.

So what does it mean? What is the meaning of the thefts and swindles played upon generous people who do nothing but help those who need help? And what is the meaning of the country-house burglaries which are rife now, but which – though there were thieves aplenty – hardly existed a very few decades ago?

You will be greatly dismayed, but probably not astonished, when I say I don't know. And I don't think anyone knows either. But I think I know that the Oxfam and Cancer Research thievings *could* not have happened, before, say, 1960, and the country-house burglaries *did* not start to happen before roughly the same time. If I am right, what has changed – and changed substantially in that time? I don't know the answer to that question, either. Very sorry.

The Times, 24 January 1995

That give delight, and hurt not

Y ES, YES, I know that everybody who can whistle
"The whistler and his dog" has already said everything
there is to be said on the subject of the new Glyndebourne.
Well, I am certainly not everybody, much less anybody,
and whistler or no whistler I am going to have my say, so
there.

Do you remember (no, of course you don't – only
people as old as I am would remember) the building of the
Royal Festival Hall on the South Bank? I was young then;
youth fades fast, but all through those four decades I have
kept that memory green; the memory, that is, of the great,
glorious, glittering shock that the Royal Festival Hall
gave – and, in the corridors of my mind, still gives.

Then I went to Glyndebourne, and got that shock again.

I have now been going to Glyndebourne since 1951; this
year I went to a most splendid *Eugene Onegin*, and a
somewhat less splendid *Don Giovanni* on my birthday,
which was spoilt only by the realisation that I have had an
appalling number of birthdays, already. (True, George
Christie had the impudence, when we were talking after
the performance, to opine that he was some years older
than I – a claim so painful, mendacious and uncalled-for
that I pushed him into the lake and did not stop to inquire
whether he had drowned.)

Exegi monumentum aere perennius. Some time ago, when
the new one was a-building, I found myself with some
friends at a garden party. Leaving, we realised that we
were very near Glyndebourne, where the old and new

were fighting it out, and we stopped there for a time. Fierce notices insisted on no entry; naturally, we ignored them and tiptoed into the tremendous mess. Soon, the guardians of the site got wind of us and – before they had time to set the dogs on us – we beat a retreat. But not before we had glimpsed another world.

I bet you didn't know that 1,750,000 bricks were needed for the new building. I also bet you didn't know that if the cubic space allowed to each member of the audience in the old Glyndebourne opera house – which held some 800 – had been followed into the new one, the numbers of the audience could be exactly double the old. No, said the Christies: there shall be leg-room, and breathing-room, and shifting-on-the-bottom-room, and lo! the Christies contented themselves with 1,200 comfortably seated.

Enough of this jabbering with compasses, rulers and even sextants; I walked into the new opera house and I was stunned by its beauty. Now before you say that I am getting sentimental, let me say something about beauty in opera houses; I consider myself a considerable expert in the subject, having spent a great deal of my life visiting even the ones in the most remote places. Basically, there are two kinds of beautiful opera house interior: the ornate, however lavish or delicate, and the geometrical, however severe or magical. And I swear by Pythagoras and Archimedes, nay, by the very squares on their hypotenuses, that the new Glyndebourne is so stupendously magical that it hypnotises the visitor into the belief that it could win prizes for lavishness.

The sheer warmth of the wonderfully chosen timbers (I dare not remember how many trees had to be felled, lest the Save the Whales organisation comes and eats us all) is perfectly set off by the architectural genius that has set the curves of the balconies so exactly that I thought for a moment the whole building would, at the press of a button, start going round. (Though there is one inexecusable *lacuna*: a number of seats give only a partial view of the stage.)

Not even such a wonderful opera house can build itself; this one, in the building of it, shames our country (and who knows how many others?) by the way its dozens of problems were met and surmounted while all over the land there were and are excuses for failure. George Christie gets not a penny from the State for this masterpiece (or indeed for the running of Glyndebourne itself), and his proudest claim – as it should be – is that the building was done inside the time allocated and the cost was not a penny over the budget. Just match him against Sir Alastair ("blame someone else") Morton, whose celebrated hole in the ground seems, every Monday, Wednesday and Friday, to be demanding more billions of money and more months of time, and giving unimpressive reasons for both.

But here is another man, a man who inherited from his father an opera house, and swore that he would be true to his trust. And he has been, as his new opera house makes clear.

This is an unpropitious time to be building opera houses, but if the Christies had waited for a propitious time we should wait for ever. Anyway the sun shone (it always does when I am at Glyndebourne, because I long ago struck a bargain with the Lord, by the terms of which I would never take a picnic and He would always provide clement weather), and wherever I looked I saw happiness, excitement, laughter, satisfaction, wonder and untrammelled praise. The singing and acting in *Eugene Onegin* came as close to perfection as anything can, and Graham Vick's *mise-en-scène* was one of the most enchanting and refreshing things I have ever seen on a stage. (Mind you, I had the shock of my life when, after the performance, I was introduced to the Tatiana, to whose beautiful and meaningful singing I had just been listening, entirely rapt, when I discovered that in years she is hardly more than a child.)

For *Don Giovanni*, I was wondering whether the few boos earlier in the season would be repeated; they weren't. (These had been provoked by Deborah Warner's staging; just another silly woman who thinks she is cleverer than Mozart.) But I must digress for a moment.

Once only in so many decades had there been booing in the old opera house, but – you won't believe this – it was entirely my fault. Those of my readers who follow my every step will know that the one work of music I detest, hate, loathe and abhor beyond anything else is *Pelléas et Melisande*, which I swear I would now walk 20 miles on stilts not to hear. Don't think I have not tried; I had heard the dreadful thing no fewer than five times when I struck and would go no more. Even then, all might have been glossed over, had it not been (I have never known where to stop) for my taking it into my head, that day, to write a monumentally savage column describing my feelings about the horror. Far away from Glyndebourne, I little knew what I was unleashing, but that night, when I was happily tucked up in bed with some decent Wagner, the floodgates had been opened: I had, in some touching way, given the *nihil obstat* for all those who had always detested the thing as much as I had, *but had been afraid to say so, in case they had been thought musical oiks.* My postbag in the next few days reinforced my views: vast numbers agreed – indeed, we were fully ten haters to one who loved it. Anyway, as I subsequently learnt, our side, released from the thrall, let loose at curtain-fall and poured out their years of misery into a glorious riot of catcalls. And that, grandpa Bernard will tell you, was how he introduced booing into the auditorium at Glyndebourne.

As I have repeatedly said, the glory of Glyndebourne is its élitism, may it never wane. I must end, therefore, with the most delightful expression of élitism I have ever seen. I return to *Eugene Onegin*, which was sung in Russian, a language few of the audience could be expected to follow;

reasonably enough, they were helped by English surtitles. But when, in the ballroom scene, M Triquet, the old French tutor, launches out on his "Brillez, Brillez" song, the surtitles were firmly switched off. Of course, all of us are fluent in French (I, for one, committed the entire *oeuvre* of Racine to memory last Wednesday and my daily chat on the phone with Gerard Depardieu sometimes goes on for an hour). Dear, beloved Glyndebourne, never blush when you do things like that. Just remember that doing things like that is the reason we love you so much.

The architects are Michael and Patty Hopkins.

The Times, 23 August 1994

Our plastic friends

I AM ON RECORD, in the case of Mr David Schummy, as saying that "salutations are due, and properly given, to anyone who can do anything better than anyone else." (Mr Schummy scored by being the world's greatest boomerang-thrower; when last heard from, he had kept the boomerang in the air, before it returned to his hand, for 36.33 seconds.)

Mind, there are no conditions as to benefits for mankind and similar nonsense; if a man stands on one leg for 17 years without a break he would be entitled to the coveted Levin Accolade for Excellence, However Daft. But I confess that I have recently come upon a contender for the prize who has made me wish that I had laid down certain restrictions, just as *The Guinness Book of Records* very rightly refuses to accept endeavours which might put people in danger.

Gulping hard, then, I pin the certificate on the chest of Mr Walter Cavanagh of New York, who carries about with him, in a specially designed wallet (I'll say it's specially designed) 1028 credit cards, weighing 35lb.

Any man faced with a claim like that will inevitably turn to his wallet and count his cards; I have just done so, and I am amazed to find that I have no fewer than 12. Reading from left to right, I make it Visa, MasterCard, American Express, BT Chargecard, Eurocheque card, cash-machine card, BT phonecard, ditto Mercury, Marks and Spencer storecard, London Library pass, Zoo ditto, and something called Centrecard, which has run out.

Yes, but 1,028? (And, incidentally, he ought to be giving a thought to the design of his wallet; if I have remembered the pound/gramme relation correctly – a most unlikely supposition – two-thirds of what he is lugging around is the wallet and only one-third is the cards.)

Never mind the quality, feel the width. To start with, if I hear myself once more saying "What did we do before credit cards?" *and getting no answer*, I shall cut several of mine in half, as one is supposed to do when disposing of the things. Actually, I have cut a lot of them in half, over the years, because if Mr Cavanagh holds the record of the number carried (well, I presume he does), I must be the champion at forgetting my PIN number. The trouble is that thanks to the doomladen letters you get about never telling anyone your PIN and never writing it down, and never letting anyone look over your shoulder at the cash-machine, I am practically pre-programmed to forget the damned thing the moment it arrives.

I tried turning the numbers into acronyms for a bit, but it was too depressing to go on tapping in PONG or DEAD. I will happily swap my current ones for, say, BEER, LOVE or CATS, like those idiots who pay astounding sums to get a car number-plate with their initials on it. Now I come to think of it, since the number-plate wheeze plainly works, would any entrepreneur like to join in me in setting up a business dealing in PIN-swaps?

Let us come back to Mr Cavanagh for a moment, as he waddles about with half a hundredweight of oblong plastic distributed about his person. How does he do it? (Let us not even think about *why* he does it.) There are, of course, very many facilities which offer cards – shops airlines, places of entertainment, restaurants – but the great majority of card-givers will, in addition, accept the world-wide umbrella cards, Visa and Access and their like. In other words, most items of Mr Cavanagh's collection are quite unnecessary.

Well I suppose most of us would have twigged that much by now, unaided. But of course he is not really worried about being arrested if, after having consumed a couple of Big Macs, he realises that he hasn't got a card to pay with. Then again, I would like to know whether he gives each of his 1,028 an outing in rotation; it would be a rotten deal if he just uses Visa or Access like the rest of us and lugs the rest about for reasons unknown.

There has been a good deal of irking with American Express lately. Some facilities are giving it up; Nico has a fierce statement across his menu, saying "We do not accept American Express cards". The reason is that although it is perfectly convenient for the *buyer* (although there is a substantial annual fee), the *sellers* are complaining that whereas Visa and Co are content with 1.5 per cent as their rakeoff Amex slices off something like three times that.

I had a monumental run-in with Amex, extending over five months, a couple of years ago (we have long since made it up), in the course of which I wrote what I think must be the rudest letter I have ever penned in my life – no small claim; I have arranged to have it read out at my funeral. Amex was entirely in the wrong, and eventually wrote me a letter of apology that stretched over six pages. I had a miniature form of such ding-donging with Master-Card more recently, but they hadn't the backbone for a fight, and paid up quickly.

Which was the first credit card – credit card, that is, of the modern ubiquitous kind? I have a feeling that it was the Diner's Club; I had one, occasioning much surprise among less sophisticated folk.

I have friends who refuse to hold credit cards; the most familiar reason is the danger of overspending. The transaction is indeed seductive; try as I may, I cannot think of those slips we sign as money, and money, moreover, which will not be demanded for weeks yet. Mind you, Reckless Jack Levin is not *entirely* soft in the head; I invariably pay off the whole sum every month, and even wait until the last few days for posting the cheque, reciting the Commination against Usury as I do so.

For all of their faults and dangers, credit cards are an immense boon. Imagine clutching bundles of banknotes, or always waiting while a substantial cheque is tactfully authorised. The credit card has to be scrutinised, too, but that is now done automatically almost everywhere; a mild whirring, a signature, and off we go.

I try to use my cards for different purposes – one for business, one for pleasure, and so on – but I always forget which is which; mind you, all the credit-card companies I use are excellent at listing everything paid for (Amex even sends you the duplicate of the signed slip).

Arnold Bennett wrote a book called *The Card*, but I don't think it was about our plastic friends, or even Mr Cavanagh's. It is possible that Shakespeare was thinking of Visa when he said "We must speak by the card, or equivocation will undo us all"; perhaps when he was skint and the head waiter at the Mermaid presented the bill, he pretended to have left his Access card at home, and Ben Jonson had to bail him out *again*. I don't think Mr Cavanagh would get far with that trick.

The Times, 9 July 1992

What's in a word?

POOR MR RATNER; his jewellery empire is troubled with financial problems; so much so that he is having to sell many of his shops. His advisers insist that his misfortunes did not spring from his unfortunate choice of words when referring to one particular item from his stock, but were coming anyway because of the recession. Perhaps; but he will nevertheless go down to history as the man who failed to bite his tongue hard enough, though even if he had bitten it in half, it would have availed him nothing, for he would have bled a second too late.

That, or something very like it, is what Gerald Ratner is thinking today, as he was thinking yesterday, and will be thinking tomorrow, and every day of his life to come, let him live for a hundred years. "O call back yesterday, bid time return." But the world revolves in only one direction, and nothing will induce it to reverse its course. I have no wish to deepen Mr Ratner's anguish, but I fear that it will be no comfort for him to know that all of us, too, remember with shame, embarrassment, agony or horror, a word we spoke and a thousandth of a second later wished unsaid.

I do not buy my jewellery at Mr Ratner's stores. When I want to drape a necklace of matched emeralds round the throat of some pretty thing, I go, naturally, to Cartier. But horses for courses; those who lack my millions must accommodate themselves in a different mode, and I certainly do not look down upon them. But then M Cartier has never stigmatised even one of his products as *de l'ordure*.

"Words, words, words"; that is all Polonius got for an answer when he asked Hamlet what he was reading. They seem innocent things, do they not? Yet they can ruin men and women, indeed they can bring down governments, spark off hideous wars, estrange friends, break up families, part lovers and lead criminals – and innocents – to the scaffold.

Or, of course, they can inspire heroism, create beauty, spread happiness, bring learning, comfort the bereaved, provoke true laughter, and – do not despise the lowliest of their functions – keep me and all the other scribblers from the necessity of earning an honest living.

In the beginning was the Word, and the Word was with God, and the Word was God. Thus spake St John, and most powerfully did he speak up for the word. There is, assuredly, no human being without words; even the dumb have their words inside them, and although there have been, and are, cultures with no writing (the Incas, for instance, and the American Indians), they still have words with which to express themselves verbally, aided by signs.

You know, I take it, of the *mot de Cambronne*? But do you know the real *mot*? Cambronne, at Waterloo, was commanding the Guards, and they were surrounded. His surrender being demanded, he replied "*La garde meurt, mais ne se rend pas*", and he has passed into history in one of the most splendid retorts in any language. Yet he consistently denied saying it, only to be disbelieved: his denial was attributed to modesty. Only on his deathbed did he tell the full truth: he was indeed told to surrender, but what he said in reply was less tremendous, though more concise: "*Merde!*" The *mot de Ratner* has the concision of the original, and indeed the exact wording; I would not be surprised to see it included in a book of quotations.

We have no knowledge of just what Eve said to Adam as she handed him the fruit, though we know what the serpent said. Whatever the words that carried the fatal message, how bitterly and yearningly did the pair of them wish those words unsaid. And little do proud mothers think, when they rejoice at Johnny's first word, what millions of words he will speak in due course, and what they will be: to bless her or shame her.

The most severe of the Trappist orders requires silence of its monks, though there has been some relaxation of the rule in recent years. Would it be a transgression for a Trappist to talk to himself? I am an inveterate talker-to-myself; people cross the road when they meet this man muttering as though surrounded by a throng of listeners. That may be one of the effects of living alone, or possibly of the belief that my own words are much more interesting than those of other people.

I love dictionaries. Sometimes I pull out a volume of the OED and sit cross-legged on the floor searching for a word, only to be found a couple of hours later, my original quest long forgotten, having wandered up many a leafy lexico-graphical lane in the meantime. I usually round off a session with another look at "haberdasher", that amazing word which is recorded as early as 1419 but has defied etymology ever since: no one has been able to trace its origins. Lady Diana Cooper once tried to convince me that she had unravelled the secret; according to her, the word came to England with an influx of German pedlars, selling ribbons, pins and other such items, who cried their wares at the street corner with the words "*Ich habe das hier!*" A likely story! (Mind you, nobody has ever found an etymo-logy for "cocktail".)

There are more than 1,100 uses of "word" or "words" in Shakespeare, and the heroic Mr Bartlett has listed every one of them in his great concordance; just think of the labour it took, without computers or any other modern aid. He was American, the compiler of *Bartlett's Quota-tions*. Now *there's* a man who could talk about words, knowing what he was talking about.

Costard, in *Love's Labour's Lost*, says to Moth, anent the pedants, "O! they have lived long on the alms-basket of words. I marvel thy master hath not eaten thee for a word; for thou art not so long by the head as *honorificabilitudini-tatibus*; thou art easier swallowed than a flap-dragon". Well and good; but the depressing thing about the famous "long word" (pure nonsense, of course) is that the madder Baconians and other anti-Stratfordians have seized on it as a concealed cipher, and tortured the poor word into shapes as mad as they.

Poor Mr Ratner; I don't know whether he will be cheered or further downcast when I reveal that if he had only had a classical education he would have been spared his shame, for if he looks up the *mot de Ratner* in the OED he will find a torrent of Latin words under his own, as "*carptus, carptura, res decerpta . . . pars carnis ascissa; crustum; offella, offula . . . pulpamentum . . .*", all of which initially concerned "to pluck off, cut off, separate", but of which the OED delicately says that "the word has taken the sense of 'dirt, filth' ". Next time Mr Ratner wants to emphasise something, let him follow Gibbon and leave the word "in the decent obscurity of a learned language". But what is the Latin for oops?

The Times, 3 September 1992

The stars above

I HAVE A MESSAGE for whichever of the saints is on doorkeeper duty at the Pearly Gates tonight. There will be a very faint tap, and the most modest of coughs, to announce a new arrival; his modesty, I assure you, is entirely genuine. But please will you let him in without questions about his ability to maintain himself financially (yes, but not lavishly or with extravagance), for it is Jacques Pic who knocks, Jacques Pic who has, shockingly, died a mere 60 years old, Jacques Pic who gave so much innocent pleasure to so many people for so long, and whatever the hour the bells must ring a peal of welcome, homage, delight, perseverance, integrity and joy. He will, however, be beside himself with embarrassment at the celebrations, trying to hide behind a cloud and begging the angels to stop the cheering. For when he can get a word in, it will amount only to "I did my best". And so he did.

Jacques Pic was the son of one of France's greatest modern chef-restaurateurs, André Pic; *his* mother, Sophie, started the great line with a simple restaurant and taught her son her *métier*. André subsequently moved the restaurant to Valence, where it still stands. Valence is a sleepy little town just south of Lyon, and he worked until he got the coveted Michelin star; then he went on to the second star, and at last the third. But then tragedy struck. Pic *père* found the strain of keeping his standards so high more than he could manage; illness resulted, and he lost the third star, then the second. Finally, he could do no more, which is where Jacques came in. Jacques had not wanted to follow his father into the restaurant-chef business (his passion was motor cars); but as the noble empire crumbled he decided that he must rebuild it. His father retired, and Jacques fought his way back: the second star was gained, and then the third.

That is where I came in.

In 1984, I made a journey in *Hannibal's Footsteps* (that was the title of the book I wrote about my walk and climb, and of the television series I based on it). I had eaten at almost all the three-star restaurants in France, as well as scores of two- and one-stars (as well, of course, at many unstarred ones), but Pic had escaped me. Valence is in the Rhône valley, and a brief detour to the foothills seemed called for. Sufferers from gout or stomach ulcers should skip the next few paragraphs.

I started with the simplest of *amuse-gueules*; a handsome slice of melon and some sweet Parma ham; Pic's own *marque* of champagne accompanied that, and of course the lingering over the menu. I weighed anchor with fillets of red mullet accompanied by quail's eggs stuffed with caviare. That was followed by an *escalope de fois de canard* in a lemon sauce, sprinkled with razor-cut shreds of the zest. Next was a row of *écrevisses* in a pastry boat, surrounded by a sea of truffles.

The interval was filled with *le trou Normand*, that blow to the palate which stuns the taste for the few minutes it needs to start working again; my *trou* was a lemon sorbet drenched in *marc d'Hermitage*, and it worked perfectly. So did the next course: a combination of *loup de mer* and salmon in a creamy vegetable sauce. But it was more than that. It was also a picture, because both the white of the sea-bass and the pink of the salmon had been cut up and "painted" on to the plate in alternate pieces; Pic had even had the sauce sprinkled with all its colours for the fish. Nothing daunted, I went on with the pigeon in wine; plump, soft and full of taste, none of the gamy flavour that pigeon can have. But now it was time to choose the cheese; I took a flavour-filled *chèvre* and half a dozen or so of the tiny, hard pellets which you eat from a straw.

Dessert loomed sweetly; before the vast range was even proffered the head waiter produced a *soufflé glacé à l'orange*, saying it was – a wonderfully meaningful word – *obligatoire*. Then there was nothing more but some raspberries and *fraises des bois* followed by a peach sorbet and the chocolate gâteau. (I had happily put my fate into the hands of the *sommelier*, and he did not betray me: a white Hermitage followed by a red one, both superb.)

Pic himself led me to a beautiful *chaise-longue*, and I subsided for an hour or so; I found the *maître* himself sitting beside me, and I murmured "*J'ai mangé des miracles*", and he blushed – he really did blush, this amazing, shy, self-effacing genius, and said "*C'est mon métier*". I had noticed.

From then on, we were fast friends, though towards the end I had to forgo the delights of his table, because whatever I did or said he would not let me pay; but when I read of his death it was a blow from which I am not ashamed to say that I wept; indeed, I would have been ashamed had I not wept.

Pic was truly unique. He shunned publicity; the very idea of a television series filled him with horror (we had the devil's own job to persuade him to take part in my Hannibal walk), and – I think uniquely among the three-star great ones – he did not advertise his latest concoction, nor did he fly to Los Angeles or Jeddah to do huge banquets for the hugely rich. He stayed in Valence and cooked, and he cooked because, and only because, he knew that he made his customers happy with his cooking.

He was even a hero to the other great chefs of France; Troisgros said of him "*Jacques Pic est le plus généreux de nous tous, dans sa vie comme sa cuisine*". And *le dauphiné*, the newspaper of the region in which Valence stands, reinforced his modesty, saying "*Il était le plus discret des 3 étoiles*". He died, of course, in harness; indeed, his death took place in his kitchen; surrounded by his *brigade*, he was doing what he had done so long – cooking unimaginable delights to make people happy and thus to make himself happy. Well, at least he was saved from pain and debility; he fell dead in an instant from heart failure. (Alain, his son, trained by Jacques, will now take over in the kitchen.)

He was, for all his shyness a merry man, and he would have had a struggle between laughter and modesty when he saw the front page on which his death was recorded; the whole of the top of the space was filled with the news of his death, pictures and all; below was the trivial matter of the Maastricht referendum. I salute a man, an artist, a grand soul and a friend.

The Times, 28 September 1992

A very big bang

WELL, POOR OLD God. Hardly had he recovered from the news that he was a hallucinogenic mushroom, than his most cherished secret – how the universe came into being – has been revealed. (Rubbing it in, Professor Turner of Chicago University said: "They have found the Holy Grail of cosmology", which is one in the eye for Tennyson, never mind God.)

The quantity of bilge that has been poured into the solar system since this "discovery of the origins of the universe" would be sufficient to wrap Alpha Centauri in melted chocolate fudge three trillion times over, even ignoring the bits that stick to the saucepan. Here, for instance, is that heroic but somewhat over-excitable expert Professor Stephen Hawking, who declares that the news is "the discovery of the century, if not of all time", an odd claim considering that there is a great deal of time that has not yet happened; wouldn't it be better to wait until it has? But if we have the Prof, we must inevitably have Patrick Moore; our plain man's guide to the universe, jollier and barmier than ever, tells us that ". . . everything – space, time, matter – came into existence at one moment, between 15,000,000,000 and 20,000,000,000 years ago".

Well, you've got a hell of a lot of leeway there, Pat, you must admit; even the British Rail timetable can be more exact than that. As it happens, Professor Freeman Dyson of the Institute of Advanced Study in New Jersey (I'll say it's advanced) can be even more exact than that; he has worked out that we are not, after all, doomed to disappear a mere 20,000,000,000 years hence (wait till I have mopped my brow in relief), but will go on, he has worked out, for a number of years which, if written out at a rate of a billion digits a second, each digit being no larger than an atom of hydrogen, we would need a piece of paper two hundred thousand billion billion billion billion times the size of the surface of the Earth. Shove off, Ryman's.

Nor do we stop there, or at least Dr Derek Raine of Leicester University doesn't. "It is very, very exciting," he says. (The excitability of scientists, particularly when they are talking gibberish, is a matter that would repay close study, and a substantial grant to Leicester University for further investigation of this curious phenomenon is essential if Britain is not to become a scientific laughing-stock.) He goes on: "The puzzle scientists have been trying to solve is where did all the galaxies, the sun, planets and stars come from?"

Well, yes, that *is* the puzzle, isn't it? Assuming, as I do, that they were not found under a gooseberry bush, if only because some clever-dick would point out that we don't know where the gooseberry bush came from, my best guess is that God has a sense of humour, and is at this moment rolling on the floor with a handkerchief stuffed into his mouth and tears pouring down his cheeks, while the whole angelic host is doubled up similarly and for the same reason. If so, just wait till the contribution of Professor Efstathiou of Oxford University reaches the celestial regions; striking a cautious note, he says of the now notorious "fluctuations" that, "It's possible these fluctuations are caused by dust on an existing galaxy", and the picture of some poor charlady from outer space being given a right rollicking for not Hoovering under Aldebaran before skiving off for the weekend will have the saints practically weeing themselves in their mirth.

Amid all this nonsense, to which I shall return in a moment, the Bishop of Peterborough contributed the only sensible words spoken since the "news" broke: "This doesn't make a great deal of difference to me", he said, adding, "It certainly doesn't make any difference to God. If anything, it makes him even more amazing". Good for you, Bish.

Just step back from the nonsense, and try to see what has actually been discovered. For some years, there has been a tentative agreement among most astronomers that the universe came into existence with the Big Bang; an infinitesimal speck of matter became smaller and smaller and more and more dense, until one day – "Pow! Bam! Crrrunch!" – and we were all off and running.

However, the Big Bang (for which, of course, there was and is no evidence at all, only a theory that fits the tiny scrap of knowledge that humanity has so far achieved) exhibited some curious features, which led to residual doubts about the theory. It is these doubts that are now supposed to have been laid to rest, and the absurdity of the conviction is demonstrated in yet one more of the comments that this business has provoked, which refers to "the minute irregularities which the Big Bang theory demands, *if the present-day state of the universe is to be explained*".

My italics, and I employ them because the present-day state of the universe is no nearer being explained than it ever has been. It is noticeable that if tiresome fellows like me ask the scientists whence came the matter which constituted the ingredients of the Big Bang, they get tetchy, even shifty. Professor Wheeler of the University of Texas displayed those very *stigmata*: "People ask what happened before the Big Bang", he said, and answered, "It is a meaningless question. There was no 'before'. It is like asking what is north of the North Pole." No, it isn't. It is a perfectly meaningful question, only Professor Wheeler doesn't know the answer. Nor do I, for that matter, but unlike him I can try to banish my own residuary doubts by speculating on the idea of the Creation, which, after all, does demand a Creator – a much more likely solution than Professor Wheeler's cop-out.

There is, in this business, a kind of impudence. However the universe came into existence, the idea of it is utterly ungraspable. When we are told that there are billions of billions of heavenly bodies which are billions of billions of miles away, and many other billions of billions are hurtling through the universe in billions of billions of directions, we stretch our imaginations until they are in danger of breaking in pieces. But we simultaneously stretch our capacity for awe and wonder, and it is that capacity which, when we are told that the secret of the universe has been found, only to learn that it has not been, fortifies us in our quest for a real meaning in the universe, armed as we are in the certainty that there must be one. Shakespeare had no doubt in the matter:

> Sit, Jessica. Look how the floor of heaven
> Is thick inlaid with patines of bright gold;
> There's not the smallest orb which thou behold'st
> But in his motion like an angel sings,
> Still quiring to the young-ey'd cherubins;
> Such harmony is in immortal souls,
> But whilst this muddy vesture of decay
> Doth grossly close it in, we cannot hear it.

The Times, 30 April 1992

The necessity of bears

BEARS, NOW; YOU didn't expect me to be writing about bears, did you? Nor did I, to tell the truth, but I have just found a crumpled cutting about two students who were camping in the Yosemite National Park, in California, when a bear appeared, a black female 8 ft high, giving every sign of eating the two youths. Well, you wouldn't expect me not to take the opportunity of reciting *à propos*, would you?

> When the Himalayan peasant meets
> the he-bear in his pride,
> He shouts to scare the monster,
> who will often turn aside,
> But the she-bear thus accosted rends
> the peasant tooth and nail
> For the female of the species is
> more deadly than the male.

The two took refuge in an outdoor lavatory – it's a good thing that California is house-proud – and remained there all night, as the bear prowled around. At daybreak, the beastie decided that there would be no breakfast for her, and trotted off to look for easier fodder.

But there is more to a hungry bear than meets the eye, not to say the claws. To start with, the animal is immensely old; it was developing 25 million years ago ("Who hath measured the ground?"). It is inexorably declining, in the face of the noise and mess of civilisation, though slowly, and now that the world has become more careful not to accelerate the decline, it is in some areas almost thriving. Nor can bears be lumped together on the principle that when you have seen one bear you have seen them all; there is a huge variety of the furry fellows, from the familiar polar bear to the enchantingly named cinnamon bear, not forgetting the sloth bear, which is presumably the one that hangs upside down with a card on its back reading "Do not disturb". And then there is the grizzly bear, whose Buffon-form name alone strikes fear into the stoutest heart: Ursus horribilis.

If you meet one, you might pray for the sight of a lavatory, though it is unlikely that you would get to it in time: the bear – horribilis indeed – can run at 30 miles an hour, and I bet you can't. It is said by the experts that the bears usually try to avoid human beings, but the human beings would be wise to take the news with some care; not long ago, I saw on television a group of zoologists who were studying the polar bear, to which end they had encased themselves in cages with very stout bars; their comrades had retired to a safe distance, and those behind bars awaited whatever might occur.

The scene was as striking as it was alarming. As from nowhere, a bear appeared and shuffled towards what it presumably thought would be a refreshing meal, where-upon another appeared, and then a dozen or so, all walking around the intrepid figures in the cages. The programme finished before the obvious question could be asked: how did the encaged seekers out of knowledge get out of their cages without being eaten?

Grizzlies are the largest, as well as the fiercest, of bears. They can weigh more than 12 hundred weight and stand 9 ft high. They are solitary creatures; in the mating season the male is very solicitous, but when birth is finished, the partners go their separate ways.

It is strange that so fierce and even terrible a creature has been welcomed into the nursery: toy bears must be among the most cuddled of all soft toys. It is almost, though not quite, certain that the Teddy bear did get its name from President Theodore Roosevelt.

The horrible sport of bear-baiting has an appallingly long lineage. There are drawings of the entertainment from the 14th century. The word "beargarden", denoting some kind of uproar, comes from the sport. There, a chained bear (or bull) was attacked by savage dogs; there is a bloodcurdling extra in the practice of stuffing the pitiable animals' nose full of pepper. Gradually, the horrors of bear-baiting penetrated the coarseness of the time and, with the Puritans leading the abolitionists, the sport declined, though not before Macaulay made his famously cynical comment: "The Puritan hated bear-baiting, not because it gave pain to the bear, but because it gave pleasure to the spectators". Bear-baiting in Britain was finally outlawed by legislation in 1835.

There are bears in the Pyrenees; I take it that these are the nearest to us, for surely the Germans can now call only on boar. The number of the Pyrenees bears is small, and getting smaller; the experts say that they are too few to breed successfully, so that unless bears can be imported and coaxed into living and breeding, they will go the way of the dodo. Moreover, there is a furious battle over a new road through the Pyrenees. Conservationists argue that that would finish off the last of the bears, but the hard-headed Pyrenean peasant is fighting for the road, which will bring, or is at least expected to bring, a good deal of prosperity to the area. I have lost touch with the story; have the bears won, or the road-makers?

We British are notorious suckers for any furry animal; we will merrily pick up a stoat or a mink and tickle it under the chin, which accounts, I believe, for the number of people in this country with only one ear or one eye. But not long ago, there was a bear story that truly touched any heart not made of granite.

In Turkey, the rules about the treatment of animals are carried out – how shall I put it? – somewhat less than rigidly, fiercely and passionately. Thus, when a troupe of dancing bears was seen, and seen being ill-treated by their owner, the British bystanders vowed to do something about it, and that something grew from a sad "Ah, poor things" to an enormous, and meticulously executed kidnap of the unfortunate beasts.

Nor could this be called meddling in other people's business; the horrible torture sustained by the animals – in particular, one bear called Black Cloud – should have been stopped long before. (The bear's handler was wont to beat the animal savagely with a pole, he dragged it literally by the nose, it was left chained in freezing rain, and its food was stale bread. Elsewhere, a row of eight dancing bears was chained almost permanently to a sea-wall. In Britain the owner of the animals would have been in prison in no time; indeed, only a few weeks ago, a man was sent to prison for hideously neglecting the seaside donkeys from which he made his money.)

The rescue project went off without a hitch, and the rescued animals have been sent to wildlife sanctuaries and similar homes. And Turkey has promised to enforce its own laws.

I have always liked the circus; I don't think I have ever taken sides in the argument over it, and nobody can tell me that the performing seals aren't enjoying themselves showing off. But at one point I jib, and that is when the bears themselves appear. My revulsion is caused not only by my suspicion that these animals have been beaten into compliance; I find it truly sickening to watch one of nature's noblest beasts dressed in frilly bloomers and riding bicycles.

The ecological fanatics, like any other fanatics, do their cause more harm than good. But you do not have to be a fanatic to think that it would be a pity if bears were to disappear entirely from the earth. True, two young men might demur – the two who started this story by having to spend the night hiding in a lavatory from an 8 ft bear. One of them particularly might demur rather more strongly, because he caught a blow from the beast, and when rescue came it was found that he needed 40 stitches. (Talk about a bear with a sore head.)

Everyone smiles at the famous stage direction in *The Winter's Tale*: "Exit, pursued by a bear." But nobody smiled at the bear in question when Peter Brook directed the play; a huge, savage creature faced us in the stalls, and we were more likely to shudder. Anyway, let Shakespeare have the last word:

> Such tricks hath strong imagination,
> That, if it would but apprehend some joy,
> It comprehends some bringer of that joy;
> Or in the night, imagining some fear,
> How easy is a bush suppos'd a bear!

The Times, 28 December 1993

Murder most foul

An IMAGE RISES into my mind as from a forgotten pool. There is a young girl, I think no more than 19. Pretty and blonde, she is holding a bunch of flowers, and she is standing on a doorstep. She has just rung the bell.

The door is opened; the man who appears is smiling, as well he might be; for it is his birthday. The girl proffers the flowers. He knows her; he is a friend of her family. He moves to take the bouquet. As he does so, she shoots him dead with a gun that had been concealed among the flowers. She drops the flowers to the floor, and leaves quickly.

A dream? A film? No, reality. It happened in Germany; not in Hitler's evil Germany, nor even in Adenauer's obstinate Germany, but in Helmut Schmidt's quiet, honourable, social democratic Germany. The Baader-Meinhof gang had scored another palpable hit.

The murdered man had some kind of national administrative post, nothing to do with armed forces or spying and such. The girl was the child of wealthy and respectable parents, and had never been involved in any crime, much less killing. She had left home, and taken up with the notorious gang. Then murder.

What prompted my memory? The news that the remaining members of the Red Army Faction (Baader and Meinhof committed suicide in prison), still serving their sentences, have become disillusioned; perhaps the murderous blonde infant is still among them. They propose a bargain: an end to the killing in return for an amnesty. I was doubly surprised. I thought the killing had stopped years ago, but I learned that the official in charge of selling off firms previously owned by the East German state was assassinated only a year ago.

The killers have expressed no remorse, and there is inevitably argument as to whether the deal should be agreed. Viewed in one light, it might end the cycle of death and imprisonment; from another angle, it could be thought a surrender on the part of the state and a victory for evil; yet another opinion is that it would actually increase terrorism, because such bargains would proliferate.

But I am more interested in the past of this story than the present and the future. Federal Germany bore the greatest brunt of what was called urban terrorism. I think there is a reason for that, which I shall come to.

Almost without exception, the murderers were young. The great majority were of upright and lawabiding descent. Very few were from broken homes. Most of them had a good education. Almost all were graduates. As far as I know, few if any have demonstrated genuine repentance over the years.

In America there were violent, politically motivated gangs (the Black Panthers were the most notorious). At much the same time, the IRA restarted its violence, which had been dormant for many years. The Spanish separatists, ETA, joined in. In Italy, the Red Brigades murdered many, but there was real poverty there. It was a time of blood, but why did Federal Germany suffer so much more than most other countries troubled by such wanton murders?

Could the answer be something like this? In America, there were deep racial canyons to cross; no wonder that those who crossed them bore arms, and used them. The IRA wanted something tangible, as did ETA, and both believed (or professed to believe) that killing the right people would in time bring them their reward. The Red Brigade could pose as fighters for social justice. But in other European countries – and most notably in Germany – *there was nothing seriously amiss*. Simplifying greatly, I do believe that, for the first time since the reign of the Emperor Caligula, human beings were murdered in considerable numbers because their murderers were bored.

Come back to the 19-year-old murderess. What did the future hold for her? More education that did not interest her, parties and dances that had already staled, a more or less arranged marriage into the appropriate stratum of society, children in which she would, or believed she would, take no interest.

What did her kind of society offer her and her equally bored coevals? A thirst, surely, for the means to reject it, and not only to reject it but to extinguish it. Many simply dropped out and entered the drug culture. But for a few, that would not suffice: the boredom had become insupportable, the society fit only for another Flood. In Paris, their counterparts were smashing windows from end to end of the rue de Rivoli, but they were serious about it, as de Gaulle realised in the nick of time. In Germany, or at any rate in the Germany of our young blonde, the tide of boredom was now a raging sea. Let us spoil a birthday; let us spoil it permanently; yes, the roses will do, will do very well.

Such murders were not ideological. There was no more ideology in the Federal Republic than there was starvation. Nobody was oppressing the young fanatics or anyone else. But that was precisely the problem. How clearly Dostoevsky would have recognised what was happening, and how he would have failed to be surprised when a German bishop commended the Baader-Meinhof group, murders and all, on the ground that they were opposed to the materialist society that they – and presumably the bishop as well – were living in.

Remember, the young murderers and murderesses did not expect, or even really hope, that their activities would ultimately bring down the hated government, which was hated because the ordinary people (ah, those ordinary people – wait till we get into power and see what we do to them) were content with their lot – as well they might have been, considering how well off they were.

If they did not kill out of boredom, why did they kill? Not for fun: an earnest mien was invariably seen on their faces, whether in the dock or on the Wanted posters. Nor, as must by now be clear, could they have hoped to overthrow the established order and establish their own. Nor in the role of the Four Just Men: they did not confine their murders to those who ran prisons or tended nuclear installations or gave evidence against them when they were prosecuted. Their murders were murder for murder's sake.

Shall we learn anything from them if the deal goes through? I doubt it. Many, after all, have served their sentences and been released, but I know of no such explanation having been offered. And indeed, what explanation could convince us? To be convinced, we would have to recognise that a girl not yet out of her teens, with presumably all reasonable hopes for the future, would abandon her future and its hopes alike, and instead commit a particularly macabre murder. Does the German language, I wonder, have an equivalent to the English phrase "The Devil makes work for idle hands to do"?

The Times, 14 May 1992

The final question

MY NAME IS Levin, and Levin is almost always a Jewish name. I am a Jew. I am not at all a good Jew – I take no part in the religion of my forefathers, and indeed I am so *déraciné* that the only clue to my Jewishness (because the myth of Jewish noses was exploded long ago) is that I am circumcised. (No, come to think of it, there is one other indelible mark I carry – whenever I hear of a Jew having done wrong I feel a stab of pain.)

And yet, exactly 50 years ago to the day, I discovered – what the world could not have believed until then – that had the Second World War been lost, I, and all my family, together with every other Jewish family in Britain, would have been murdered, for no reason at all other than that we were Jews. And not long after that, I learnt that approximately six million Jews *had* indeed been murdered, again for no better reason.

Surely, this is a phenomenon that requires from all of us the most searching examination?

Of course; but you will find, to your great astonishment, that every attempt to understand what this truly incredible event means comes up against a wall of incomprehension. It happened, and it happened as I said; but we cannot understand *how* it happened, and *a fortiori* we cannot understand *why* it happened.

By coincidence, a reader sent me a letter a few days ago, asking me to solve the mystery. This is what he asked:

My dilemma lies in the question, how can a civilised nation condone mass murder? We know that the Germans were and are a highly cultured and civilised people ... Nothing separates us other than geographical boundaries. If one refuses, as I do [*and as I do too* – B.L.], to accept the premise that these crimes were a secret known only to a few (and no one, German or otherwise can deny the public vilification of the Jews after 1933), then this question must be addressed. I do wish that some of those who were involved in the programme of genocide would stand up and explain their "rationale".

So touching was my correspondent's letter, that I replied immediately. This is what I said:

I cannot give you an answer, because I have never found one. I have a substantial shelf of Holocaust studies, many very profound and detailed, but that question has never – as far as I know – been answered. And the Germans *and* the villains themselves have failed to answer. One day some scholar will find the answer, but that day is not yet.

One more quotation, very relevant; it comes from a letter in the *Sunday Telegraph*:

There are no degrees of mass murder: Mao is not a greater criminal than Stalin because he killed twice as many people. Mass murder is an absolute crime and there are no degrees to it.

What, however, makes Hitler's mass murder of the Jews unique is that he tried, and well nigh succeeded, to exterminate *all* the Jews, men, women and children in his grasp. Every person of Jewish descent from Paris to Kiev, knew that he and his family were condemned to ill-treatment and death. Whereas every Russian knew that there was a one in 10 chance of his being sent to the

Gulag . . . *every* Jew in occupied Europe knew that he and his family were condemned to torment and death.

Arbeit macht frei. I think that of all the words and in all the languages since speech has existed, those words are the three most wicked. They are German for "Work makes freedom", and what makes them uniquely evil is that they were framed over the arch of the gate of Auschwitz, where countless human beings died, and died deaths as horrible as death itself can be.

Arbeit macht frei. Germans have always been credited with efficiency and thoroughness; they proved it at the gate of Auschwitz-Birkenau, where a complicated internal railway system had been built to bring the doomed to the gas chambers. (The trains, unlike Mussolini's, ran on time.)

Arbeit macht frei. All over the East, and for years, those crematoria smoked. They smoked just like coal, to make heat; surely they thought that there was no difference between those coal-fed chimneys and the familiar fuel burnt in countless hearths to warm countless drawing-rooms?

Arbeit macht frei. Just what did the Russian scouts think when they pushed open the gates of hell? Of course, they would have been to a great extent inured – after all, Stalin was not in awe of the Queensberry Rules, and by now his soldiers weren't either, even if they ever had been. But what the Russians saw – the heaps, the mounds, the pyres, the *mountains* of naked, murdered corpses – what did they make of it?

Arbeit macht frei. Do you know that there are aged Jews in Britain and the United States and Europe (not many left in Europe) who, taxed with the terrible Jewish conundrum – where was the Jewish God when the millions went to the gas-chambers? – rejoice in God's bounty for sparing a few? *Arbeit macht frei*, indeed.

"What hast thou done? The voice of my brother's blood crieth unto me from the ground." Yes, six million such voices, and yet we still cannot understand how, in the centre of civilised Western Europe, we have nothing to say but "now art thou cursed from the earth, which hath opened her mouth to receive thy brother's blood". All the avenues along which we went, thinking that we might find the answer, were one by one found wanting; shaking our heads, we finished as ignorant as we started.

What will the future think of us? What will our descendants say of us? One answer is almost too terrible to offer. Did you watch, on BBC television the other night, among the massive series of Holocaust sights and thoughts and horrors, the part given to the Jews of Hungary?

For a time, Hitler had left the wily Hungarians alone, and at one point in the struggle, it looked as though Hungary's Jews might escape the plague. Alas, they did not, and went to their deaths with the rest. But the Hungarian-Jewish march of death was recorded by the cameras, and that is what I am drawing your attention to, if you did not see it. The commentator spoke of the huge march through the middle of Budapest; he recorded the dreadful fact that the endless line contained 400,000 men, women and children, and then the cameras took over. What they showed was a tidy, orderly, evenly paced march, with very few Nazis and guards. And I must ask my question, though by now I hardly have the strength to do so. It is: why didn't they run away? There were 400,000 in that march, and they marched to their deaths neatly and tidily. Yes, if they had broken step and run for it, many would have been immediately shot, others would have been caught and killed, others would have been denied refuge; but *four hundred thousand*?

It is not for us to rebuke the dead: indeed, I think I have already gone too far. Would *you* change places? Would you even try to understand the dilemma?

I return, inevitably, to where I started. I do not know how or why the greatest evil in history grew and flourished in such harmless-looking soil. (As my correspondent said, "We know that the Germans were and are a highly cultured and civilised people".)

But I ask again: what will posterity say? That such things must never happen again? Easily said, easily said. What will the grandchildren of a few more generations understand? And a few more generations still? How many generations must pass for the Holocaust to be one with Nineveh and Tyre? What do we actually know about William the Conqueror? Nothing but that he came here in 1066? Yes, the Holocaust was unique (and pray God it remains so), but will the children of a century hence feel as we do?

Arbeit macht frei. If a child studying the German language were asked by his teacher what the words mean, the studious child would not only translate it correctly but would think it a very useful and honourable motto. And if the child was told the other meaning of the words? What then? Would the child understand what he was being told? Or would he dismiss it as something that happened a long time ago?

There is no answer to my questions. But I am still a Jew, and I still cannot understand why Jehovah chose to save the Jews of Britain but not of elsewhere. One day, we may find the key. Until then, we can only give thanks, and sing the most beautiful of all the Hebrew melodies: "Kaddish". A pity that it is the prayer for the dead.

The Times, 27 January 1995

And a partridge in a pear-tree

GOD REST YE merry, gentlemen, let nothing you dismay! Until, that is, a Serb cuts your wife's throat and burns your house down with you in it, or you starve slowly to death in Somalia, or are tortured in Burma by order of the government, or you are a Hong Kong citizen facing the knowledge that in a few years you will be handed over, with no assertable rights, to one of the most ruthless bandit states in history, or you are sleeping nightly in a narrow doorway in the Strand for lack of more comfortable accommodation (perhaps a wider doorway in Regent Street), or you are a Muslim being murdered by Hindus or a Hindu being murdered by Muslims, or you are being buried alive by an Indonesian earthquake, or you are in the next Russian plane to be shot down by a Georgian rocket for no particular reason, or you are a crooked politician in Italy or Japan (where *all* the politicians are crooked, especially the prime ministers) and you realise that you haven't enough ready cash for the appropriate bribes, or your German-Jewish grave was desecrated last night by Nazi daubs, though come to think of it, that would be the least of your worries because you would know nothing about it.

These are hardly Yuletide sentiments, I realise, but unfortunately that is the way the world is going – not appears to be going, but this time actually is. Many years ago, Pandit Nehru spotted something very remarkable, which nobody else had seemed to notice; he announced, having realised it, that there was no war going on anywhere in the world, not so much as a skirmish over a few disputed boundaries. The wonderful metaphor that Nehru's sharp eye had seen and introduced, naturally turned into a hope that it might become permanent.

Some hope; it was not necessary to be a cynic to feel that the pause in the rattle of the drums reminded us that most of the time there *was* a war – many wars – going on, and anyway the interval was hardly long enough for a dash to the bar and a puff on a cigarette before the curtain went up again. Nor did it last long; the news of it had just sunk in when the Vietnam war broke out, and it dragged on so long that it might have been designed to ensure that no such sentimental moments would be countenanced in the future. But for a moment, when the music stopped, once in the world's history the mounts of the Four Horsemen of the Apocalypse could be seen placidly munching hay in their stables.

War was resumed; much of it civil war (a more inapposite name for anything in history could hardly be imagined), and the Four Horsemen heaved themselves into the saddle. Yet war itself, these few decades, has had to c⌐ ⌐ place to horrors that civilised men and women could not have imagined; when did you last read a daily newspaper lacking an account of a rape? (Rape, incidentally, of women, men and children indiscriminately.) Cruelty has acquired a new dimension altogether: knifing, bludgeoning, stamping, burning.

A peaceful family giving a barbecue party in their garden is attacked for no establishable reason by a gang of drunken hooligans, and when the mêlée ends the father is found to be dead – kicked to death, as it proves. The Single Issue Fanatics, notably the "Animal Liberation Front", find smashing windows, wrecking lorries and burning buildings too tame for their hatred of mankind, and now yearn to find a suitable human being to kill. A seven-year-old girl slips away from her mother's care for no more than five minutes – *five* – and when the five minutes are up she is found ravished and strangled.

When the Soviet empire collapsed in well-deserved ignominy, how many of us had any idea what would follow? We believed, and had a right to believe, that it would burst asunder overnight in a frenzy of hope, vigour, imagination, fraternity and self-help. And yet, in a matter of months, that monstrously tortured nation, freed from its 70-year-long prison sentence, which deserved the sympathy, the plaudits and the sustenance of the world, was being racked with internecine hatreds, with hopelessness, with savage fighting over the levers of power, with even more savage real fighting for even less reason.

When Tito died, and a few years later there trickled out the truth of his monstrous thieving and even more monstrous sybaritic lifestyle (enough, you might think – though wrongly – to shake Fitzroy Maclean's admiration for the murderous scoundrel), I laughed as loudly as anyone; I recall that I took up my entire space that day for my laughter. Well, he would be a nonpareil merry fellow who could laugh about what Yugoslavia has become today. For that matter, would you stake your life, or even your goldfish's life, that the ridiculous Greek squealing about the name of Macedonia (the *name* itself, not disputed terrain) will never come to shooting?

What is there in the sulphurous air of our time that such madness – enough to excite the envy and admiration of a Whirling Dervish – stalks the world? So difficult is the answering of that question that there would be no shame in trying the man with the signboard announcing that The End of the World Is Nigh, to ask him how he knows, and whether he can put a more precise time on the event. Is it really beyond possibility that there *is* some kind of governor of the world – call him God or Time or Hubris or Over-Population or the Ozone Layer (but not Gummer, I trust), and that our stock of centuries is at last running out? Only a few weeks ago we were supposed to tremble at the news that an asteroid is rushing towards the earth, and will sooner or later crash into us with a force that will destroy the entire caboodle. I say that we "were supposed to tremble"; plainly, we did not. Perhaps we should.

The older I get, the more I yearn to give up trying to make sense of the fury that seems to rule the world, poisoning the wells of peace, trampling on the green shoots of kindness, driving mad the leaders of the nations, ignoring the cries of the suffering, shutting the doors of freedom. If there *is* a judgment to come, why are so many behaving as though they would welcome it, fiery furnaces and all?

I say that I go on trying to make sense of the world, and wish I could stop trying. But why shouldn't I stop? I can find any number of desert islands – islands of the imagination, of quiet, of learning, of simplicity, of Mozart and Villon, Erasmus and Shakespeare, Rembrandt and *Les Enfants du Paradis*. Did you know that my hero, Sir Karl Popper, does not now take any newspaper? Why cannot I follow his magnificent example? Assuredly the world can get on without me; can it be impossible for me to get on without it?

Now: are these just the grumblings of a man who is getting older and doesn't like it? I don't think so; I have not painted the picture more sombrely than it deserved, and I would go so far as to say that I have understated the darkness. So what is left? Nothing?

Ah, no, that cannot be the answer. Tomorrow is Christmas Day, and although I cannot participate fully in the prayers and ceremonies of the Christians, I do know that Christmas is more, much more, than the exchange of gifts, the merriment round the table, the carols however truly beautiful. Even if we leave out the centre of the season, there is still just enough peace on earth – battered, scarred, bedraggled, limping – to squeeze into the hearts even of those

who had begun to believe that there can be nothing more
to come. I counsel myself against despair, and amaze myself
to find Macaulay, of all people, helping me:

> *Then none was for a party;*
> *Then all were for the state;*
> *Then the great man helped the poor,*
> *And the poor man loved the great:*
> *Then lands were fairly portioned;*
> *Then spoils were fairly sold:*
> *The Romans were like brothers*
> *In the brave days of old.*

Tout casse, tout lasse, tout passe. Even our unquiet day
must sleep, though its dreams must be dreadful beyond
imagining. But while it sleeps we can look out of the
window at the stars, and from them learn again the lesson
we forget and remember, forget and remember, forget and
remember: that there is a world elsewhere.

Can the horrors of the wickedness abolish beauty? Can
they destroy art? Can they overthrow love? Can they drag
out from the human heart its infinite capacity for holding
anything and everything in its embrace, with no questions
asked and no sinner turned away?

Oh, no; and clad in that armour, we can read the words
without flinching: "I tell you naught for your comfort.
Yea, naught for your desire; Save that the clouds grow
darker yet, And the sea rises higher". It is important,
indeed it is crucial, to recognise that the "real" world is
just as dreadful, mad, violent, wicked and incorrigible as
it seems; the worst danger we run is to believe that things
aren't really as bad as all that. They really are as bad as
all that, and more so. Call back defiance: the words we
must embroider on our banners are "Holdfast is the only
dog".

The eternal verities are not changed, not even damaged,
by the wickedness and the despair alike; come the three
corners of the world in arms . . . Provided that we do not

try to deny the terrible reality, there is no shame in retreating to the Schubert quintet, to Shakespeare's sonnets, to the Rondanini pietà. Whatever Christmas means to us, from nothing to everything, it will last for ever. And love, the beloved republic, may weep, but will abide.

The Times, 24 December 1992

Index